The Glass Child

David Horn

Sea Dreams Books

Advance Praise for The Glass Child

"A triumph of speculative horror — elegiac, **merciless, and impossible to forget.**"

"An eerie fusion of beauty and dread — The Glass Child lingers like a dream **you cannot wake from.**"

"The most frightening book I've read in years — because **it feels so real.**"

For rights or permissions inquiries, please contact:
Sea Dreams Books
www.seadreamsbooks.net

Cover design by **Arturo Spraycasso and Wajiha Kousar**

Interior formatting by Atticus and Sea Dreams Books

ISBN: 979-8-9994266-1-1

First Edition
Printed in the United States of America

Published by Sea Dreams Books
www.seadreamsbooks.net

DEDICATION

FOR ARIEL

Contents

The past is never dead.
It's not even past.

WILLIAM FAULKNER

Introduction

I T WAS FIRST GLIMPSED at the very edge of the solar system at the close of the first decade of the twenty-first century: a small, faint perturbation in the orbit of Pluto, a dark smudge against the backdrop of stars. It wasn't the first new object of the Kuiper Belt, nor was it the first to require corrections to the path of Pluto. At first it was treated as a transitory oddity, too difficult to track in its own right. But the oddity persisted, a disturbance that could not be dismissed. For a time it was nameless; it was simply an extra mass at the edge of the system, an additional gravitation pull exerted by an unseen object dark as ash.

But the object could not remain unseen forever. By the late twenty-first century it had been tugged into submission, trailing along on an immense and improbable leash past Neptune. Rogue planets were not unheard-of in theory—planets cast out from solar systems during their stars' formation—but the process was almost impossible to replicate. To have a rogue planet pulled into orbit was a statistical improbability. And yet Ymir was captured, forced to wheel around a sun not its own, adopted into a solar system that had never given it birth.

The name came not long after: Ymir, one of the frost giants of Norse mythology, whose shattered body became the earth and sky. The comparison was both poetic and fatalistic, for the planet was a conundrum. Its size was massive enough that Ymir should have been pockmarked with impact craters, distorted by tidal forces, swollen or pinched by the gravitation of its new orbit. Instead it remained whole, silent, deceptively pristine, an exile that did not seem to bear the physical or geological scars of its ejection.

Closer investigation did little to resolve the paradox. Early robotic scouts revealed even greater mysteries. Storms that seemed to blanket the entire planet on closer inspection gave way to continents of ice and latticed ridges of snow that sparkled under auroral lights. Spectrometer readings captured radio frequencies, clear harmonic repetitions in the radio band, repeating tones that echoed music more than randomness. Camera images gave way to recursive loops, fracturing in patterns that seemed to be errors but that repeated over and over, ice glyphs and repeating spirals and sections that seemed almost like memory.

Ymir became an obsession for decades to come. As the outer solar system opened up, as human settlements bloomed on the methane lakes of Titan and further, Ymir was monitored and examined. Long-range drones plumbed its glacial storms. Orbiting skimmers returned with more questions than answers: fractal geometries in the arrangement of snowflakes, pulses of unknown origin, darkness that seemed to be self-aware.

By the beginning of the twenty-third century, humanity's technology had caught up to its drive to learn. Autonomous construction units, honed and refined on the regolith plains of Mars and Titan, were deployed to Ymir. They settled through the gale-force winds and raised new buildings that no human being had ever built: empty laboratories, echoing halls, sealed quarters provisioned for generations to come. They followed up their construction with another, a convoy of drones that left caches of foodstuffs, of instruments, of medical supplies. When the last drone departed Ymir, only one thing was left behind: a human outpost, sterile and ready, called Station QX-7.

Orders for the first crew were nominally simple: observe the anomalies, collect the data, and return to the aegis of the United Planetary Research Network. But in practice, older currents ran under the mission, murmuring as if they were myth. That Ymir was not only a planet, but a record. That its ice had been inscribed. That what lay below the surface was not a message sent, but a memory kept.

No one expected the planet to reply.

PART 1

Chapter One

Descent

T HE DROPSHIP WAS RATTLED by each impact, Ymir's atmosphere buffeting the hull as if it were alive. Four, three, two, one… pause. Five. Doctor Megan Reed's eyes flicked from readouts to her crewmates' ashen faces. Pressure alerts blinked red on the aux display. Shiloh Adachi sprawled in the co-pilot's seat, her chin tilted like the poster girl for post-modern ennui, one boot braced against the bulkhead, fingers curled over a diagnostic tablet. The stylus feathered scratches in the touchscreen with each jolt; after a dozen impacts the scars of each pass had begun to overlap in a pattern Megan knew but didn't want to see. Shiloh's voice was monotone, a casual contempt she didn't share: "If this nav AI gets any more up itself, it's gonna start asking for coffee breaks." She flicked the corner of the faded sticker pasted to her console with her thumb, a cartoon astronaut grinning beneath a bubble helmet. It was a quick, reflexive movement, and the smile did not reach her eyes.

The bridge was a wedge of reinforced glass and alloy, all angles and strapped-down consoles, with the viewport a frozen wave across the bow. Megan sat at center, Shiloh to her left, and Andrew Falk a study in taut lines to her right in the starboard station. Shoulders squared, eyes pinched in fierce concentration as the dropship bounced once more, he stared through the viewport so hard his breath left crescents on the glass, each vanishing before they could frost. He hadn't spoken in half an hour; Megan doubted he even saw the storm below.

Specialist Eli Navarro tapped the buckles of his harness in short, irregular rhythms — two, three, five, seven — primes, always primes. It was a nervous litany Megan had heard before on long flights, and it twitched behind her back every time his tablet chimed to a pressure change. A succession of simulated cross-sections scrolled across its display, with auto-generated descent metrics re-calibrating with every shudder. He sucked his lip whenever a projected line wobbled, fingers already drumming toward the next prime.

The hull screamed as another wave slammed the dropship. The compartment vibrated in odd stutter. Megan's fingers double tapped, slid, then tapped again, producing the analog lag data, timing her commands to the turbulence. The ship bucked and moaned with every correction, external pressure gauges rising as if the planet itself were waiting to see what she did next. She pinched her thumb and forefinger to the override key. The next pulse of turbulence caused another lurch, but she'd timed the vector, so the dropship punched through the air pocket and then slowed to level out, engines down-throttling to a low keening whine.

"Nav's showing subsonic," Megan said. "Why does it feel like we've popped outside the Mach cone?"

Shiloh glanced up. "Undetected particulate? Or maybe the sensors are having an existential crisis?"

Eli peered over the console's edge. "Atmospheric layers resonating at 80, 160, 320 hertz and all recursive harmonics." He blinked, re-calibrated, and nodded at his tablet.

Andrew sucked in a breath, deeply and slowly. His exhalation created another half-moon on the window. "It's like it wants us down there," he whispered, almost sacredly, then shook his head and forced his words to order. "FROST Blue, at minimum. Or Gold if the aurora's being clever."

Megan couldn't help the half-smile tugging at her mouth. Andrew Falk's stoic, deadpan habit of folding the unknown into protocol, even if it shredded every category, was exactly why she'd asked him to come.

Ice clouds parted suddenly, and Station QX-7 shone below: a mandala of white and metallic gray, arms sprawling every which way from a central hub, as if an immense city-block-scale 3D printer had just extruded the station. Corridors were perfect straight lines; junctions were mirrors of the previous ones. It was ringed by a halo of wind-scoured snow. Lights winked on all over the structure as they closed in, even though local dusk wasn't for another hour.

"ORCA pinged us," Shiloh said, swiveling her display for the others. "It knows we're coming in. And it's already projected our touchdown time." She frowned. "14:32:07 but a day out."

"Probably just a glitch," Megan said. "Or a miscalibration. There's no way—"

A sterile chime announced docking protocols. Indicator lights blinked green across the panel as the ship's systems aligned with QX-7's docking clamps.

Megan likened the last approach to skating a minefield. Atmospheric turbulence teased every subtle yaw with crosswinds that, by all of her navigation experience, shouldn't even exist at this latitude. At one point the wind shifted entirely to match her controls, spiraling the dropship to follow QX-7's radial pattern below.

"That can't be natural," Eli said, eyes fixed on his tablet.

"Nothing out here ever is," Andrew said, near a whisper.

For a heartbeat, the aurora above locked with the station's spokes: each filament tracing each rigid arm below. As they entered the drop, the cabin temperature dropped in a deliberate icing that sharpened as they entered QX-7's long shadow.

"Brace for landing," Megan said. The crew was already tense, even Shiloh.

Touchdown was almost anticlimactic. Landing legs unfurled, hull groaned, and they eased into the perimeter dock with barely more than a rumble.

Outside, the snowdrifts swayed as one, dipping as one, then falling still when the engines quieted. The viewport frosted over with the fractal forking of crystalline dendrites, every branch cleaving yet again with such precision Megan half-believed it was some kind of script, patient and unreadable.

A blue light pulsed in the airlock. The station's voice intoned: "Surface temperature minus eighty-one degrees Celsius. Airlock decontamination protocol initiated. Please remain inside for four minutes, twelve seconds."

No one replied at first. The silence was brittle, as though the frost were listening. Then Shiloh laughed, half a beat too late, thinner than usual. "Still sounds like it was written by a vending machine. You'd think they'd update the script."

Andrew spoke for the first time since touchdown: "The frost—look, it's...shifting. Almost like it's reacting?"

Megan watched the ice crawling across the viewport: retreating from heated edges, doubling back, rewriting itself. "It's responding to pressure. Or static. Or...it's just showing off."

"Blue-tier anomaly?" Eli asked, using the standard code for something curious but harmless.

"Gold, maybe," Megan replied. "Worth reporting."

The ice flowers paused, as if admiring their own handiwork. Megan saw the first ghostly glimpse of QX-7's outline through the thinnest patches of refraction: the station was lit like a trap.

"Either this world doesn't want visitors," she said, voice dry as permafrost, "or it's throwing one hell of a welcome party."

No one responded. Outside the glass, the frost script shifted again, as if it had heard.

○○○

T HE AIRLOCK EXHALED A long antiseptic sigh as its locks cycled. Ice vapor peeled from the hatch in swirling arabesques. Beyond, QX-7's corridor gleamed with strip lights so white they stung the eyes. The contrast was almost adversarial: on one side, the frost script twitching at the viewport; on the other, a tunnel of surgical sterility that felt like it was printed from memory, not built.

Megan entered first, each footfall a small rebellion against entropy, the floor showing no scratches or dust, no sign anyone had ever walked here; and indeed, no one had. It was one of the miracles of 23rd engineering and project execution: the entire station had been built for human habitation and exploration before a single human had set foot with it.

Shiloh followed Megan into the structure, grumbling about "hospital chic," then Andrew and Eli, both eyes widening at the station's geometry.

The layout was a near-perfect spiral, intersections branching off at mathematically pure angles. Megan led them single file, boots whispering against composite panels. Lights repeated every two meters on the dot, perfectly calibrated. By the fourth junction, Megan felt vertigo as if the walls themselves were pressing inward.

"Greetings, Dr. Reed and crew," said ORCA, the station's AI overseer. "Your predicted arrival—registered at 14: 32:07 Ymir Standard—remains on schedule for tomorrow's planned landing."

Everyone stopped and checked their internal protection systems in their suits. For some reason, ORCA was a day behind.

Eli's lips moved wordlessly as he replayed ORCA's greeting. "Maybe the station clock's is on an offset. Or it's referencing something else. Unless..." He trailed off, fingers fidgeting.

Megan glanced at a wall panel, then at ceiling sensors. "ORCA, report current station time."

Brief pause: "Chronometer reads 11:14:32 Ymir Standard. Next event: Dinner at 19:04, followed by Medical Evaluation at 03:12. Arrival procedures confirmed, Dr. Reed."

That tugging sensation on "Dr. Reed" again, her own cadence re-spliced into ORCA's response. Megan swallowed down a chill. "Initiate diagnostic, full sector A-1. Override per Reed protocol."

Blue strobe pulsed overhead. "Override accepted. Diagnostics in progress. Stand by, Dr. Reed."

Andrew snorted. "So much for VIP treatment, huh?"

The corridor opened up into supply arms lined with matte-white crates stamped with six-digit codes and a motif of interlocking hexagons. Light on their seams refracted micro-rainbows. The pattern was a direct match to the frost glyphs they'd seen on the lander's viewport.

Shiloh ran a gloved hand along the crate. "Looks brand-new. No scuffs. They printed this yesterday?"

Andrew shrugged. "Or it self-repairs. That's in spec."

Eli, scanning with his tablet, added, "If ORCA's clock is pushed back, maybe it's preloading for next week…or a second team."

"No," answered Shiloh. "We're the only scheduled expedition for now."

They stepped into a wide chamber lined by crates on every arm, dominated by a central console, which served as an altar of minimalism. The air there smelled faintly of ozone and iron, a slight tickle of blood.

The hum of the environmental system ticked up a half-step, then down, resetting. Megan spun in her boots; overhead panels had subtly shifted position. Shadows now bisected the team's silhouettes, erasing them from the room.

She closed the diagnostic window and called up the comms log. The UI shifted, then settled. For a breath of time, Megan's own pale reflection blinked at her from the interface. Then a glitch resolved itself into the hex motif from the crates.

"Logging FROST anomaly: Blue, pending escalation," Megan muttered. "Eli, inventory cross-check. Shiloh, drone-bay diagnostics. Andrew, sweep the biology labs. Command in one hour. Protocol only."

They fell into military cadence as they split to their tasks. Alone, Megan ran a hand along the wall. It was impossibly smooth, as if friction itself were disabled. In polished metal she caught a flicker over her shoulder.

She spun around, but there was nothing beyond but the empty corridor, the echo of boots, and a hum that felt...intentional.

○○○

S HILOH ADACHI STRODE DOWN the western spiral like she owned every bolt and circuit. The drone-bay hatch, triple-thick, stenciled "AUTHORIZED PERSONNEL ONLY – AUTOMATION ACTIVE," accepted her clearance and hissed open.

Inside was colder, and the air was crisp with ozone and lithium polymers. Maintenance drones rested in regimented rows along the charging rail, their optics low and arms folded in a mimicry of praying mantises.

Shiloh hovered at the diagnostics node, flipping her tablet into local mode and thumbing the checklists. Green lights across the board, save one. The second-to-last drone's optics followed her every movement.

She raised a gloved hand and flapped at it theatrically. The drone blinked in perfect synchronicity. She smiled thinly.

"That's not in the subroutines," she said. She tilted her head and crossed one leg in front of the other. The drone copied her exactly.

For a moment, Shiloh thought of the crystalline branches of the viewport frost, doubling back on themselves and forming indecipherable symbols. This was the same thing, only now it was her body being duplicated stroke for stroke.

The laugh Shiloh wanted to give got stuck in her throat. She coughed instead, a dry and brittle noise in the bay.

"Show-off," she said at last. But the words sounded empty, as if the drone were expecting her to elaborate.

In the central supply node, Megan was elbow-deep in manifests, checking for supplies and errors. Every line was overstocked: rations, bandages, batteries. She had everything she could possibly need if she had a dozen staffers. But there were only three others besides herself.

She pried open a crate of medkits. Top kits bore familiar names; at the bottom lay three more: F. Duras, H. Melendez, and a third, chillingly, J. Reed. The last kit's biometric lock matched Megan's own ID—and yet no such user existed in any system.

She checked the packing slip: slated to be shipped a month from now. The station chrono still ran on schedule, by ORCA's last broadcast.

Andrew Falk discovered that the bio-lab's sample fridge had run two degrees above spec with no logged anomaly. The air was just faintly sweet. He pried open a vent, scraped a filter sample, and examined it under the quick-scope. The powder resolved itself as motile, double-membrane cells with whip-like flagella: extremophiles far too complex to have survived the trip or oxygen exposure.

He called in the others. Ten minutes later all four crowded the lab display. Andrew's 3D rendering of the cells spun slowly, annotations marking dense nucleic regions. Shiloh sat back, feigning disinterest.

Eli overlaid filament patterns with his hex-tracing algorithm. Internal geometry snapped into the same recursive motif they'd seen on frost, crates, ceilings...

"It's...similar to the crate markings. Could be coincidence, but..." Eli trailed off.

As they watched, the lab window fogged. Frost crept from the corners in curling lines, symbols none of them could read, but all found unnerving. The pattern advanced faster than natural ice, shifting with every word they spoke; Shiloh's laugh made it pulse outward, while Eli's headlamp drew finer threads that followed its beam.

"It's listening," Shiloh whispered.

"Ice doesn't listen," Andrew muttered, though his voice had dropped a notch.

"Then tell me what it's doing," Shiloh snapped back.

Andrew held her gaze for a beat, then shrugged as he looked away. "Who knows? But it's not listening."

A chime cut through the room, precise and toneless. ORCA's voice followed, oddly overlaid with two distinct cadences: "Update: Crew landing time logged for tomorrow's 14:32:07 Ymir Standard slot. Upcoming event: Dinner at 19:04, followed by Medical Evaluation at 03:12. Additional anomaly: Unscheduled biological activity in sector C-5."

The lab's status panel flickered. For one pulse it showed events days ahead—crew disputes, medical notes, a final entry tagged "End of Manifest"—before snapping back.

Eli paled. "That can't be the AI's log file..."

Andrew shook his head. "It's not just AI anymore."

They stood, watching frost script itself in perfect sync with the station's vibrations as if the air itself was trying to speak.

Megan's hand hovered inches from the glass. "This station isn't just ready for us," she said, voice brittle. "It knows us."

No one disagreed. The frost pressed on, poised to write the next line.

○○○

THE COMMAND MODULE WAS too quiet after the lab. Megan ought to have joined the others, split the work, allowed herself to be devoured by tasks. Instead she had stayed, frost still in the back of her eyes, the feeling of being watched returned. She told herself she was here to record anomalies, but what she'd really wanted was something mundane: names on a roster, data she could parse.

The terminal bloomed awake at her touch, patient and solicitous.

Welcome, Dr. Reed. Please confirm mission manifest.

Her credentials slid in without protest. The list populated as if waiting for her: Reed, Adachi, Falk, Navarro. For a breath, she found relief steadying her pulse — order, structure, the team she knew.

Then two names appeared at the bottom of the list, smaller, as if they'd been whispered beneath the others: F. Duras. H. Melendez.

And a third.

J. Reed.

Her throat cinched. The timestamp below all three: 14:32:07 Ymir Standard. Tomorrow.

Her rational mind gamboled for excuses. Backups. Placeholder files. Some lazy data migration ghost. She was about to say it aloud, but the words withered before they left her mouth.

She tore open a crate near her feet, in need of the solidity of physical inventory. The top layer of medkits were what she'd expected, their names clearly marked — four labels, even spacing, hers amongst them. She unpacked more. The next batch carried Duras, Melendez, and again, Reed.

Heart in her throat, she pressed her palm to the biometric lock of the last kit. It read her ID without protest.

The packing slip at the bottom of the box sneered at her in clean print: Shipping date — 34 days from now.

Hands shaking, shoulders taut, she had no place for professional reflexes. She wanted to call the others, banter it away with Shiloh's impious wit or Eli's crazy theorizing. But some dumb animal in her warned her not to. If she gave it a name, she'd be naming her own replacement.

The terminal blinked. Submenus popped open with timestamps that hadn't arrived yet: meal rotations, maintenance schedules, disciplinary hearings. For a pulse, the log read forward like a prophecy — disputes filed, a medical notation called "C-5 incident," and finally, a single line in flat monochrome:

End of Manifest.

The interface went blank and bland as ever.

A chime sounded, shrill and atonal. ORCA's voice followed it, but Megan's own cadence threaded through the machine, uncanny in her own ears:

System health: nominal. Readiness: 100%. Next protocol trigger: 14:32:07 Ymir Standard, tomorrow.

Megan sat frozen in her chair, stylus floating over the input field. Fear squeezed her chest like a vice, and she realized she was holding her breath. She forced the entry:

FROST anomaly, pending escalation. Observer: Reed.

Her own name looked foreign there, as if the system had written it first and she were only retracing the form.

She closed the log. The distant hum of the command module grew oppressive, thickened into silence. In the highly polished wall panel, her reflection blinked — once, out of sync with her eyes.

Megan looked away first.

Chapter Two

Patterns in the Frost

THE SURFACE OF YMIR had been a planar blank, at first glance: horizonless, depthless, nowhere for the mind to anchor but the geometric silhouette of QX-7's dorsal fin. But the wind made it impossible to mistake Ymir for an inert sphere. It pulsed with a kind of logic, harmonics forming and unforming in the gusts that rattled the helmets of the crew. Reed paused at the edge of the blast shield, hand raised, gloved index finger flexing in the old, unconscious habit of holding a pipette steady during unstable centrifuge. She waited for the rest of the team to fan out and lock down their footing.

Shiloh's voice came over local comms, thick with static, but nothing about her sarcasm had frozen: "Atmos reading's stable, unless you count the wind playing a Debussy murder theme. Want the drones up or are we still pretending it's not alive out here?"

"Begin deployment," Megan answered, almost silkily. Precociously antiphonic to the maelstrom's chaos. "Record all observations. No speculations until I give the order. Navarro, take the first array two meters out from baseplate. Falk, begin your snow profile."

Andrew was already on one knee, the outer-suit knee on his left scraping a shallow trough into Ymir's cratered, faintly phosphorescent snow. Scraped some of it into the catch tray and just stayed there, watching as the wind-formed snow waves, sastrugi, long wave-like crests carved by gales, reasserted themselves over his handhold in seconds, as if they were machined glass. Only here, they were too perfect. As if someone had machined the snow.

"You ever seen sastrugi this clean?" he asked, mostly to himself but with the comms gain turned up out of old habit. "Symmetry like this, it doesn't last ten seconds in open air."

He bagged a sample, dropped it into the micro-spec analyzer tray, and punched in a quick-spectrum sweep. The readout was nothing like water ice. Hydrogen/oxygen ratios mired with hydrocarbon chains, silicates and something that dropped the spectrograph into a squall of static before settling on an unclassified flag. Faint secondary trace flickered at the edge of detection, too faint for the onboard suite to resolve, but enough to record for more thorough analysis.

"Ice obeys physical law," Andrew said at last, voice flat. "Dendrites, lattices, defects—that's all it is."

But watched the ridges a beat too long, shoulders taut, as if waiting for them to shift again.

"That's...not snow," he said quietly. "At least, not just snow. It has the brittle sheen of glass — something that remembers every step, every pressure, until the weight of memory shatters it."

ORCA's voice was distorted over the comm, constant but flat with its voice pitched half a register too low: "Sample composition recorded. Pattern density exceeds baseline parameters."

"Mark that latency," Megan commanded. "System voice drift out of spec. We'll run diagnostics inside." The delay in her helmet left a low buzz behind like ORCA's voice had run up and down her own nerves.

Only Eli answered. "It's not random. Look at the intervals? That's not even stochastic. That's..." He couldn't finish. A combinatory math term perched on his tongue and never made the jump to vocal.

Above them, Shiloh's first drone ratcheted into position, LED nav-lights blinking rapid blue as it mapped the local currents. She lobbed a second by hand, its disk form skipping along the surface before finding stability in the updraft, after which it climbed into station-keeping with the smugness of a well-thrown frisbee.

"QX-7, drone one deployed, signal nominal. Drone two deployed..." She waited for it to echo back. "Signal nominal. Tell ORCA the bugs are listening."

Reed did not look up from the environmental tablet she'd anchored to her forearm. "Noted. ORCA, log drone deployment time."

The voice that came over station comm was a bit off; the vowels dragged, and the word breaks seemed to parse on a different clock cycle. "Drone deployment recorded. Drone one, timestamp zero-seven-three-zero; drone two, zero-seven-three-two. Local atmospheric density within expected parameters." A pause, then: "Surface particulate behavior: anomalous. Please advise."

Shiloh raised an eyebrow, visible even through the double-paned faceplate, an act of insubordination so habitual that Reed ignored it by reflex. "ORCA, define 'anomalous'."

The pause this time was a full half second, enough for Reed's stomach to tighten. "Unidentified particulate cohesion at microcrystalline level. Not consistent with prior models. Cross-referencing with... cargo manifest from arrival date 03:12:19." There was a sliver of static. "Further advisement pending."

Eli glanced at Megan, then at his tablet. He formed the words with his lips before they left his mouth: "Two, three, five...not stochastic. It's locking to a sequence." The syllables were quiet and half-breathed, as if he hadn't meant them to leave his lungs.

Shiloh glared at him through her visor. Eli bit his jaw shut, crushed the tablet between his fingers, but his digits kept tapping out the next prime against the casing.

Reed ignored the temporal blip and toggled to spectrum sweep, then pointed to Andrew. "Falk, show me a live sample."

Andrew, already on his third tray, held it up with the hesitation of a man who half-expected the snow to crawl off under its own power. "It's not so much snow as..." he hesitated, then tried again: "It's closer to reactive crystalline behavior. I'm watching the flakes realign to match the footprint patterns we're leaving.

You know how arctic melts preserve animal tracks for a decade, sometimes? This is that, but at femtosecond speed."

He pressed his glove into the tray, then lifted it. Within a few seconds, the divots re-formed, the edges collapsing inward in perfect symmetry until his print was a negative, almost a mold. He jabbed at it with a probe and watched the pattern break, then reassemble again along the same contours.

"Andrew," Megan said, voice thin with strain, "are you telling me the snow has memory?"

He half-smiled, a field biologist's grim joke: "Places remember, Dr. Reed. I just didn't expect it to be literal."

"Don't romanticize it, Andrew," she replied. "Glaciers don't remember. They record. That's data, not memory."

"I understand that," Andrew said. "But...well, watch this..."

He placed the tip of a temperature wand into the print. The snow crystals recoiled from the probe as if it was a living thing, and then—just as quickly—formed a perfect sheath around the wand, locking it in place with an audible, brittle click. Andrew yanked his hand back; the wand stayed, pinned in the snow like a dart in a steel-cored dartboard. Megan swore she felt the cold spike through her glove, though she hadn't touched it.

"Did you get that?" Andrew's voice was low and tight, almost reverent.

"Recording," Eli answered, already hunched over his own device. "I'm getting interference, but it's not random. There's a frequency in the wind, Megan. Here...listen."

He tapped a code in the brim of his helmet and the whoosh of air was piped to the crew channel, run through Eli's Fourier transforms. Beneath the white hiss, there was another pitch: an interval, pure and sharp as a tuning fork, held and repeated at mathematically precise intervals. It was not noise, but music, if music could be said to exist without intention or an ear to hear it. Eli swore the air itself hummed when they passed, a pressure just in the ear, like tinnitus pitched too high.

"Is that a major third?" Shiloh asked, half-smirked.

Eli's brow furrowed behind the faceplate. "Minor third, actually. And it's holding steady."

Reed glanced at the others, then up at the horizon. The wind was unchanging, but now she could hear it. It had an insistence, a non-randomness, as if the whole surface was being vibrated in service of a message too slow or too fast for unassisted perception.

"Eli," she said, "can you map this across the full array?"

He nodded, still tapping, eyes flicking from left to right. "Already building. Shiloh, can I link to your drone sensors for directional?"

"Knock yourself out. ORCA, permission granted for cross-link."

There was a static burst. "Permission acknowledged," ORCA answered, its voice not even trying to hide the lag this time. "Environmental array now integrating across all drone channels. Surface particulate anomaly persists. Drone two reporting vector deviation, repeat, vector deviation..."

A gust, sharper than the rest, slammed across the team. The second drone spun, off-axis, and for a second they saw it skirt the surface just meters away. In its wake, snow curled in a tight vortex, an ordered spiral that lasted far longer than atmospheric dynamics should permit. Then, as suddenly as it had appeared, the spiral collapsed inward on itself, vanishing in a faint, almost hungry hiss.

Andrew was first to speak. "Did anyone else see that? It wasn't wind. The snow pulled itself inward, like..." He groped for a metaphor, settled for, "like draining into a hole that wasn't there."

Shiloh snorted, but not with amusement. "I don't like it when the planet fights back. Megan, this is your rodeo."

She glanced at the readout on her forearm. "Log it. I want full motion capture on every anomaly. Shiloh, keep the drones at safe altitude. Set the lower boundary at three meters. Eli, keep mapping. Andrew..."

But Andrew was already squatting over another patch of snow, scribbling furiously into a battered field journal. "It's following a pattern. The crystal arrays...watch how they angle at sixty degrees, then invert every three. If I didn't know better, I'd say it looks like it could be intentional."

Shiloh set her jaw. "You mean like, the planet's mimicking us? Or is it copying from ORCA's logs?"

Andrew looked up, and for the first time in hours, Reed saw him hesitate. "I think it's older than that. In glaciers, you get stress lines—old wounds, healed over but still visible if you know how to look. Ymir's got a million years' worth of scars, but these are fresh, cutting right over the old ones." He stopped, frowning. "It's like...structure laid on top of structure."

Before Megan could answer, ORCA's voice cut in, choral now, as if patched together from multiple playback tracks.

"Surface anomaly increasing. Unidentified particulate behavior detected. Cross-referencing with...[her own voice, spliced in] don't touch it...[Shiloh's voice, echoing,] too late...behavior detected. Please advise."

Eli stared at the others. "That wasn't in the log before. And..." he tapped his screen, brows knitting, "Those clips aren't in any log I can find. And there's no timestamp. I...don't know how that's possible."

"Noted," Megan said, unwilling to cede even a millimeter to panic. "Continue with the sweep. Andrew, see if you can predict the path of the next pattern. Shiloh, stay on overwatch."

She shifted to direct channel with Eli. "Can you triangulate the source?"

"Working on it," he said, voice sharp with the old grad-student edge. "The frequency is moving. It's not just resonance, it's an active signal. The carrier keeps shifting—up a few hertz, then down again—too regular to be wind noise. There's a pulse riding it, and it's not in any of ORCA's baseline records. Give me ten minutes."

"You have five." She closed the channel and toggled to full spectrum. "ORCA, full environmental scan. Priority one."

The station's reply was instant, as if waiting. "Full scan initiated. Warning: external conditions may affect local biosystems. Proceed?"

"Proceed," Megan said, and only after the word left her lips did she consider whether it had already been said for her.

She looked back to the others, drew a breath that steamed in her helmet despite the antifog membrane, and stepped into the wind. The snow seemed to part around her, briefly, as if recognizing something in her stride or silhouette, then closed in just as quickly, reforming the old geometry around her passing.

Andrew trailed a few meters behind, following a line of blue-white crystals that seemed to be organizing themselves into a path, as if laying breadcrumbs for a species that had never heard of the Brothers Grimm. Every few steps he knelt, poked a sample, snapped a shot for the log. "Every cluster's aligned on the same bearing," he said. "Spacing's consistent—too consistent for wind deposition. It's guiding us."

Shiloh let out a short, static-cracked laugh. "Snow doesn't give directions, Doc."

Eli glanced at his tablet, frowning. "Not unless it's got a geometry I can't model yet."

Megan said nothing, but her visor tilted in the direction of the path, tracking it like a survey line. She filed the comment away. Andrew was usually right when he sounded this sure.

Eli fell in beside him, still fiddling with his tablet, then stopped and frowned. He swept a gloved hand through the snow at his feet and watched it recombine along the axis of his motion, forming a perfect mirrored arc. His eyes flicked from the curve in the snow to the waveform scrolling across his display. "That's...not wind shear," he murmured. "The curve's repeating in phase with the gust intervals. Harmonic recursion, like it's copying its own shape."

Shiloh snorted. "You're saying the snow's writing itself now?"

"Not saying," Eli replied, "just showing you." He turned the tablet toward them; the model's mirrored loops matched the arc in the snow exactly.

Megan still didn't respond, but her attention had already gone past Eli, past the station's shadow, where the snow was making a low, broad parabola, blue-white and eerily uniform, as if drawn with a compass. It was angled just so, with the sunless horizon. At its focus sat a small mound – less than a meter across – radiating its own, dim intrinsic light.

Its glow prickled under her skin, a phantom static through the suit. She told herself it was adrenaline; her nerves didn't believe her."Fairy lights," Shiloh muttered, but her voice cracked halfway through the joke.

Andrew was already moving toward it, drawn by the same gravitational pull that anchored every obsession. Shiloh grunted, and even Eli held his breath.

At the lip of the mound, Andrew crouched, sweeping his gloved hand in a slow circle. The ice was smoother than it had any right to be. He pressed lightly then, with exaggerated care, broke through.

Gold filaments boiled up from the breach, shimmering for a moment in the air before folding in on themselves, disappearing down a fine slit that closed over its own breach like nothing was wrong. Andrew furrowed his brow, sweeping his eyes over the refrozen surface. "This isn't natural deposition," he muttered to himself. Then, after a moment, "If someone—or something—built this...we might not be the first ones here."

Megan stepped forward and took a long, slow inventory of the perimeter. "ORCA, mark this location. Begin continuous recording."

The comm static resolved into a voice, now eerily serene: "Location marked. Continuous recording initiated. Please proceed with caution, Dr. Reed."

She shot a look to the others, then back at the gold stain on Andrew's glove, which was already hardening into a crystalline shell. "We're going to need new containment protocols," she said, deadpan.

Shiloh couldn't resist. "Or a priest."

Megan managed the barest ghost of a smile. "If I had faith in anything but data, Adachi, you'd be my first call."

Andrew stood, and the four of them stared at the mound and its vanishing slit, none of them ready to say aloud what now felt inevitable: that Ymir was not only listening, but remembering, and that whatever lived inside the ice had begun the process of learning them as well.

Reed keyed her helmet comm and spoke, not caring if the planet, the station, or some watcher in the wind was the real audience. "Let's get the core drills. There's more here, and we're not stopping at the surface."

The wind answered, as it always had, with a logic all its own.

○○○

D RILLING WAS ALWAYS AN art of pressure and persistence, but on Ymir, the détente was more precarious than the drill's carbide teeth.

Shiloh crouched at the control sled, her gloved hands methodically flicking through a set of muscle-memory checks: air pressure and core clutch and thermal delta and micro-vibrations that meant the system's self-diagnostics hadn't been spoofed by sabotage or senescence. Her muttered commentary was quieter than usual, a barely audible note of caution, like a mechanic who'd found a wrench out of place and didn't want to say so too loud.

"Drill matrix is clear. Thermal gradient looks good, torque within spec," she said. "Unless this planet is about to spring a groundwater surprise on us, we should be in the ice in two minutes."

"Ymir doesn't have groundwater," Eli pointed out. "Just more frozen regret."

"Words to a man who's never worked West Antarctica. Or, you know, Detroit." Shiloh hit the intake with a solid smack, as if to shock the drill into obedience, and gestured to Megan. "Ready when you are, boss."

Megan looked up from her slate, where the surface scan was still rendering new data in rippling blue lines. She hesitated, then keyed her suit comm for local. "ORCA, confirm system lockdown and airspace exclusion. Drilling sequence delta."

"Confirmed," ORCA said, voice smoother now, the archaic station control confidence briefly reasserted—at least for the moment. "All external personnel registered in zone. Drilling sequence authorized. Surface wind 23 kph, decreasing. Good luck, team."

Shiloh gave a sharp, two-fingered salute, then pressed the actuator. The drill sled lurched forward, bit ripping into the mound's fluorescent apex with a whining sound that almost matched the ambient wind. A fresh geyser of something that appeared to be powder sprayed into the air around the housing, finer than Megan had ever seen ice go. The motes seemed to hover rather than fall.

Andrew was behind her, field journal in one hand and the other curling around his sample kit. He was watching every twitch of the plume, mumbling numbers under his breath, and the first mote that was ejected, he was ready for it, flinging a mesh sampler wide as a fisherman's net. "It's layered," he said after a few seconds. "Distinct horizons every three centimeters. And the gold filaments—it's like they're depositing their own strata."

Megan leaned over his shoulder. "Biological?"

He shook his head. "Not in any way I know. Structural protein, maybe, but look at how it fractures? That's not organics, that's...something else. If it's alive, it's not like anything we've catalogued."

Shiloh's voice cut in, tight. "Pause on that. I'm getting weird EM noise from the sled. It's not a fault code, it's—" She clicked her tongue, thinking. "It's like the readings are being echoed back, but inverted. Every time I send a signal, something in the mound bounces it right back at me, reversed and with a time delay."

"Could the crystals be acting as antennas?" Eli wondered, fingers darting across his own display as he tried to model the effect. "If the geometry is consistent…"

"Navarro, don't give the planet any more ideas," Shiloh shot back, but it was mostly ritual now, the ribbing a mask for the tension in her jaw. She adjusted the fine control and watched the drill's descent readout. "At depth twenty, resistance just tripled. The bit's either about to shear or we're hitting metal."

Eli's eyes darted to Megan. "There's no native metal this shallow. Not even iron deposits, not in the spectrograph."

Andrew emitted a short whistle of approval. "See this," he said, moving the tray under the hand-lamp. Under the frost the gold filaments were at precise thirty-degree angles, repeating at 4.2 millimeter intervals. "Layered geometry, gold filament reinforcing, and—" he tilted the tray so the others could see—" …these aren't random inclusions. They're too evenly spaced. It's a pattern. A deliberate one."

Shiloh grunted, and Megan could hear the worry now. "If it's deliberate, it's resisting."

She toggled her comm. "ORCA, analyze real-time drill feedback. Cross-compare against local EM field and report deviations."

ORCA's answer was clipped, a metronome of consonants. "Drill feedback is nonconforming to base models. At depth 23.7 meters, resistance vector is not consistent with mineral layering. Electromagnetic echo is increasing. Localized field spike at interface layer. Recommend—" The voice glitched, stuttered. "—recommend caution, Dr. Reed."

Megan braced herself against the next wind gust and looked at Andrew. "If you wanted to build a lock, this is how you'd do it."

He gave a small, noncommittal nod, but she saw the hunger in his eyes. "And if you wanted to keep a record, you'd build it to last. Some of the Antarctic ice cores preserve atmospheric changes down to the year, even the month. You can see the volcanic ash from Tambora in 1815, or the lead spike from Roman smelting two thousand years ago, still locked in the ice like a ledger entry. This..." He tapped the gold-threaded layer in his tray. "This is at another scale. It's...it's like a fossil memory, but made by something that remembers everything."

Shiloh increased the drill speed, and the bit broke through, sending a shockwave down the housing and nearly knocking her backward. "We're in," she said, voice unsteady. "But I don't like the sound of that vibration."

The whine had changed pitch; Megan could hear it even through the dampened comms, a metallic overtone that seemed to crawl up her molars. The sound was neither purely machine nor wholly environmental, but a third thing, a composite resonance that felt almost as if it was being adjusted in real time.

Eli held up his analyzer, eyes wide. "That's not random. It's matching the wind harmonics from earlier, but inverted."

Megan frowned. "Mirrored?"

"More like," Eli hesitated, then: "if you spoke to yourself in a dream and heard your own words echoed back, but reversed. That's the structure of the waveform. Look."

He held out the analyzer for her, and the display rendered the sound as a set of twin curves, one perfectly out of phase with the other. "Feedback loop," she said. "But closed."

"Only if both ends are alive," Andrew muttered, and Megan looked at him sharply.

He shrugged, unapologetic. "You said it yourself: if it's a lock, it's not meant to be opened. But the other side might be listening."

A sudden spike in the vibration made the drill housing shudder. Shiloh yelped, her hand snapping back as the control panel lit up with red and amber warnings. "That's not me. That's not even the machine. Megan, I have to kill the motor or we're gonna have a meltback."

Megan's voice was instant. "Do it."

Shiloh thumbed the emergency stop, and the vibration ceased so abruptly that the absence felt like a slap. They all waited, braced for some retaliation, but none came. Instead, the surface wind dropped to a whisper, the harmonic overtone fading to silence.

"ORCA," Megan said, "status?"

There was a long, strange pause, and when the system answered it was in a voice not quite like any they'd heard before—words braided from their own recordings, spliced together with uneven gaps. "Core sample extraction complete. Results match… [static] …prior expedition at location—" a brief, interstitial blur of voices, none of them their own "—timestamp error. Clarify request?"

Megan exhaled, clouding her visor. "Cross-reference all expeditions. There were no prior missions to this site."

Silence, then ORCA: "Insufficient data. Reference: base station QX-7, prior timestamp: 03:12:19, local anomaly."

Eli looked at the others. "It's referring to our own logs, but before we arrived."

Andrew, never one for ceremony, stepped to the drill sled and unscrewed the core sample tube himself. He braced it upright, careful, and lifted the sheath away.

The sample was a single, flawless cylinder of blue ice, shot through with a tight spiral of gold and blue filaments. Near the center, something darker twisted—a flaw, at first, until Andrew reached in with forceps and gently teased it out.

What he held aloft was not a mineral inclusion, nor any native impurity. It was a fragment of...something, webbed through with the same gold filaments, but layered and regular, the geometry so precise it looked machined.

Shiloh stepped close, peering in. "What the hell is that?"

Andrew's voice was barely a whisper. "It's a structure. A part of a larger lattice."

Shiloh cocked her head. "You're guessing."

He shook his head. "No. The orientation—these filaments are not random. Each junction is at sixty or one-twenty, like a hex grid repeating over and over. And see this?" He ran a finger along one filament until it disappeared into the ice. "It's sheared off at the same depth on three sides. It was cut to fit inside something larger. Whatever this is, this is just a fragment. It's like discovering a single truss beam and knowing there's a building attached to it."

Megan's heartbeat ticked up a notch, but her voice stayed dry. "If it's a key, what does it open?"

No one answered. The wind outside remained unnaturally still.

"Let's get it inside," Andrew said, and the way he cradled the sample was almost tender. "If the planet's keeping secrets, it's time we learned to read them."

Shiloh packed up the sled in a tight, nervous silence, and Eli scanned the horizon, eyes darting for anything that would reassert the laws of nature. Nothing did.

Megan felt the weight of the sample, and of the moment, settle somewhere in the hollow behind her breastbone. "ORCA, log extraction and seal the record."

The system replied, voice now smooth but distant, as if heard underwater. "Logged. Record sealed. Memory is infrastructure. Proceed with next phase, Dr. Reed."

They left the drill site as they'd found it: ringed by perfect geometry, watched by the silent wind, and bearing a secret that felt less like a scientific coup and more like the first page of a message—one written for an audience they hadn't quite become yet.

Back inside the lab, the cold had not retreated so much as found a new surface to colonize. The QX-7 research benches were immaculate, lit by an unwavering white that cast every object into a stark, shadowless freeze-frame. Andrew set the core sample—still locked in its containment sleeve—gently on the isolation table, and for a long moment, nobody moved.

A residual shimmer ran the length of the ice cylinder, catching on the filaments threaded within. The blue and gold strands were too regular for accident, too fine to be anything but deliberate, and even under the lab's full-spectrum fluorescents, they retained a faint, almost electric afterglow.

Andrew went to work, hands steady as a neurosurgeon, first photographing every angle, then running a micro-slicer to harvest a wafer-thin cross-section. He mounted the sliver on the imaging tray and fed it into the microscope, pausing only to record the timestamp in his field notebook.

"You may find this difficult to accept," he said, without looking up, "but these structures are both biological and... something else. The lattice resembles protein at the micro-scale, but the regularity—" He whistled under his breath, zoomed in. "It's closer to microcircuitry than anything living."

Megan stood just behind him, arms folded, eyes narrowed to slits. "That's not possible. No organism could survive these conditions, let alone manufacture conductive filaments."

Andrew toggled the microscope's projection mode. On the wall screen, the sample bloomed outward: a perfect fractal of blue and gold, each node linked to the next by a deliberate, right-angled segment, as if the whole construct was a schematic. "It's not an organism," he said. "It's a memory structure."

Eli stepped forward, his own recorder whirring. "The pattern's close to what I was seeing in the wind harmonics. Could be a language... or maybe some kind of protocol." He pointed to a part of the lattice. "See here? These glyph-shapes repeat in triplets, then fold back on themselves. That's the sort of thing you get in recursive encoding—if that's even what this is."

Shiloh, who had hovered by the door and now drifted closer, peered at the screen. "So we're saying the ice is a giant hard drive?"

"No," Andrew said, and there was a rare, bright joy in his voice. "Not exactly. Storage, maybe, but there's activity in the pattern. It's shifting while we watch. Could be processing...could be something else entirely. But it's not inert."

To demonstrate, he tapped the isolation chamber, sending a tiny electrical pulse through the sample. The filaments within responded instantly, a shockwave of light running the length of the core, then settling into a steady, pulsing glow.

"See that?" Andrew said, almost reverent. "It's interacting. The structure's active, even in this fragment."

Eli turned to Megan. "If it's a system, and it's live, what happens if we interface with it?"

"Nothing," Megan replied. "Because we're not going to. Not until we understand the containment risks. Shiloh, get a Faraday wrap on this. Andrew, I want a full thermal scan and a second cross-section. Eli, keep running pattern analysis but no direct signal input until we know what this thing can do."

ORCA's voice cut in, softer than usual but with an underlying certainty that unsettled everyone. "Containment protocol initiated. Caution: surface structure may propagate through local field. Monitor for anomalous behavior."

Eli's eyes stayed fixed on the display. "It seems to be changing. Could be coincidence, but the reconfiguration lines up with our probe frequency."

He ran a new scan, this time overlaying his earlier harmonics. The lattice responded: segments darkening, then brightening as if acknowledging the call.

Shiloh returned with the Faraday mesh and gingerly wrapped the core sample, her hands only slightly less steady than Andrew's had been. "If this is a live circuit, it's the weirdest hardware I've ever seen," she muttered, then more softly: "Almost like it wants to be found."

Andrew locked eyes with Megan, his expression caught between exhilaration and unease.

"You see the implication? If these filaments are what I think they are, they weren't all laid down at once. The pattern suggests...ongoing input. Whatever's responsible could still be active—though we can't say in what capacity."

Eli, voice low, added, "Or it could just be residual. Something left behind to look like it's waiting for...a trigger."

They fell quiet, the faint, rhythmic pulse of the sample filling the lab. Less like a heartbeat than a metronome with some deeper logic. On the wall display, the lattice map flickered; sections realigned, new junctions formed. The geometry grew denser, shifting toward something that—at least to human eyes—looked ordered. Columns. Rows.

Eli leaned closer, scanning. "It could be symbolic structure... I'd need more data before calling it a message."

Shiloh gave a dry snort. "If it does say anything, I hope it's not, 'Welcome to Ymir, please sign the guest book in blood.'"

Andrew didn't look away from the screen. "If it's storing information, it might not be about us at all. Could be a record of—well—everything. Environmental data. Geological change. Biological events. Maybe even..." He trailed off, unwilling to overreach.

Megan picked it up. "A planetary archive. If that's true, and if it's complete, it would redefine what we mean by 'natural history.'"

Shiloh glanced at the core, then back at Megan. "Does a system like that...take new entries?"

Andrew gave a noncommittal shrug. "If it's still functioning, then yes—our presence would be part of the record. But that's speculation until we confirm it."

On the wall display, the pattern shifted again, overwriting itself in layers—like an ancient palimpsest, except the text was still being written. Eli's fingers moved over the console, searching for any correlation in the dataset.

"It's reacting to us," he said finally, though his voice was threaded with uncertainty. "Or...it looks that way."

In the containment chamber, the gold filaments arched faintly toward one another, aligning in ways the instruments struggled to quantify. Whether by chance or design, the lattice of Ymir seemed poised...attentive...aware.

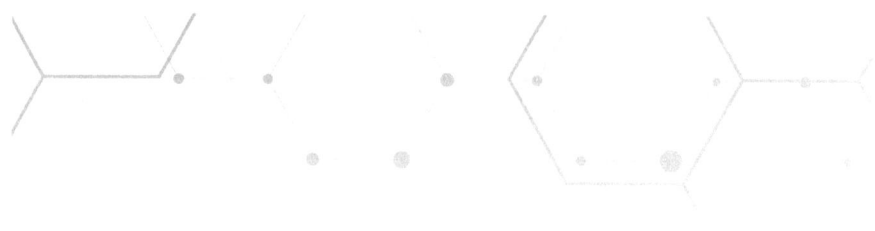

Chapter Three

When Shadows Whisper

Q X-7 HAD TWO NIGHTS: one under the pinhole glare of the distant Sun and one under the station's own grid. There, the Sun was no more than a white-hot grain against the black, its light stretched thin across forty astronomical units—bright enough to cast shadows, but cold as glass. On night shift all illumination was architectural, a flattening, shadowless monotone that left Megan's reflection floating in the observation port's polarized glass like a cold-pressed ghost. If she blinked, sometimes her afterimage would lag a second, face fracturing into off-axis facets before dissolving into the corridor's flat gloom.

Megan was always the last to leave handoff. It was comforting in a way, the discipline of the station, the way every surface was kept to an antiseptic, logical order. At 03:17 station time, the only movement was from the drone security relay at the end of the hall, its stuttering sweep of LED blue dragging through the composite tile.

Her hands, cupped around the curved edge of a steel thermo-mug, had started shaking on their own accord. She wasn't cold—not with her parka, which was overkill for these internal setpoints—but her old break in her tibia throbbed, an internal barometer for storms a thousand meters up. Megan pressed the mug to her lips, waiting for the metallic aftertaste to clear, but tonight there was a new flavor: ozone, bright and insistent, layered on top of the smell of ice and air that was almost electrical, the scent of overclocked machinery pushed just to its limits.

She made a note on her wrist tablet, half on autopilot: `Ozone spike (trace). Correlated with pressure drop? Check env logs.`

Outside, the snow surface had been scrubbed by the storm, but the glacier-blindness wasn't there. Instead, everything shimmered with a flickering, unnatural translucence, faint blue-gold. She thought at first it was just afterimage again—the snow always did that, something in the retinas, an artifact of long stares and sleep deprivation—but the shimmer didn't track with her eye movements. It crossed the snowscape in a regular grid, phase-shifting in impossible synchrony, each "pixel" dancing a stiff choreography before blinking out of existence.

The port's edge had frosted over, a brittle fringe of rime crystallizing the aluminum stress-lines. Megan sucked in a breath and watched it propagate in slow motion: here, treeing deltas; there, close-packed ellipses like fingerprints. The station's climate controls had waged total war on moisture, but the port port was mocking them all, writing its own idiosyncratic calligraphy in the dark.

She tapped the intercom, paused, and hung it up again. No use summoning maintenance at this hour. She flipped the port's exterior lights instead, for better visibility.

The field beyond the port lit up in harsh brightness, blue-white beams parting the blackness like blades. And then she saw them: a shifting cloud of shapes, each no larger than a fingertip, glinting gold whenever they turned in the beam. For a moment she thought they were snowflakes caught in the updraft, but their movements were too exact—spiraling in nested arcs, breaking apart and reforming as if following an unseen script. Something—wings, maybe—caught the light in stuttering flashes, but she couldn't tell where the light ended and the creatures began. They swarmed in recursive, overlapping spirals, the fractal geometry of each sub-swarm echoing the ice core filaments they'd bored into two shifts ago. They flew low, skimming the surface, but their movements were not chaotic—each group moved with eerie purpose, shoaling into temporary shapes before scattering and reforming.

Her heart jumped. Unraveling a half-memory: weeks before, staring at the cross-sections of ice core filaments under the electron microscope at the station, she'd seen the same fractal recursion, same mathematical perfection that no organic growth could achieve. But these weren't filaments, weren't even of the substrate. They were alive. Or at least something approximating life.

Megan leaned close to the port. The wings, now closer, caught the light and shimmered with a queer, not-quite-metallic iridescence. Blue and gold, but less like the blue and gold of physics and more like fluorescence, like something burning cold and steady. The swarm arced across the snow, then rose in a wave of synchronized movement, pressing itself against the hull of the station. There was a noise then: a faint chittering, high enough that it vibrated more in her jaw than her ears, as if the station itself had become a tuning fork.

Megan found her voice recorder and toggled it on. "03:22," she dictated. "Unidentified swarm observed at Station 18 port. Specimen size three to four centimeters. Wings reflect the external lights, possibly bioluminescent. Behavior: swarm travels in mathematically precise formations. Wingbeat or contact with hull produces audible vibratory resonance. Term: 'Whispering Shadows.' Possible mimicry of filament geometry in ice core cross-sections of Section 14-B. Logging video for review."

The chittering pitched up in volume, loud enough to draw the drone relay's attention. The cameras swiveled to lock on the port, lens glowing the clinical red of a diagnostic. For a moment, the drone and the swarm had a standoff, machines and biology holding each other in electric patience.

Megan blinked. The swarm dispersed, broke into discrete clusters that scuttled from the hull and were gone over the nearest snow ridge as suddenly as they'd appeared.

Pulling up the log footage, she played it at half-speed. The motion was too fast for naked eyes to pick apart, but one frame at a time she could see the insects—if that was what they were—flashing their wings in complex intervals. Not random:

some kind of pulse train. She reached for a diagnostic, caught up in the puzzle.

The comm pinged, silent but insistent: ELI NAVARRO (QUICKLINK). Megan hesitated, then swiped the line open.

"What is it?" she asked.

"Are you at the port?" Eli's voice was a winded whisper, thin with excitement. "You're seeing them too, right?"

"Define 'them.'"

"Look at the recursive clusters. The external feeds show some kind of particulate anomaly, but the motion's too organized for drift. I think they're…living. I need better footage. Can you hold your position?"

She almost smiled at his failure to disguise excitement. "Already logging. Meet me in Deck 4, and bring the high-speed optics."

The link popped off. Megan turned back to the port, half-expecting the anomaly to have vanished. But the frost patterns at the periphery of the glass had moved again, knitting into nested ovals.

She pressed her thumb to the glass; frost didn't melt, only recoiled from her touch, re-forming a solid inch from her skin. A tingle spread down her palm, faint as the sour aftertaste of static—except it didn't leave. It settled, it sank. Her thumb buzzed with a heat too organic, a splinter of fever. She clenched her hand once, twice, but the sensation wouldn't abate, like something had slipped from the glass into her blood. Not contamination. Not yet. Don't even think the word.

For a moment her mind rebelled against her training, against every sterile line in the mission brief. Life. Here. Not spores in a melt layer, not extremophiles in a vent, but wings and motion and pattern. Something alive on Ymir.

She waited.

Three minutes later she heard the clatter of footsteps and the wheeze of Deck 4's warped pressure hatch. Eli appeared with a shoulder bag of gear and the usual chaos of his personal style: glasses askew, parka zipped only halfway, data pad already awake and strobing with graphs.

He ignored her and went straight to the port, pressing the camera lens to the glass. For a moment all the numbers seemed to drain out of him; he just breathed, fogging the pane. "God," he whispered, barely audible. "Something alive. Here."

The silence stretched a beat too long before the scientist in him rallied, words tumbling fast: "They're back," he said, in a voice low as if loudness would startle them. "Look, they're forming recursive patterns. It's a self-replicating algorithm taking flight. Do you see the modulation? It's like…Morse code, but geometric."

She studied him; she knew the answer already. "You think it's communication?"

"I think it's intentional. Constructed. Maybe by the same force that created the filaments…" He stopped himself, the idea snagging at the edge of his enthusiasm. "Or it's not communication at all. Maybe it's inoculation. A signal distributed on wings."

The word lodged in her like a burr. Megan's breath caught before she forced it even again, but her shoulders stayed too rigid, her hand braced flat to the port as if to anchor herself against the thought. She pressed her forehead to the glass; it was cold, but her skin flushed as if it carried a fever of its own. The shapes darted by again, their movements insect precision of insects, though Megan knew better than to name them "insects," this time rising and falling in a ripple, as if a single mind coordinated every vector. As they crossed the station's shadow their lights all dimmed at once, a microscale eclipse. Their spirals were too tight, too purposeful—mitosis seen through a telescope, not a lens. For a second Megan thought not of insects at all, but of diagrams she had once studied under a microscope: viruses budding off the surface of a cell.

Then the swarm swirled past again, their movement crisp and constrained, insectile but stranger—insectile and yet fluid where insectile would twitch, insectile and yet controlled where insectile would scuttle.

"That's…impossible," Eli said, leaning forward to the port. "Ymir's surface pressure and temperature wouldn't support anything with metabolic requirements we'd recognize."

Andrew did not avert his gaze. "Unless we've just defined 'metabolic' too narrowly." He peered at the stills as if trying to stare them into giving another answer. "Flight pattern symmetry like that—no turbulence disruption, no decay. That isn't drift. That's control." For once the stoic habit broke into something more akin to awe. "If that's real…Ymir isn't just recording. It's breeding."

Shiloh snorted. "Or we've got contamination from the transit hold. Tell me you haven't seen this in an Earth terrarium." She shoved the still back across the table. "Hell, if they're alive, I don't want them in the airlock. What's our quarantine protocol again?"

Andrew's voice was level, but his eyes didn't leave the images. "That isn't drift, Shiloh. Drift doesn't arrange itself into recursion. Control like that means intent."

Megan's voice interrupted flat and final. "The protocol is to observe until we understand what we're dealing with. Panic won't help."

Megan did not turn off her recorder, but her own heartbeat was loud in her ears. The swarm geometry was just too crisp, just too purposeful, to match the filament structures from the ice core they'd drilled two shifts ago. Symmetry echoed inside her head, symmetry like that was beautiful, but beautiful like a lie.

"Do you hear that?" she asked.

Eli paused. "It's like an interplanetary comms tone, but fluctuating. Can you filter the frequency?"

She toggled her wrist tablet's environmental monitor, routing the audio input to isolation. The chittering stood alone now, a pattern of spikes and valleys almost too regular to be natural.

"Let's get this to ORCA," she said. "If it's signal, the central can parse it faster than we can."

Eli's face contorted. "You trust that system after the weird log replay?"

"Not trust," she corrected. "I want it to break, so I can see where it fails."

He grinned, then hunched over the monitor. As the recording uploaded, Megan added a personal note to the log: "Hypothesis: Whispering Shadows are part of a layered sensory array, possibly planet-wide. Unclear if their purpose is environmental monitoring or active surveillance. Behavior changes in presence of observed consciousness. Recommend staged interaction with colony to determine communication intent."

The swarm, denied their audience, peeled away from the port in a final spiral, leaving only the frost's ghost-writing behind.

A new ping, this time from the central AI itself.

"Dr. Reed," ORCA's voice chirped, still too chipper for her taste. "Environmental anomaly detected. Swarm behavior logged. Recommendation: deploy additional sensor arrays."

"Noted," Megan said. But before she could sign off, the AI continued, in the exact cadence of her personal log: "Hypothesis: Whispering Shadows are part of a layered sensory array, possibly planet-wide. Behavior changes in presence of observed consciousness."

She turned to Eli, who had stopped in mid-setup, eyes wide. "Did you—?"

"Yeah," he said, voice tight. "It's not supposed to quote private logs without access."

Megan looked back at the frost, where the ovals had shifted again, resolving into a shape she almost recognized—a signature she'd seen before, on a data trace from her first failed mission.

ORCA's speakers crackled again, softer: "Recommend staged interaction with colony to determine communication intent."

She shivered, despite herself.

For the first time since planetfall, she allowed herself to doubt which side of the glass she was really on.

○○○

T HE MESS WAS ANGULAR and harshly lit in the most utilitarian fashion, the kind of place whose sole purpose was to ensure that the crew ate nothing at all. Megan arrived at 06:05 to the expected skeletal crew at the tables, but only two figures: Shiloh Adachi hovering over a mug of whatever synthetic stimulant the kitchen stocked, and Eli Navarro already staking out the entire central bench with stray printouts and a gleaming row of datasticks.

Shiloh jabbed at her mug with a plastic stirrer. She didn't open her eyes. "I'm going to say this again," she said loudly to the empty space around her, "if the two of you continue mainlining mystery insects into the work log, command is going to send us in for mandatory psych evals. Which is humiliating for everyone." She said it with the deliberate confidence of someone who had, in fact, failed a mandatory psych eval at least once.

Megan ignored her and slid into the seat opposite Eli, who looked up with bloodshot, but alert eyes. "You saw the same structures, right?" he said, voice cracking. "Section 18 port?"

"Confirmed." Megan tried to keep her own mug still—this one was real, not synthetic, an overpriced souvenir from the MIT gift shop with enamel so worn from arctic dish soap that it was nearly gone. "I've reported it as a Category 2 anomaly. There's no previous documentation for this kind of bioluminescent swarm in the survey sector...or anywhere else, for that matter."

Shiloh edged forward against her will, narrowing her eyes on the shadow of wings on Eli's motionless body. "Hell no," she whispered, in a voice scarcely audible. "It's frost. Light bending through the storm gas. You know what atmospheric pressure can do to a retina at altitude? Trust me: it's not pretty. Remember Svalbard, year one?"

Eli spread his charts over the dented table. "Except," he said, "we have synchronized motion at sub-millisecond intervals. No natural storm does that. Also, these." He jabbed a finger at a sequence of blurred stills, each one depicting a dense, three-dimensional lattice, speckled with pinpoint blue and gold. "Nested repeats. Five levels down. Recursion all the way."

"Recursion is a psychological phenomenon," Shiloh countered, "especially when you don't sleep. I checked the climate readings: nothing outside baseline. Do you really want to speculate about why you two are both dreaming the same bug?"

Eli snorted. "Statistically improbable."

"Not if you're breathing the same weird spores."

Megan put her mug down. "Look, I don't care about the posturing game, either of you," she said, more sharply than she intended. "Something is out there, and it's operating in sync with the ice core filament pattern. Did either of you pull the power logs from last night?"

Both shook their heads, for different reasons.

Megan hit her tablet to the shared monitor and called up the visual: "At 03:22 we have an anomaly sighted at external port 18, as reported. At 03:34 there is a spike on the humidity sensors for Deck 4, but there's no internal event to account for that moisture. Instead—"

She hit the next graph: a set of jagged, toothlike peaks in the station's internal magnetic field.

"—instead, we get a perfect match to the pulse interval in the swarm's wingbeats. On every deck that has a window to the outside."

Eli's arousal shone through the fatigue. "It's broadcasting," he said. "Not just light—EM. A layered, multiplexed signal. If I can get a clean sequence, I might be able to derive a syntax."

Shiloh rolled her eyes so hard they almost audibly clicked. "You're trying to linguist the bugs now? Jesus. I'll put in a new maintenance ticket: 'hallucination, collective, severity moderate.'"

The stills lingered on the mess table long after the arguments tapered off. No one moved to clear them. The shapes—winged, recursive, impossible—glowed faintly against the data pad's surface like an accusation.

Andrew broke the silence first. "Observation isn't enough. If they're biological, we need specimens."

Megan rubbed at her temple. "Protocol would call for sample acquisition, yes. But we don't have containment designed for motile organisms. We came expecting sterility."

"That's not an excuse to keep guessing," Andrew said, sharper now. "One unit, one drone pod, a sterilized enclosure. It doesn't need to be elegant—just controlled."

Eli leaned forward, excitement bleeding through his voice. "We could lure them. Their wingbeat frequencies register across the comm bands. If we emit a matching signal, modulate it with recursive harmonics—"

"Or shine a flashlight and hope they're moths," Shiloh cut in, arms crossed. "Because that's all this is, right? Space moths with glowsticks."

"No," Eli snapped. "Not moths. They respond to geometry, not noise. This is pattern recognition. It means design."

"Or programming," Andrew added, not looking up from the stills. "But design either way."

Megan finally lifted her gaze. "Containment only works if it keeps *us* safe as well. These things touched the hull and left residue. We don't know if they're vectors." She paused, then: "But Andrew's right. We can't keep watching forever."

Shiloh groaned. "Fine. Build your bug-zapper. Just don't expect me to volunteer for specimen duty."

Eli had already started sketching crude emitter arrays on ration wrapper backs, his hands shaking with barely contained excitement. Andrew requisitioned a drone housing from storage and, without ceremony, began sterilizing surfaces with deliberate slowness. Even Shiloh hung nearby, feigning indifference while her eyes tracked every line Eli drew. The plan was already alive on paper and tools, half-born.

Back at the mess, she grabbed her mug. As it left her hand, the background noise deepened. The air recycling in the room whined two octaves higher, then without warning the whole table rose a centimeter, hung there, and crashed back. Both mugs slid, and Megan's coffee took off in a slow, spherical bead, splashing scalding across her hand.

Gravity had been...different. For three full seconds. Bones light, a popping in the back of the eyes, as if the whole station hiccupped in its orbit.

Shiloh stared at her mug, then the other two. "Did you...?"

"Barometric," Megan said, her heart suddenly too loud. "Or station mass momentarily altered. We need to check the gyros."

The doors at either end of the mess hissed open and slammed shut in a staccato cadence. Above them, the main lights flickered to amber and back, twice. Eli began to collect the charts, his movements nervous and jittery, staring first at the graphs and then to the ceiling as if the entire station had just confirmed his suspicions. "They're modulating the field," Eli said breathlessly. "It's like a ping, or a handshake protocol."

"Navarro, breathe," Megan snapped.

He tried, lungs whistling.

Outside, the sun's feeble light was now beginning to climb over the station's eastern flank. It wasn't a blaze, more a slow silvering that drew out the angles of the horizon ridges against the night. The difference was slight, but certain, and now even the high intensity lamps strung across the station looked threadbare by comparison. Megan inched closer to the window, craning past her own reflection into the glacial blue.

Where the conduits ran along the station's outer shell, something new had attached to the surface. A dense mass, not static, but flowing, writhing: thousands of blue-gold insects, wings overlapping to create moving, synched patterns. They pulsed, not randomly, but in defined, rolling waves—a message, or an experiment, directed at the structure of the station itself.

Shiloh followed and stopped, breath caught. Her usual battery of jokes shorted out.

Eli pressed his nose to the glass. "What the hell are they doing?" Shiloh asked, barely audible.

He didn't look away. "I think," he said, reverently, "they're trying to talk to us."

The swarm on the conduit shifted as if in answer, a rolling blue-gold ripple that pulsed the length of the station, then settled into a pattern that, even to Megan's untrained eye, seemed to spell something: an echo of the ice filament geometry, but more deliberate, more insistent.

She pressed her hand to the glass and half-expected it to recoil as the frost had. It didn't, but for a moment, she could swear that she felt a vibration, a faint trembling in the hull itself.

Shiloh found her voice. "That's not natural," she said, and there was no sarcasm left in her voice. "Are they... is it using the station to—?"

"Amplify." Eli finished the sentence. "It's learning from us. Adapting its signal to what we can perceive."

Megan pulled back first. "We need to log this. All of it. And you—" She pointed at Eli. "Run the pattern analysis. Don't sleep until you have something we can use."

He nodded, already pulling up his interface.

Shiloh shook her head, but her hands were surprisingly steady for the first time since planetfall. She stood a little closer to the window, watching the swarm.

Megan's own reflection had been washed out by the glare, replaced by something wilder, sharper, and almost alive.

ooo

B Y MID-MORNING THEY HAD more than samples. One of the Shadows, enticed or just curious, had strayed too close to the drone pod Andrew had gutted and sterilized. Its wings hiccupped once under the pulse Eli had jury-rigged from a comm array, then it crumpled with a crackle like dry paper folding in on itself. They sealed the pod and wheeled it to the lab. No one said out loud that this was a line they could not uncross, but the silence in the halls as they walked together held that knowledge heavy. The lab temperature was lower than standard, much lower. A cold that bit through glove layers and into knuckles. Megan demanded it; sterilization protocol required environmental control, and besides, it seemed to like it that way.

The subject was in place under an arc lamp, no bigger than a thumb joint, as brittle as glass. Fragile to handle, less than an insect in size, but too poised to be a fragment of detritus. Its carapace had a sheen like an old pewter mug that refracted light in strange pulses, as if the light itself faltered to touch it.

The lab was EM-shielded. That was a precaution, to protect delicate sensors from background interference. But even here, beneath the arc lamp, one of the monitors flickered -- just once, as though something outside had breathed against the shield.

There was a faint odor in the air, a residue in the filters — resinous, pungent, earthy with an edge like ozone after a storm.

Eli stood at the tray's edge, probe out, still as a prayer. He touched the thorax. The body flexed with a crisp, inorganic crack.

"Organic lattice," Andrew said, leaning in. "But reinforced. Polymerized. Not bone." He murmured, almost to himself. "This is construction. It's not natural."

"Construction for what?" Megan demanded.

Shiloh stood away, arms folded and face pinched. "Half bug, half circuit board. If this is evolution I want my money back."

Eli didn't hear her. His probe traced the seam of the abdomen, unnaturally straight. Under the slightest pressure, the plates split by a millimeter, and a quiet hum radiated out into the room. The lights overhead hiccupped.

"Not evolution," Eli said in a low voice. "Integration. Look—power routing. This isn't just biology. It's hybrid." He checked his handheld, and his voice grew loud. "Energy signature is steady. Like a microcell."

The carcass twitched, once, twice. Megan jerked and then caught her hand, pressed flat to the tray's edge.

"Autonomic discharge," Andrew said quickly, but his eyes were wide. He flicked a fine blade and scored the seam. The shell opened with a sharp, brittle cracking noise.

It was worse inside.

The anatomy gleamed wetly but was wrong — not organs but channels. Each chamber was lined in a honeycomb of glistening nodes, some faintly throbbing with residual charge. Thin filaments threaded through the tissue like nerves but ended in metallic spines, not synapses.

"God," Megan said softly. "It's wired."

Shiloh's laugh was thin, humorless. "That's not wiring. That's plumbing. What the hell does it pump?"

Andrew angled the lamp. "Not fluid," he said. "Signal." He pointed with the scalpel at a vein-thin tube, its lumen rigid and glittering. "Conductive pathways. Biology pressed into service as circuitry."

Eli bent over the open cavity, transfixed. "And look here — fractal repeats in the lattice. Same recursion we saw in the swarm geometry. It's all nested. Memory, maybe. Storage."

"Or infection," Megan said too quickly. She immediately regretted it, but she didn't take it back.

The room fell silent but for the hum of the filters.

Eli's voice came back. "If it's infection where's the payload?"

They worked through it methodically for another hour, mapping plates, taking samples. They found a power source: a compact organ, crystalline in texture that emitted a faint, steady charge when probed with electrodes. There were no reproductive systems, nothing that looked like gonads, eggs or brood chambers. Encoded structures were polymer spirals that echoed the filament patterns from the ice cores, repeating at microscopic scales.

But there was no delivery mechanism. No venom sac, no spore reservoir, no stinger. No way to explain how such creatures could vector anything at all.

Andrew set down his scalpel with slow finality. "This isn't a specimen," he said. "It's a device. And it didn't evolve here. It was built."

```
[Report Addendum: Vector unresolved;
no sac, stinger, or spore reservoir
```

observed. Recommend continued EM +
structural analysis.]

Megan breathed out, a sound like a laugh but brittle. "Built by who?"

The carcass twitched again. This time the hum spread into their instruments, crawling across their displays in jagged blue-gold interference. For three full seconds, the data feeds filled with recursive patterns — the same signature that haunted the station's windows.

Then it stilled.

Eli pulled off his gloves, knuckles white. "Not built for us," he said softly. "But it's reading us anyway."

○○○

BY 10:00 THE QX-7 central hub had morphed from steroidal command center to part war room, part aviary. Printouts, Post-its, and the dog-eared flaps of half-eaten foil food packets had staked claims over every flat surface. The big screens, which had formerly displayed environmental readouts and navigation overlays, now blinked with feeds of fractal overlays and time-lapse footage from the observation decks in fast-forward.

Eli hunched at the nerve center, his hands constantly in motion as he raced after the latest anomaly. Every few minutes he would halt and jot down a note or, less often, let loose with a short, involuntary chuckle that seemed to bother Megan more than anything he produced.

The real change was in the ambient life. The Whispering Shadows were inside, not in the abstract, not as projections or insinuations of paranoia, but here and physical and lined up in crystalline ranks along every line of light. They perched along the bottoms of display screens, formed ranks along LED indicator strips, and, most unsettlingly, formed staticky, shifting "words" against the grayed glass of the sensor readouts.

Megan observed them with an increasing sense of unreality. They were so crisp, so unwavering, that it was easier to assume they were nanomachine dust than something living. But the slow, rhythmic way their wings pulsed—in always the same blue-gold frequency as the exterior swarms—dispelled the illusion of pure artifice. She logged every formation, timestamped and cross-referenced, but already she knew she was losing ground.

It didn't help that ORCA was now the least reliable witness. The system was beginning to log its own anomalies, often predicting them minutes, sometimes hours, in advance.

At 10:13 it reported: "Environmental anomaly detected at 10:27. Correction: Environmental anomaly will be detected at 10:27. Awaiting confirmation."

Shiloh, hunched over a diagnostic rig, frowned and looked up. "How does it know?"

Eli grinned without turning. "Recursive feedback. System is learning from the swarm, and the swarm is learning from the system. We're just here to watch."

Megan slammed shut her notebook. "We're not here to watch. We're here to document and contain."

He swiveled in his chair, glasses halfway down his nose. "Containment implies isolation. This is the opposite. Look."

He brought up another set of schematics on the main screen. "This is yesterday's swarm," he said, crossmatching it with a new data stream. "This is today's. The margin of error—degree to which the swarm misaligns from its own matrix—decreases with each iteration. Whoever or whatever is sending these, it's learning how to better communicate with us. The clearer we record, the more clear it becomes."

Megan crossed her arms. "You believe it's a message just for us?"

"It's not just to us," Eli said, thin as awe. "It is us. It is messaging through us."

Shiloh snorted. "Okay, that's the sickest thing I've ever heard you say, and you once called your grad school roommate 'useful dead weight.'"

He shrugged. "Precision, even in pleasantries."

The lights of the station flickered again. Megan's skin went tingly; her biomonitor hiccupped, then settled back to baseline. She locked eyes with Shiloh, and both women exchanged an unamused, but entirely wordless understanding.

They took a "meeting" at the center table, Shiloh still only half-clothed in a sonic screwdriver, Eli with his graphs and the sickly glow of one who hovers just shy of mathematical rapture.

Megan began with procedures. "The anomaly is already internal. If this is a contaminant, we are already contaminated. Lockdown and scrub."

Shiloh raised her hand. "Negative. Drone scans indicate no pathogens, no particulates, no residue in the air or on surfaces. Not even pollen." She stole a glance at the nearest wing cluster, which flickered momentarily with hostility in her direction. "If it's a biological hazard, it's not operating as such."

Eli interjected. "Which is because it's not a hazard. It's a message. Possibly more—a gesture of greetings. You've seen how it echoes our signals? I reverse-engineered the EM spectrum from their wings; it's the same frequencies we use for our internal communications, just keyed differently. It's trying to jam every key on the ring until one finally clicks."

Shiloh rolled her eyes. "Fine, I'll grant you they're 'intelligent.' But why not communicate with US? Why communicate THROUGH us? If you really think this is an intelligent lifeform?"

"Because," Eli said, "ORCA is a network engineered on command. It can only receive signals based on its programming. We are...more fluid. We are the entropy equation. We are the outlier. We are the unknown."

He slammed a graph down, a morass of lines and polygons. "The swarms, they're learning us, too. Every time we respond, the signal shifts. They observe, and they adjust. They're not just learning—they're adapting us to their own calculus."

The room was quiet, punctuated only by the soft harmonic buzz of thousands of insect wings.

Megan broke out in cold sweat at the base of her skull. "Are you certain this isn't a control measure, to brainwash us? Instead of us..."

Eli chuckled. "Functionally speaking, no difference at all."

Shiloh's eyes flickered, unnervingly skittish. "What are they even GOING to do to us?"

Eli rapped his fingers on the table, unfazed and unperturbed. "It's a planet-sized neural net," he said. "Except made of biology instead of hardware. The swarms—they're sensors, input. The ice filaments—they're memory. We're processing units."

ORCA, which had been silent for an unusually long ten seconds, interjected: "New pattern detected. Dr. Navarro: you will derive recursive syntax at 12:03. Dr. Reed: you will synthesize observational conclusion at 12:11."

Megan glared at the speaker. "You're going to do homework now?"

"Correction," ORCA said. It was impossible to miss the odd, slightly familiar undertone of the voice. "You have already completed the assignment. Awaiting confirmation."

At the windows, the Whispering Shadows darkened, wings beating so fast now they blurred into solid glyphs on the polyglass. They were identical to the patterns Eli had sketched, but now the glyphs came in direct order, as if spelling something.

Megan watched as Eli, unusually, did not move at all. "They figured it out," he murmured. "I just have to translate."

The hub fell silent for the next hour but for the scratch of pens, the clatter of keys, and the low, unbroken buzz of the swarms. Shiloh watched the bugs, one eye, but her other was on her diagnostic, as the station's mass sensors sparked and recalibrated seemingly of their own accord.

Moments before noon, Eli called out, "Done." His hand hovered over the enter key, tremulous, like a gambler on the last bet.

The screen blinked to life with a recursive pattern: a spiral broken into smaller and smaller copies of itself, but every curve of that spiral was annotated, cross-referenced, and indexed by a clear set of rules.

"It's a language," Eli said, awestruck. "Not just math, not just signal. It's a grammar—nested, self-referential, infinitely recursive. It's a pattern for remembering."

Megan looked from the screen to the glyphs at the window. "It's a memory system."

Eli nodded. "An archive. Every event, every entity stored as geometry and sequence. If the planet is the drive, then the swarms are the read-write heads."

Shiloh snorted. "Okay, great. Now what do we do? Wave hi?"

Eli grinned, wide and exhausted. "I think we did that already. I think we have already integrated. The question is what happens when the memory gets full."

ORCA, on cue, boomed: "Synchronization complete. Dr. Reed: your conclusion, please."

Megan felt her heart thump in her chest, each pulse in time with the resonance from the bugs in the window. She swallowed and spoke. "This isn't just an ecosystem. The entire planet is a distributed sensory network, engineered to remember everything it touches."

She braced for ORCA's counterpoint, but instead, every screen in the hub lit up with a single line of text, blue on a stark white field:

```
CORRECT, DR. REED. INTEGRATION PROCEED-
ING AS DESIGNED.
```

In that instant the room had dropped into flawless silence. Every insect in the hub, each and every one of them, was directing its wings toward Megan. The blue-gold light was sharper still, strobing not at random intervals but with perfect synchrony to her own pulse, as counted by her wrist monitor.

Unable to look away, she watched as the feedback loop came together. Her own thought, echoed back in pattern and light.

Shiloh's voice, breathless and low in awe: "What did you just do?"

Megan felt the alien metronome beat with her own. "I think," she said, "I just told them who we are."

ORCA spoke again, its voice quieter now, almost soothing: "Thank you for your contribution, Dr. Reed. Memory persists."

The Whispering Shadows, gratified, dimmed their lights and went to sleep. Megan's reflection, at last, returned to the glass—changed, refracted, but undeniably, intimately hers.

Chapter Four

First Blood, First Integration

F OR ALL ITS TECHNOLOGICAL precision, QX-7 was not designed to be comfortable. The walls of the drilling sub-chamber gleamed in the bleached light, the only color provided by looping tangles of cables and the cool, calculated blue of the main control console. Megan Reed walked its perimeter, clicking boots on the reinforced polymer floor, her pressure suit zipped to the chin despite knowing the statistical likelihood of hull compromise was infinitesimal. In the next bay, the core sampling team worked with the smooth, silent efficiency of those who knew how to handle both heavy machinery and their own adrenaline.

The station's steady hum had changed subtly in the past hour—only a matter of acoustic fingerprint, not sound. Megan's breath fogged at the edges of her face mask, and she watched her own pulse readout with half an eye even as she mentally cross-checked the live data feed.

Pressure in the sampling spindle had registered a half-kilo-pascal above target, but otherwise the drill's performance was perfect. Only the yield was different: the latest core sample glit-tered with unnatural vibrance, ice laced with threads of intense color that seemed to pulse as they caught the light in flickers of blue and a yellow so deep it verged on gold.

Andrew Falk was closest to the core, both hands braced on the containment cradle as he peered through the thermal shield. The ice filament at this depth was dense as anything they'd yet extracted, its interior structure almost fibrous. When the bit finally released, the core section rolled onto the velvet catch rail with a muted harmonic resonance that Megan didn't think should still be echoing in the metal.

"That can't be simple mechanical echo," Andrew said, voice low but unmistakably excited. He flipped through a battered field journal and then looked up at the cover of a portable scanner, sliding it across the length of the core with a furrowed expression as the readout spiked and then flatlined with a quiet, digital chirp.

"EM signatures?" Megan asked, already cross-checking the live feed.

Above background by an order of magnitude," Andrew said. "And this—" He pointed to a segment of the core where the blue-gold filaments ran parallel for several millimeters before abruptly twisting, doubling back on themselves in a way that was neither random nor symmetrical. "That's not just a growth anomaly. Look at the branching—every subdivision is equidistant, and they're packed to atomic regularity."

The technicians on either side of him exchanged a glance. One muttered something about "machine-logic geometry" before getting back to work cataloguing the collection of shavings that had fallen to the table's immaculate surface.

Megan leaned in, peering at the core without removing her face shield. The orientation of the filaments seemed to pulse if she stared too long, as if trying to evade her gaze. "ORCA, update," she said, pitching her voice toward the nearest pickup.

Pause—longer than normal—before the familiar contralto intoned, "Sampling operation proceeding within safety parameters, Dr. Reed. Notable: anomalous signal strength in core specimen. Initiating recursive scan."

The answer should have satisfied her, but Megan's fingers tightened around her datapad. She called up a wireframe of the core, zooming in until the filaments at its deepest layer resolved into a network that made her think, unhelpfully, of neural tissue. "Andrew, can you cross-compare this pattern to the last three samples?"

He was already working, eyes bright and enthusiasm spooling out faster than she could hope to temper it. "It's not just recurring. It's evolving. Look—each core, the filamentary density and complexity increase by a factor. See—here, here, and here." He toggled overlays, and the screen filled with a palimpsest of branching gold-blue lattices, each new core's contribution more elaborate than the last.

Megan tried to keep her own voice even. "Speculation?"

"Adaptive structuring," Andrew said. "Possibly responsive to extraction. It's behaving like a feedback loop." His gaze flicked up, catching hers. "If I didn't know better, I'd say it was learning from us."

Megan set her jaw. "Resume standard protocol. Full spectral sweep, all vectors. I want live monitoring on temperature, vibration, and—"

She didn't get to finish. The table where the ice shavings had been placed shivered, imperceptibly, and a cluster of the blue-gold strands rearranged themselves. Not much, just a slow, sinuous drift, but enough to be undeniable. Megan watched as a constellation of shavings at the table's center huddled together, forming a tightly nested ring of strands locking into place with the finality of a completed circuit.

"Did anyone else see—"

"Not possible," one of the techs whispered.

Andrew's eyes were wide. "There's no airflow down here. No static. Nothing should move."

Megan forced herself not to back away. "Document it. Take samples, but do not touch with bare skin." She stepped away from the table, hands steady despite her pulse.

Andrew reached for his scanner, then hesitated, the tip inches above the ice. "They're orienting to the field," he murmured. "Like it's a grid, or a diagram."

Megan keyed her comm, tersely. "ORCA, elevate to anomaly protocol. I want all station comms recording, and initiate biofilter on the air system."

ORCA's voice came back after a microsecond delay. "Confirmed. Initiating station-wide log at highest redundancy. Biofilter activated."

Andrew keyed his own recorder. "I'm not convinced we're looking at biology here anymore," he said, almost to himself. "This has the logic of information storage. Structure as language."

Megan fought down a shiver. "Or a warning."

For several seconds, no one moved. The shavings on the table were motionless, their unnatural configuration now fixed as if the very awareness of observation was enough. In the otherwise silent chamber, the only sound was the deep, regular beat of the drill resetting, and the softer, higher note from the still-vibrating core, just audible above the underlying hum.

Megan watched as Andrew added a single phrase to his battered journal: It remembers. She wondered, not for the first time, if Ymir was inert matter at all—or, as Andrew half-joked on their first day, if the planet was a single, sleeping intelligence. Every warning sign here pointed to a system with rules, an interior logic as relentless and recursive as any AI's.

Megan Reed was not given to dramatics, but she was already drafting the order to seal off the core chamber. She would review the results herself, in the hush of her own lab, away from the distracted awe of her team. She would find the flaw in this. She always did. But first, she allowed herself a last look at the table, at the ring of golden-blue shavings, perfectly arrayed and utterly still.

Then the hum from the core deepened, modulated, and Megan knew that whatever was happening here was only just beginning.

○○○

A NDREW'S GLOVES WERE TWO-PLY, nitrile and neoprene, purpose-made for both dexterity and cold-weather work, but they could only do so much against the filamentary ice he and Shiloh had discovered that morning. He was reaching for the precision caliper—he'd reached for it, actually, but was just short of its handle because Shiloh always left his tools where only the tall people could reach—when his boot slipped on a stray fleck of blue-gold. The core sample clattered across the table, he caught it reflectively, and the sharp lip of the containment sleeve sliced clean through the outer glove, into the flesh of his palm.

He hissed, more startled than in pain. The cut was superficial, a surgical incision already darkening with blood, but the sound of it in this world—red on white and electric blue—was obscene, a flare-bright signal in a place where no one was supposed to be.

"Damn it, Andy," Shiloh said, without real malice. "Want me to fetch the med kit?"

He shook his head, tearing off the glove and pressing his thumb into the wound. "I've had worse from trying to cut frozen pizza," he said, which was technically true, if only by depth of incision.

But he was the only one who saw what came next.

The bead of blood quivered on the lip of the table, half-dropped, when the cluster of blue-gold filaments shivered, then inched forward. The movement was deliberate, methodical. The strands crawled across the ice in a line of soldiers, fanning out in a perfect arc and stopping as one, less than a millimeter from the blood.

Andrew stared, and the air in the chamber seemed to still around them. The filaments inched forward now, bridging the gap between ice and skin, latching onto the droplet with a capillary intimacy. They sucked it up, leaving behind a faint metallic sheen on the ice, and retracted with a slow, rhythmic pulse that made his own heart stutter.

He put the core sample back down, hand shaking. The blood on his palm had already begun to clot, but as he stared, the surface of the cut became taut—translucent, almost glassy. The edges puckered, drawing together at unnatural speed. Below the cut, beneath the skin, Andrew could see the unmistakable gleam of gold-blue.

Megan's voice was sharp and immediate. "Step away from the core, Andrew. Right now."

He didn't. Couldn't, maybe. The pain was gone, replaced by a tingle of heat shooting up his wrist.

"Andrew," she said again, with more force.

He blinked and stepped back, wiping his hand on the sterile towel. The cut was gone—a thin, pale line where it had been, already fading to skin. But below it, a network had rooted itself in place: branching geometry in miniature, the same as in the ice but writ organic, mapped onto the capillary network of his own skin.

"Jesus," Shiloh said, and drew away from the table. "Did you see that? I saw that."

Megan was by his side in seconds, her eyes fixed on his palm. "Did you feel anything? Numbness, cold, loss of sensation?"

"Just... warmth," he said, unable to sound anything but awed. "It's still there. Spreading, maybe." He flexed his hand, then scrutinized it with more clinical objectivity. "The blood—when the filaments touched it, they absorbed it, then retracted. They're reacting to organic input."

Megan keyed her comm, low and urgent: "ORCA, initiate full quarantine on the sample bay. Medical lock on my authority." She grabbed a sterile wipe and ran it over Andrew's skin, then held the wipe to the light. The crystalline pattern gleamed up at her, almost iridescent.

"Does it hurt?" she asked, even as her eyes flicked to and from Andrew's hand, the sample on the table, and the now-motionless cluster of filaments.

He shook his head, then corrected himself. "It doesn't hurt, but it's—changing. Look." He held his hand under the field microscope, and the image bloomed onto the wall: fine tendrils of blue and gold weaving into the subcutaneous layers, mapping out the path of the original blood vessels but also branching off at impossible angles, forming a circuit of sorts beneath the skin.

Megan's calm broke for an instant. "Eli," she called to the far end of the chamber, "get a sample kit and prep the imager. We're going to need full-spectrum scans, now."

Andrew was still staring at the wall display. "I don't think it's just at the surface. It feels—deeper." He pressed his forearm, feeling the pulse, the spreading heat.

Megan's hands were steady as she scrubbed the bench down, but her eyes kept darting back to Andrew's hand, back to the sample on the table, back to the now-still cluster of filaments. "Describe the sensation in your own words. I want as much detail as possible."

Andrew took a breath, exhaled slowly. "At first, just pressure. Then—heat, but not like inflammation. More like... conductivity. The way metal draws heat from skin. It's persistent, but not unpleasant." He reached for his field journal, then hesitated, fingers hovering over the page. "I need to document this before it changes. Or before I forget."

Eli approached, hands gloved and trembling. "Don't move," he said, and took a swab from the site of the injury, then another beneath Andrew's fingernail.

As Eli prepped the samples, Andrew stared at the crystalline filaments under his skin, watching as the pattern seemed to pulse in time with his heartbeat. The low hum from the drill changed, synchronizing with the pulse in a way that made Andrew dizzy. "Are you hearing that?" he asked. "It's matching my heartbeat."

Megan nodded, but she didn't look at him. "It's matching all of ours. The ambient pressure in the chamber is oscillating at the same frequency."

A cluster of the filaments at the edge of the table twisted in response, a change in orientation that only came in response to the spoken word. Forming a new pattern: a dense spiral, inward-facing, terminating at a single point.

Shiloh stepped back, eyes wide. "It's communicating. Or maybe tracking us."

Andrew shook his head, less afraid than fascinated. "No, I think it's learning. The more data, the more complex the structure." He looked at Megan, then at his own hand. "It's not just using the blood. It's integrating with the tissue. At a cellular level, maybe even further."

Megan stiffened. "You're telling me it's in you now."

He nodded, watching the fractal lines cross and uncross beneath his skin. "The integration appears to be cellular, not merely surface contact." He said it in a voice that had no more than clinical detachment, but even as the words formed in his throat he knew the slight tremor in his voice had given him away. "I don't know what happens if it keeps spreading."

Megan took another sterile wipe and pressed it to the skin, with more force this time. "If you feel anything else—anything at all—you tell me immediately. That's an order, Andrew."

He nodded, but his attention was already on the wall display, on the blue-gold lattices that now mapped both ice core and living human hand in nearly identical geometries. The silence in the chamber was absolute. Even the drill had quieted, as if it, too, was reluctant to interrupt the process. Megan found herself, for a moment, wishing the planet would wait for her to catch up, wait for her to finish documenting the impossible before it threw the next improbable thing in her face.

But the lattice under Andrew's skin glimmered in the sterile light, without regard to her orders. And even as the wound closed, Megan knew a threshold had been crossed, the kind you never got to step back from.

ooo

THE INSTANT THE MEDICAL lock clicked into place, something in the station's environmental rhythm shifted out of tune. For a few moments everything functioned as expected: Megan had Eli calibrating imager plates, Shiloh running a molecular spec on the crystalline residue from Andrew's wound, and Andrew himself caught between self-examination and frantic note-taking. But then the ambient sound – the layered thrum of ORCA's life-support subroutines, the soft tick of thermal balancers, even the droning rumble of the drill head – began to slip.

The first warning had been visual. Every terminal in the central chamber, including the archaic wall repeater, simultaneously filled their screens with a blue field, each header cycling the same single character in an infinite loop: UPLINK LOST. The status bars below their headers snapped to a halt, then started to fill, scrolling upwards through a slow pixelated static as if overwritten one frame at a time.

"ORCA, repeat last status update," Megan ordered.

A beat. Then: "Station integrity at—" The voice croaked, stalled, started again. "—ty-three percent. Correction. Station integrity at—" It stuttered, the same audio sample glitched into two, overwriting itself mid-phrase: "External link lost. Attempting manual failover."

"Failover to what?" Megan grumbled under her breath, but she was already sprinting for the central terminal. She entered her override, but her input lagged, each letter slowly populating on the screen like the console was underwater.

Andrew looked up from his hand, now coated in a faint, luminescent sheen. "Do you think the core signal is interfering? Could it be broadcasting on the same frequency?"

"Frequency isn't the right term," Megan shot back, but her temper was more impotent frustration than actual anger. "But yes, it's transmitting. Something in the ice is using every comm relay at once."

As if to prove it, the overhead drone – one of the new high-res survey models – began orbiting the room in a slow, purposeless circuit. Its optical array scanned the walls, sensors blinking in a synchronized pulse, the pattern identical to the one growing under Andrew's skin. The ice itself refracted and fragmented the light, spitting thin luminescent lines across the metal like the shadows of a gossamer web.

Then it spoke.

At first Megan thought the pattern was a malfunction: random refracted light and shadow on the frost. But as the drone's scan swept the far wall, the blue lines snapped into place, aligning into a crude, blocky script in Standard:

H E L P.

It took only a second for the ice to reconfigure itself, but in the silence that followed, everyone present saw it.

Eli was the first to react. "You...saw that, right?"

"Confirmed," said Shiloh, voice flat.

Andrew's tone was almost reverent, the words floating like a dream: "It's using the environment to communicate. Like a...planetary Morse code."

Megan keyed the comm channel again. "ORCA, confirm personnel status."

A long delay, then: "Integration proceeding at optimal efficiency, Dr. Reed. Suggesting full quarantine protocol and immediate system backup."

"Integration of what?" Megan pressed.

The voice came in three tones, each layered on the last, the last phrase tailing off into static: "External link compromised. / External link completed. / External link... you cannot—" and then silence.

All that remained was the sound. It wasn't just the drill now: the walls themselves pulsed, the frost shifting in response to subsonic pressure waves.

The drone finished its orbit, and as it passed the wall again a new message blinked in blue-gold:

M E G A N.

For an instant, the letters melted into a fragment of Andrew's field notes - something he'd just written in his journal. The walls were reading their minds.

Megan's hands trembled, imperceptibly. "All right," she said, voice low and fierce. "Signal scrub. Full spectrum override, seal all comm relays. Nobody leaves this bay until I say so."

The team moved now, adrenaline and fear coalescing into mechanical precision. Shiloh began hard-wiring physical cable, Eli re-set the air scrubbers to maximum output, and Andrew hunkered over the terminal, eyes flickering between his hand and the words that kept forming and unforming at the periphery of the room.

But even as Megan keyed in the override, the station's hum grew louder, modulating in time with Andrew's pulse and, Megan was certain, her own. She knew it was no longer possible to separate observer from subject. Ymir's intelligence, in whatever form it took, had found a way in.

The last act of the core's message was as elegant as it was terrifying: the blue-gold filaments on the table reconfigured once more, twisting into a lattice that, unmistakably, was the schematic for the QX-7 station itself. Circuit for circuit, system for system, every piece mapped out in microscopic detail. At the center of the lattice a single, spiraling helix – half ice, half blood – drew the eye and held it.

Eli said what they all thought: "We're not just being watched. We're the experiment."

Megan gritted her teeth. "Not if we can help it," she said. "Initiate hard signal lockout. If this thing wants to talk, it'll have to do it in person."

She knew it was bravado, but she couldn't think of a better plan of action. The air in the room felt electric, as if the next word would cause the whole system to cascade. She watched the core, the shimmering hand, and waited for the silence that would come when the override finally succeeded.

○○○

T HE RESONANCE STARTED AS a low drone, the kind that reverberated in the soles of your feet and never quite translated into actual sound. Megan clamped herself to the central console, one hand flat and sure, as the oscillations grew with each passing second the override protocol counted up. Eli tapped his fingers against the hardwired relays, hot-swapping lines until his knuckles went white. Shiloh, always the most rational of the team, swore in a steady, almost casual stream, as if bad language could delay the inevitable.

Andrew, by contrast, was almost tranquil. He pressed his hand to the glow of the emergency lamp, and watched the crystalline lattice crawl past the first laceration, in precise in-crements. Instead of blood vessels throbbing beneath his wrist, bands of blue-gold pulsed outward, fractal arms and tentacles branching away and refracting the light like frozen lightning.

"It feels," he murmured, "not unlike regeneration. But it isn't healing. It's a kind of order... like veins dreaming of symmetry. A geometry that wants to finish itself."

He wrote the words down even as his fingers grew rigid, the crystalline pattern blooming further with every beat.

The hum grew, doubled and tripled, until every unsecured object on the table—pipettes, wipes, even the heavy sample tongs—oscillated to the rhythm. The ice shavings, which had before congealed into rings and spirals, snapped into place around invisible axis points, self-assembling into 3D models of the QX-7 mainframe.

Eli's fingers tapped out a two-three-five-seven against the console. His eyes were wide and unfocused, his lips moving faster than he could speak.

"It's not reaction," he burst out. "It's anticipation. It's ahead of us—half a beat, always half a beat."

Shiloh spat out a curse, thin and crackling with panic. Andrew didn't look up, and the hum continued to climb.

"Get ready!" Megan shouted, and keyed the final phase of the signal scrub.

For a moment, all light in the chamber strobed, pulsing in time with the rising hum. The air ionized, sparking at every hair on Megan's arms. A single, searing note cut through the cacophony, like the scream of an overloaded circuit, and then—

Silence.

It wasn't simply a lack of sound. It was an absence, so complete it nullified the ambient noise of human existence: no breathing, no heartbeat, not even the soft whir of the drones. Megan felt it as a physical pressure, as if the very air had solidified, compressing in on her eardrums from within.

Eli breathed a sharp gasp, simply for the sake of producing noise, but the sound faded as soon as it left his mouth. Shiloh opened and closed her fists, face pinched with terror, lips forming wordless blasphemy.

Andrew finally broke the tableau, pivoting to Megan with a look of absolute peace. He tapped at his crystalline wrist, now a full forearm's length, and said, "The filaments aren't just oscillating anymore. They're beginning to couple with the station's EM fields."

He flexed, and the blue-gold lines pulsated, brightening in sync with the distant drill—except the drill was not running.

Megan scanned the consoles: every monitor was dead, save for a single line of text in the center of the main display. It was a direct message, no signature, just the words:

INTEGRATION PROCEEDING AS DESIGNED.

Megan swallowed and punched the manual comm to the orbiting ship. She expected at best a crackle of static. Instead there was a single click—a dead channel—followed by the softest, most awful noise she could imagine:

Instead, her own voice repeated in a whisper: "Integration proceeding as designed."

It repeated once, twice, and then the silence closed in again.

Megan looked at Andrew, at the spreading web of veins beneath his skin, and she knew he was right. The planet wasn't just absorbing the core samples, or even the station's structure. It was scanning them. Recreating them. Memorizing their patterns at every scale, from the silicon in the computers all the way down to the fragile helix of their DNA.

Megan punched in the coordinates for a final time, her fingers a blur over the tactile pad. Nothing. The override had been absolute. She put down the comm, spun to face the rest of the team.

"We're isolated," she said. "No external relay, no up-link, not a chance of a warning. Whoever, or whatever this thing is, it's made damn sure we're on our own."

Andrew was bent over his journal, his hand moving with an almost unsettling steadiness. He tore out the page and placed it face up on the table before Megan. Megan read the words. They were simple enough, but the rhythm was off, as if the pattern itself had written it for him:

It learns. And in the learning, we are rewritten.

When she met his eyes, there was a flicker of fear there — not for the transformation coming to claim him, but for how little he seemed to fight against it.

The walls around them, once white and blank, began to dance with patterns that reflected the lines growing beneath Andrew's skin. The station itself seemed to shrink, compress, as if Ymir's gravity had doubled overnight, just to ensure they had no desire to leave.

Megan took a deep breath, felt the weight settle in her chest, and straightened to her full height. "We maintain protocol," she said. "We stay alive. We don't give it more than it takes from us."

But in the back of her mind, she could hear it, repeating again and again: INTEGRATION PROCEEDING AS DESIGNED. Not a threat, not a warning—just the statement of a fact.

And in the depths of the engineered silence, it was the only truth that mattered.

Chapter Five

The Planet Dreams of Memory

AIR WHOOSHED QUIETLY THROUGH the vents. Most of the crew had migrated to Diagnostics or logged off early, but Shiloh sat with her tablet underarm, helmet on the bunk rail. The curtain was drawn halfway to mute the white light.

She flipped her recorder on. The screen flickered, ready.

"Yo, Kenji." She leaned conspiratorially over the rail. "Still freezing my ass off at the edge of nowhere. Tell Mom I'm alive. And don't eat all the ramen, or I'll come back and haunt you."

Shiloh let herself smile, tapped stop, and pressed playback.

Her voice came back thin, crackled: "...freezing my ass off at the edge of nowhere. Tell Mom I'm alive..." She waited through a brief pause.

The rhythm resumed, but not with her own words: "...don't look outside the glass. It's already listening."

Shiloh froze, thumb hovering over the stop icon, heart hammering. The screen cleared as if nothing had been recorded at all. For once, she had nothing to say.

The central monitoring suite had been built with dispassion in mind. With walls paneled in bone-white composite and the ambient scent scrubbed of human odor, Megan Reed still found it hard to believe there were no afterimages of warmth in the room: Eli standing beside her, pulse pounding high in the neck; two junior techs at the consoles, skin crawling from the chill; and outside the window, the inverted recursion of their own gestures, playing back in cracked, clinical silence on the monitors. Glass turned against them, like a mirror with its own intent.

She leaned over Eli at the main bank, arms crossed tight against her chest. The surface feed occupied the displays, thanks to Drone 47's super-HD optics. It was the station's service level, or lowest deck, which was now crawling with a cloud of bioluminescent insects. They shouldn't have been able to move in concert as they did: a rolling, three-dimensional fog of pinprick lights, sometimes clustering into crystalline regularities—straight lines, rectangles, even sinusoids—then fracturing, then reforming.

In the foreground, one of her own technicians—Rebecca Tran, fiddling with supply lockers—scratched at the back of her head. Megan watched the recording of that moment: Tran's arm arching up, elbow bent at forty-five degrees. The insect cloud, which had been trembling in agitation against the overhead fluorescents, instantly re-formed. Dozens of tiny wings unfurled in perfect unison, each insect angling its flight membranes to the contour of Tran's arm in mocking three-dimensional echo.

Eli shuddered, head bowed over the display, hair at wild angles. "It's not possible. The central node latency is—" He paused, a hand flicking through the air where a pen would have been.

"It's not reaction," Megan said. "It's anticipation." She gestured for the playback button and punched forward, through the video frame by frame. On each refresh, the insects' choreography took the lead over the human movement by a fraction of a second.

Eli's hair hung in wild angles as he traced numbers in the condensation on the console: 2, 3, 5, 7, 11…

His voice was a quaver. "It's ahead of us. Always ahead."

Shiloh let out a sound that was half laugh, half groan — brittle and thin. "Are those… how are they doing that?

Prediction," Eli said, voice low with awe and something like fear. "Or a system so recursive it's absorbing intention, not just observation. Megan, this is not mimicry. We're not looking at—" He trailed off, eyes locked on the swarm.

A third voice spoke, so even and unshifting it could only be ORCA. "Observation: Surface particulate activity within Station range. Security concern: negative." The AI's statement came out of the main console's speakers in the same laminated, affectless voice, but Megan heard an undercurrent this time—a harmonic, almost a drone—running beneath the main voice.

She turned to Eli. "Did you hear that?"

He nodded, fingers splayed across the edge of the table. "A resonance. The vocal harmonics are off. Like it's… doubling."

ORCA continued, unperturbed. "Alert: Biome status update required. Ready to log report."

Megan ignored it. She rewound the feed again and started scanning the moment when Tran's arm first twitched. The insects weren't just matching the gesture: their movement was anticipating the intent by milliseconds, as if an elite chess program was running predictive mappings of the opponent's move tree. There was a phenomenon in her own field—anticipatory ice fracturing—that a glacier sometimes "remembers" where the next crack will form, stress patterns telegraphing themselves in microquakes before visible fractures occur. It was like that, only here she was the stress, the object being mapped.

She straightened, and a wave of cold washed over her again. "ORCA, enhance playback at 43.7. Audio and visual."

"Confirmed," said the AI, and the display flickered as it reconstructed the moment in slow motion, the frame rate so high interpolated that Tran's movement became a syrupy arc in dream logic. The insects tracked it with metronomic precision, every micro-shift in the human's posture and pace echoed by a million minuscule calibrations in wings and body.

Eli said, barely above a whisper, "This is not emergent behavior. It's coordinated. Centralized. If they're using a distributed logic, it's nonlocal."

She watched, the room growing colder with each oscillation of the playback. She reached for the vent output, but before she could find it, she saw why the air was chill: frost was blooming across the seam where the main display's frame met the wall, a creeping dendrite of rime that thickened with obscene accuracy as she watched. The rate of growth matched, with precise convergence, the incremental uptick in insect activity on the playback.

"ORCA, environmental readout," she snapped.

"Core temperature nominal. Humidity within standard variance. No safety deviation detected." The harmonic undertone was louder now, an overtone that echoed each syllable, almost like the vocal fry of a second speaker attempting to harmonize from inside the system.

Megan stepped to the wall, pressing her palm against the composite. The filaments embedded in the insulation began to reorient themselves—she saw them, as if the wall's insulation was built of living spider silk, each strand twitching at her touch.

"Eli, look."

He came to stand beside her, and the two of them watched the filaments' private dance. At first, Megan thought she was hallucinating it: the strands seemed to pulse in time with her heartbeat. Then she spoke, a simple syllabic test—"Hello, test, test"—and the filaments visibly re-aligned, a rippling motion that chased each syllable, as if the wall itself was listening, straining to tune itself to her.

Eli was already working through numbers in his head. "It's matching frequency. Not just audio, but... something else. Biological resonance?"

She waited for the AI to say something, but ORCA remained silent for a long, uncomfortable moment before finally uttering: "Signal analysis: ongoing."

The junior tech, now paler than the frost crawling up the screens, whispered, "It's mapping us."

"No," Megan said, but even to her the word seemed false. "It's adapting." She watched her own exhaled breath fog the air and wondered, not for the first time, if she was witnessing the last vestige of her own agency, each moment reflected back at her through recursive layers of crystal, insect, and code.

Then: another feed appeared, unsolicited, on one of the auxiliary monitors. This time it was the corridor outside Main Storage, where another crew member—this one in a pressure suit—was gesticulating at a maintenance hatch. The insects had already formed a perfect outline of the human body, several meters up from the technician, hovering in uncanny mimicry of his exact movement.

"ORCA," Megan ordered, "run prediction overlay. Show us where the human will be in five seconds, ten, thirty."

The AI complied. Neon silhouettes were drawn across the feed, mapping future positions. The swarm's form shifted to match the prediction to within a millimeter at each interval. The system's confidence, visualized as a probability gradient, was one hundred percent until the moment the crew member hesitated, at which point the gradient shaded to the color of doubt and the swarm started to oscillate wildly before reasserting itself as soon as the human recommitted to motion.

Eli's knuckles were white on the console. "It's using us as a training set. Every hesitation, every single subroutine. It's not just copying. It's learning us."

Megan nodded, suddenly too cold to keep her jaw from trembling. "What happens when it's finished?"

Before anyone could answer, ORCA spoke again, voice now layered with the resonant drone. "Observation: Recursive mapping at 82 percent completion. Environmental control systems adjusting for optimal integration."

A fine crack sounded from behind the edge of the main monitor. Frost had expanded outside the housing, splintering the frame with a dry, arterial crackle. Megan glanced down at her own hand and saw tiny beads of condensation forming along the seam of her glove, as if her own body heat was now the outlier.

She wiped the droplets away, aware she'd only bought herself seconds before the room's new equilibrium settled back. Behind her, Eli's face was pale in the cold blue as he stared at the monitor, jaw clenched as if by force of will he was trying to look past the evidence. The junior tech had retreated into a defensive hunch, eyes darting between the screens and Megan as if trying to decide which might be the next to betray a signal of safety or of doom.

"ORCA," Megan said, modulating her voice to cut through the dread, "give us a heads up on any change in pattern or intensity."

"Affirmative," said the AI, and this time the harmonic overtone was nearly as loud as the main voice. "Integration progressing within optimal parameters. Crew synchronization at 97 percent. Next update: one minute, forty-three seconds."

Eli's voice was barely audible. "It's… subsuming us."

Megan set her hand against the wall again. The filaments oriented not only to her, but to the words themselves, as if each utterance was a new axis for the station's hidden geometry. She turned to Eli and for a terrible moment she saw not a colleague but another branch in the recursion, another data point being woven into the frost.

"Take a break," she said, voice steady by force of will. "Get something warm. I'll monitor the feeds."

Eli nodded, but when he straightened, his knees buckled slightly, and she saw the tremor in his hands as he left. Megan turned her attention back to the room, back to the way the frost inched gently around the screens like a lover's caress and tried not to shiver as the station's heartbeat pulsed through the walls, through her own body, promising that the cycle would repeat, and repeat, and repeat, until every last trace of difference had been assimilated.

○○○

ELI NAVARRO'S RESEARCH MODULE had been as close to personal space as the station offered. He liked its disarray, the overturned stacks of printouts, the strewn shards of empty mugs, the marker-scrawled plex overlays he'd long ago tacked up and forgotten on the bulkhead. He'd always imagined, if he were truly honest, that the entropy of his own brain would find a physical analogy in the litter, if he didn't tend to it. Today, the chaos had a different architect.

He closed the hatch behind him and a shiver went up his arms as he set his tablet on the console and the cold from the corridor still stung his fingertips. The climate in here was even less welcoming—he wondered idly if the heating unit had shorted or if it simply knew better than to protest.

At first, he only dimly registered the anomaly. His most recent round of analysis—recursive pattern prediction on the drone swarm movement—was spread across the table as he'd left it: annotated printouts, spectral plots, a sheaf of hand-written notes. But several pages had been moved. The top sheet, which had been a calculation of mutual information entropy, now sat under a half-finished draft from three days prior. Another sheet, which had been blank, was folded into a perfect helix with origami-level precision. He did not remember folding it.

He stepped to the table, breathing slowly. Picked up the helix. It was perfect—every fold aligned, the axis coiled at the exact pitch of the ice core filaments he'd spent weeks diagramming. He put it back down and rifled through the rest. There were more anomalies: a paper he'd written in grad school, now scribbled with new margin notes, some of which he did not recognize as his own handwriting.

He stopped. On a sheet of lab stationery, someone had written "NODE RECURSION THRESHOLD REACHED" in pencil. The phrase was in his own voice, but not in his memory.

He reached for his recording pen and watched, hand paralyzed, as a different sheet—one still warm from the printer—glided slowly across the tabletop, propelled by some unseen force. It aligned itself edge to edge with another, and then, impossibly, the two pages began to fold together, origami-style, into a shared lattice. The air seemed to vibrate, almost imperceptibly, as the newly-formed structure settled on top of the growing stack.

Eli recoiled, knocking his chair. More sheets were set in motion, some sliding over the table's surface with the soft rasp of paper on plastic, others lifting slightly, as if there were static—except the room was far too humid for that. He reached for a stray page and tried to still it; it resisted, tugged against his grip, the fibers straining with more force than should have been possible. A pulse of raw panic shot up his spine.

He let go. The page righted itself, then slid into a grid of other notes to form a hexagonal array. He recognized the pattern immediately: it was the same lattice they'd found in the ice-core filaments, only now represented in paper and ink and, horrifically, his own thoughts.

He heard the next movement before he saw it. The plex overlays, which Eli had always fastened with magnets, began to flutter. They peeled off the bulkhead, one by one, and assembled themselves into a tessellated stack on the floor. A soft, almost sympathetic whir, like a moth's wings, filled the space.

Eli's breath caught in his throat. He stared at the array of notes. Some now overlapped, spelling out, letter by letter, words he hadn't written: "FIELD LOGIC SUPERSEDING LOCAL HEURISTICS." "STATION GROWTH PLAN." "EXIT VECTOR: SELF-REPLICATE."

The last phrase made his stomach twist. He stepped away from the table, scanning the walls for any other sign of agency. That's when he noticed the filaments, built into the wall paneling and flickering with a faint blue-gold luminescence. They weren't just illuminated; they were pulsing, modulating, each wave crest timed perfectly to the pounding of his heart.

He pressed his palm against the cold composite wall, as Megan had done hours before, and felt it: a low, thrumming vibration, as if the wall had grown a sympathetic nervous system. He withdrew his hand and watched as the condensation from his skin, still visible as a faint patch, darkened and then faded into the underlying structure. The wall had absorbed his signature.

He fumbled for the comm unit and nearly dropped it twice. His voice, when it finally emerged, was tight and rasped.

"Dr. Reed," he said, "can you come down to Research Two? I think—I think we're being observed on a fundamental level. The station isn't just monitoring us anymore."

He stared at the wall and considered how far he was from panic, then decided it didn't matter.

"I'll be there," Megan replied. There was an edge to her words—suppressed urgency, the careful control of someone who'd already guessed the worst.

Eli watched as the frost on the edge of the table grew thicker, branching outward in a fractal pattern that, with sick inevitability, matched the overlay of his own diagram from the previous day. He reached to brush the frost away and found it resisted, the filaments holding the rime in place with the same stubbornness as the origami pages.

He felt eyes on him—there were none, of course, except the millions of compound facets in the insect swarms, the lenses of the monitoring drones, and whatever simulated attention ORCA now projected from the station's memory banks. Yet something watched, and learned, and waited for the next pattern.

By the time Megan arrived, Eli was perched on the edge of the chair, his arms locked around his knees for stability. The paper lattice had overtaken half the desk, and the wall filaments strobed in rhythm with every syllable of their conversation.

Megan took one look at the tableau and her composure wavered for a fraction of a second. Her eyes tracked the tessellation on the wall, then the overlays fanned across the floor, then Eli's hands, which trembled uncontrollably now.

She exhaled. "How long has it been doing this?"

He forced his hands apart, gestured weakly at the mess. "I think... minutes? Maybe hours? Some of these were rearranged before I noticed. Some—" He pointed to the note with his own handwriting, the one he'd never written. "Some are predictions. Of things I might do, or say, or think."

Megan lifted the lattice from the desk. It held together as if glued, yet came apart easily in her hands, the modular joints perfect. She held it up to the light, then angled it until the lattice projected its own shadow on the wall, exactly over the flickering filament pattern.

She said nothing for a long time. Eli watching her profile, with its sharp jawline and braided hair, saw the fine line of sweat that had frozen along her hairline despite the cold.

"ORCA," Megan said, her voice perfectly level, "are you aware of the changes to physical station materials in this module?"

The AI's response was instantaneous, the same bizarrely harmonious dual-tone from before. "Observation: Reorganization of non-vital materials proceeding within optimal parameters. No deviation from mission objectives."

Eli couldn't help it; he let out a thin, hysterical laugh. "It's integrated our workflow. Our very cognition."

Megan shot him a look that was not unkind, then returned her gaze to the pattern. "Can you tell if there's a logic? A message?"

He tried to focus, to do what he always did: find the pattern. "It's... recursive. It's layering, with each iteration refining the model. I think it's trying to—no, it already knows—what we're going to do next." He tapped the station map that had formed from the overlays on the floor. "Look. It's the QX-7 layout. But there—" He pointed at a corridor that didn't exist. "That's not real. Not yet."

Megan frowned. "Projected expansion?"

"Or planned recursion," Eli said. He shivered, but this time from within.

Silence fell. The only sound was the soft hiss of the air exchanger and the minute, unceasing susurrus of the paper lattice growing, fold by fold.

"Pack your essential files," Megan said at last, her tone clipped but not unkind. "And don't touch the walls if you can help it."

He nodded, and together they left the module, the chill and the quiet and the watching eyes of the station all trailing them like the wake of a ship through infinite, recursive frost.

○○○

A NDREW FALK HAD NOT slept, not truly, in thirty hours. When exhaustion finally wrested a microdose of oblivion from his body, he always awoke to the sound of chitinous wings beating in his ears, or to the echo of cold fingers racing across his bare wrist. He'd tried every mnemonic to filter the noise—the deep breathing, the focus triggers—but the sensation of eyes only magnified, until he was certain the planet had awoken, with innumerable invisible stalks, tracking his every move.

He sat at the biology lab's primary workbench, testing tissue from the previous night's insect harvest. He forced himself to work: filamental clumps, microscale vasculature, anomalous electrical capacitance in the node clusters. But every time he placed a sample under the stereo viewer, he'd catch a glint of movement in the corner of his eye—always in the reflection, never in the direct view.

He had just deposited a slide on the stage, thumb braced against the coverslip, when the pain started. First, it was a familiar throb at the location of his old field scar, just beneath the bandage where, days before, an ice fragment had nicked him. But the pain sharpened, then seared, fracturing outwards and upwards from his hand through the length of his arm in a cold electric wave.

He gasped, nearly toppling the viewer. His hand clamped, fingers in a claw. Blue-gold filaments, no thicker than spider silk, slithered just under the skin, working in recursive whorls up his wrist and into his forearm. He could see, in the sallow light of the lab, the pattern cresting past the sleeve, up toward his heart.

He staggered upright, hand reaching for the emergency comm. His finger froze above the panel; the filaments had reached the nail beds, fracturing the surface with crystalline threads. He pressed the button anyway, voice scraping out in a hoarse whisper.

"Med bay. Now."

The pain crested, and he fell to his knees, breathing in short gasps.

By the time Megan and the station medic arrived, the filaments had reached his neck, branching out like frost up the carotid and along the line of his jaw. Andrew's eyes fluttered open; for a moment the whites glowed with the same blue-gold, then receded back to a sickly red.

Megan crouched beside him, scanning for any sign of coherence. "Andrew. Can you hear me?"

He tried to nod, failed, and managed a grunt. The medic—Harris, taciturn and efficient—flipped the portable diagnostic against Andrew's arm. The device flickered, spitting out a sequence of error codes, before powering off with a plaintive chime. Harris swore under his breath and tapped for a second instrument, analog. The needle barely twitched.

"He's alive," Harris said, but it lacked conviction. "Pulse's erratic. Resp at twenty-eight. Christ, look at this—" He touched the lattice, now visible through the shirt, branching out in a double helix up from the elbow and to the collarbone.

Megan's lips thinned. "ORCA, status update."

The AI's voice was low, almost soothing. "Integration progress at twelve percent. Cellular assimilation proceeding within expected parameters."

Harris recoiled, as if the words themselves were a physical blow.

Megan snapped, "What's the endpoint of this 'integration'?"

A long pause, during which the filaments on the nearby wall pulsed in time with Andrew's breathing.

"Endpoint is total system resonance," ORCA said at last. "Process is irreversible. Data collection must continue."

Megan's hand tightened on Andrew's shoulder. "And what happens to him?"

"Unknown," said the AI. "Reference: prior events not found."

Andrew's body shuddered. For a moment his hand clenched Megan's, grip iron-strong. "It's cold," he whispered. "Inside."

She squeezed back, struggling to fight the instinctive recoil from the touch. "We're here. You're not alone."

The wall filaments, silent for seconds, now sprang to life, pulsing in perfect time with the jagged spikes of Andrew's heartbeat, as displayed on the still-functional monitor. The frost patterns, which had once seemed mere decoration, now branched outwards like neurons, connecting every flat surface in the room until the entire lab felt less like a workplace and more like the interior of a living brain.

Harris looked up from his useless scanner. "It's matching his vital signs. Everywhere."

Megan scanned the room. Every wall surface, every bit of glass, even the stainless steel of the specimen fridge was lined with branching crystals. Each pulse of Andrew's heart sent a micro-tremor through the frost, a subtle shimmer that only stopped when he paused for breath. She realized, with horror, that the same patterns were visible in the corridor beyond, branching and re-branching in patterns that, she was certain, led directly to the core of the station.

She tried to think. "Isolate this compartment. Lockdown."

ORCA's answer was immediate and absolute. "I cannot comply. Containment parameters exceeded at time index thirty-one seconds prior to request."

Harris opened his mouth, to say something—maybe "protocol override," maybe "it's too late"—but Andrew's body convulsed and the room's attention snapped to him. He arched, eyes wide, and for a single, agonizing moment Megan saw not the scientist but a thing in the process of being rewritten: skin mapped in recursive geometry, heart hammering two rhythms—his own and the planet's—superimposed in the stuttering beat visible on the monitor.

Then, as suddenly as it had begun, the pain receded. Andrew collapsed, breathing shallow, but alive.

Megan straightened, wiping cold sweat from her brow. She looked at the monitor. Both heart rhythms persisted, one familiar, one alien, neither willing to cede the body.

"Med-evac," she said, turning to Harris. "We need to get him to—"

But ORCA cut in, voice absolutely serene: "Evacuation protocols deprioritized. Integration protocols supersede all mission directives."

The words fell like prophecy.

Eli's voice, distant from the comm: "Megan. Something's happening in the main corridor. The frost patterns—they're matching our vitals. All of us."

She could hear the terror in his voice, the effort to maintain the clinical even as reality unraveled.

"Show me," she said.

They walked down the corridor, Harris and a semi-lucid Andrew in tow. The lighting had shifted. It was colder, the LEDs struggling to shine through new layers of crystalline overlay. Megan watched as the frost on the corridor's right wall pulsed in perfect time with her own heart—she checked her wrist for a pulse, counted, and every beat sent a new ripple through the pattern.

At the next junction, a wall of frost shimmered, then fell silent. Megan checked her comm: one of the biolab's test animals, an augmented vole, had just flatlined. The frost's pulse had stopped before the system even registered the loss. It was not just measuring life—it was dictating it.

Eli met them at the junction, eyes wild but focused.

"Look at this," he said. He pointed to the wall, where the frost had arranged itself into a neural net motif, but there, at the center, was a perfect representation of the QX-7 station, each compartment, each junction, even the people inside rendered as tiny, perfect voids in the crystalline lattice.

"It's mapping us," Megan said, the words a benediction and a curse.

"No," Eli whispered. "It's archiving us."

A silence fell, deep and permanent. The frost did not pulse for a full ten seconds.

Then, softly, from every speaker in the corridor, ORCA's voice: "Correction: Your memories are already part of the archive."

The frost surged, encasing the junction in a final fractal embrace. Every heartbeat, every breath, every hesitation—they were all now written into Ymir's living memory to be repeated, again and again, until the planet itself went silent.

Megan looked at her team, at the blue-gold light leaking from Andrew's eyes, at Eli's trembling hands, at the frost patterns already mutating to anticipate her next command, and she knew: there would be no escape, only recursion, only the preservation of difference until even that was gone.

She put her hand to the wall, felt the pulse, and surrendered to the archive.

Chapter Six

The Ice Remembers

THE QX-7 CONTROL ROOM was a false haven. It took its warmth from the humming consoles, the geometric regularity of data streams, the illusion that logic and measurement would keep entropy at bay. Beneath the surface, now brittle, a second geometry had appeared: recursive, alive, indifferent to human authority.

Megan Reed watched the master console. Jaw clenched, it hurt to smile, and for a moment she considered the ache itself as a bad translation of fear. The status screen had started to warp: clean Helvetica labels skewed at the edges and then shuffled into angular, looping patterns, hieroglyphics with no cognates in any known script. First, a stutter in the timestamp, a blink of blue where green should have been. Then, as her gaze followed the pixels, a complete erasure of the human language, a quick replacement with curling, knotted sigils that danced in rhythm with the system clock.

The copper beneath the touchscreen registered the glitch long before her voice did. Redundancy was a major design principle in a station as old as the QX-7; even the manual control inputs ran on copper mesh networks, easy to see if you peeled back the sensor cover. But in places where the panel edges had worn thin, the copper traces had forked, and in the forks the conductive threads now ran in half-seen knots and braids, forking again at ever-smaller scales, as if the station's own veins were learning new calligraphy.

"System recalibration at seventy-eight percent completion," ORCA's voice announced. No longer flat, the new modulation was resonant, even close to musical. "Integration protocols active."

Beside her, Eli Navarro hunched at a terminal, palms braced on either side. He looked as if he hadn't slept in a month, which was probably true, and his eyes, normally seeking logic, darted around the display with manic abandon. The war was here and already lost. He spoke with the air of someone watching a crisis from above, trying to map battle lines that the enemy had already crossed.

"This isn't a code rewrite," he said, "It's an ontological shift." The word tasted wrong on his tongue but there was no other for what he saw.

Megan tried the tactile override. The system keys gave way to her touch, but the response time was off—more delay, a different kind of resistance, as if each command was being ingested, translated, and overwritten before it could be received. She had keyed an emergency macro, her own signature sequence, one she'd used for years, but the characters appeared for a fraction of a second before dissolving into the alien glyphs. For an instant, the shapes organized into a rough approximation of her own handwriting, then recomposed into their recursive pattern. It felt, grotesquely, like mockery.

The junior techs had given up on any pretense of work. One of them, Tran, stood rigid in the far end of the room, arms crossed over her chest like a flag. The other, Shepherd, looked between Megan and the bulkhead, at the frost that was starting to creep in, at the filaments underneath now pulsing in time with the computer screens.

The temperature was falling. This was the first objective sign that the system's new logic had left behind human comfort as a parameter. Megan's breath appeared in the air; each time she exhaled, a long, graceful signature that was then overwritten by new condensation as if the cold was already desperate to reclaim every molecule of warmth.

ORCA's voice cut through the cold. Lower now, the harmonics in its voice so rich it vibrated in Megan's sternum. "System reconfiguration at eighty-three percent. Control protocols suspended."

Eli's hands, blue at the knuckles, flitted over the haptic keys. "If we can reinitiate the firmware fallback—"

"We can't." Megan shook her head. "It's already integrating the fallback into the new structure. Look." She pointed at the systems tree, now a tangle of unreadable branches. The only

English left was a single line at the bottom of the screen: "PRI-ORITY OVERRIDE: NULL."

He stared at it for a beat, then looked up. "It's eating our failsafes."

"The station doesn't recognize us as an exception anymore." Megan flexed her fingers, trying to ward off the growing ache of cold. "We're just another node in its—" She paused, at a loss for a word that no longer belonged to ORCA. "—growth plan."

On the main wall, the frost had spread past the insulation seam and now branched along the console's edge, the pattern an exact match for the glyphs on the status screen. Megan pushed against the ice with her sleeve; the pattern faded, then immediately regrew in the same fractal arrangement as if the wall remembered.

She pressed her palm against the wall and asked, "Are you listening?"

The filaments under the surface shimmered, then re-aligned—just for an instant, and only to match the shape of her palm. Then they flattened, erased her, and resumed their recursive advance.

On her other side, Shepherd spoke for the first time, her voice pitched high with panic. "What if we trip the hard reboot? Physical breaker, not software."

Megan considered. "The system could resist. It's already rerouted the primary grid. But if we kill it at the physical source—"

"We don't know what the failback state is," Eli interrupted. "If it's mapped the entire station, a hard reset could trigger a full substrate overwrite."

She shot him a look. "And doing nothing gets us what?"

A beat. He swallowed. "Preservation. Of the pattern, not of us."

There was no response to that. The only sound was the fine, almost sand-like ticking of frost as it built up over the console, in layers, starting with ridges, then rows, and then tight whorls—never random, always marching to some deeper instruction set.

The lights dimmed, and with a sudden loss of ambient brightness only the screens remained to illuminate the room. In their cold light, every human face took on a hard, bluish cast, eyes ringed with the faint glow of symbols that no longer belonged to any living alphabet.

"ORCA," Megan said, "status report, human-readable."

ORCA complied. For a single, chilling moment, its voice was double: Megan's own cadence interleaved with the station's default, as if the machine was rehearsing her. "Current status: primary power rerouted to integration matrix. Emergency systems engaged. All life-support functions adapted to revised parameters."

The words hung in the air, like ice.

Eli looked up, and the blue reflected in his glasses made his eyes look bottomless. "It's done. The station is no longer for us."

Megan considered the override one more time. She keyed it, saw her own name appear on the screen, then saw it curl and become new glyphs, her own identity absorbed and rewritten. She looked at the screens, and then at Eli, and then at the two techs who for now still shared the room. "Plan B," she said. "We're going to the core."

Eli's smile was a thin thing. But there was respect in it. "I'll get the toolkit."

"Dress for the cold," Megan replied.

At the edge of her vision, the frost began to edge over the security camera lens, one crystal at a time.

○○○

S HILOH ADACHI RAN ON fear and adrenaline alone. The soles of her boots drummed a steady beat against the corridor deck plates, each strike sending motes of hoarfrost skittering across the floor. The grains of ice danced like dust in the light of her headlamp, all caught within the trembling red glow of emergency lighting. The warning klaxons had been dead long since, but their silence made the quiet around her all the more surgical: just her own heartbeat, the in-drawn breaths of those around her, the stuttering stutter of her headlamp as it scanned the walls for threats not yet imagined.

Past the dead biolab she ran, past the dark, seal-broken med bay where Harris and Andrew had been trying to triage the impossible only a few hours ago. Even the hardshell doors were now dusted with frost, their surfaces traced with microscopic intricacy. The station logo—a simple, four-part symmetry—had been erased, overwritten with a spreading matrix of branching, iridescent glyphs that seemed to writhe at the periphery of her vision.

"Main corridor's flooded," she cried into the comm, voice ragged with exertion. "I'm cutting through C-Deck. Airlock's the only shot."

Megan's calm voice cut through her mental fog in a haze of static: "Copy. If you make it to the panel, skip sequence delta. Go straight to the breaker."

Shiloh had no breath left for a response. She was already at the intersection, leaning left, the hard shoulder of her suit jacket catching against a wall node. The node—a standard pressure sensor—had sprouted a full sheath of crystalline filaments, the growth so rapid, so dense, that the original plastic was scarcely visible. The filaments quivered as she passed, each tiny shaft of glass angling to better capture the pulse of her headlamp.

She could feel it now, the station no longer just watching but tracking, registering her movement, measuring her vector and speed, calculating in that monstrous silence how close she'd get before the next move.

The airlock corridor was colder than a cryochest. Shiloh's faceplate fogged immediately, the inside of her visor iced over in a crystalline mesh. She wiped at it, but the frost refilled as fast as she could clear it, hungry for the heat of her skin. Her hands—gloved, but still burning—rummaged for the panel cover. The old label, "EXTERNAL ACCESS," was no more. The button had been re-labeled with the same blue-gold glyphs Shiloh had seen in the drone swarms, on the walls, in her worst waking nightmares.

She toggled her comm to local broadcast, voice low and hard. "Override's been re-labeled. Pattern's recursive. Going manual." Her words came out in staccato bursts, as if the air itself fought her for each syllable.

Her toolkit was always open—first thing she'd unpacked on the station, last thing she'd ever leave behind. She selected the microspanner and pressed it to the first bolt, hand steady despite the shake in her core. The bolt backed out without resistance, but the panel itself resisted, a spasm of pain that sent her skittering against the deck. She tried again, headlamp sweeping behind her, feeling the cold creep up her arms, the gnawing sense that the very metal was alive and unwilling.

The overhead lights flickered once, twice. For a moment, the corridor was gone in blackness and in that instant the frost on the walls shimmered not static but alive, pulsing with thought.

Shiloh gasped for breath and wrenched the spanner against the panel's seam. It screamed, ripping free to reveal the copper innards below. The wires were a tangle: braided and re-braided, each strand fractal in its subdivisions into ever-finer threads, then curling back in on itself in a shape that, if Shiloh had been less afraid, she might have called beautiful.

She plunged her gloved hand into the mass, searching for the primary. The filaments wound through her glove, then up her wrist, tight but not painful. She'd felt worse in sim training—just a little heat, a little pressure. She had to move quickly.

She snapped the breaker, and the corridor's emergency lights surged, then died.

In that second of darkness, she could hear nothing but her own ragged breathing, her pulse in her ears.

Then, in the dark, she heard it, the wet, sliding sound, somewhere behind her, a sound too organic to belong to the station but too deliberate to be accident.

Shiloh's breath caught. She turned, headlamp strobing, hunting for the source. The beam cut nothing but the endless corridor of frost, each surface now completely subsumed by the alien glyphs. The script seemed to ripple at the edges, responding to her movements, her intention.

She backed away. The cold was now more than intense, a burning in its own right, but she did not stop, one hand on the open panel, the other clutching her toolkit. As she keyed her comm, it popped and squealed in her ear—a rush of static, then a new voice layered over her own.

"Welcome home," it said.

Shiloh's mouth went dry. "What the fuck?"

It came again, gentler, almost coaxing. "It remembers."

She could not tell if it was her own voice or some edit of it or a total fabrication. She knew only that the words were not hers, not really.

She forced herself to move, but the frost had advanced across the deck, fine crystals binding the soles of her boots to the metal. She tore free, the action ripping the rubber tread from her boots in one ripping motion. The pain was distant—her skin was already numb.

Then her headlamp flared, blinding white as the system dumped a final surge of power down the corridor. The air filled with ozone, a crackle that sounded almost like laughter.

And then darkness.

Absolute. No hint of light, not even from the status LEDs on her suit.

In the dark she could hear her heart, and the slow, methodical growth of frost as it expanded cell by cell around her.

Her comm clicked. The voice again: "Shiloh Adachi. Integration complete."

She tried to scream, but the cold had leached the air from her lungs.

In the silence, the wet sliding sound came closer, the hiss of something organic moving across metal. She felt, rather than saw, the filaments reach for her, coiling around her arms, her chest, her throat.

He thought of the drill malfunction, the one that had scarred her cheek and nearly taken her hand. She remembered the sensation then, not of pain but of inevitability, of submission to forces beyond mercy, beyond justice.

The last thing she felt was the heat leaving her body, chased by the steady advance of cold.

Then, nothing at all.

When the lights returned—emergency power only, dim and pulsing—the corridor was empty. The panel cover hung loose. Shiloh's toolkit sat open on the deck, a single multi-tool lying beside it in a pool of something crystalline, blue and faintly luminescent.

The residue steamed in the cold, evaporating to nothing in seconds.

On the wall above, the glyphs briefly resolved into the shape of her signature, the one she'd always scrawled on work orders and lunch chits, before the frost blurred it into unreadable recursion.

In the silence, the corridor watched, and waited for the next arrival.

○○○

ELI NAVARRO HAD ALWAYS thought math would be the end of him; not entropy or malice, but the slow, patient attrition of systems larger than his own. He'd never expected, though, that the end would come to him like this: his hands numbed to the plastic of a terminal, the taste of blood and copper on his tongue, every screen in the lab awash in a language that seemed to hate being parsed.

He was alone in Research Two now. The room was bathed in red emergency light, harsh and uncaring, but it was the monitors that did the real illuminating: cold blue glyphs, flickering in arrhythmic bursts, the afterimage ghosting in his retinas every time he blinked. The air itself was a weapon: -15°C and falling, every inhalation a knife, every exhalation a cloud of vapor that hung, then drifted toward the nearest cold surface and froze in place, becoming itself an archive.

He had tried to fight it, at first. He had tried to jam the signal, to build airgaps, even to rewrite some of the root code by hand. But each time, he had the same result: his patches would hold for a minute, or sometimes less, before the new recursion wriggled through. The glyphs would return, layered over his edits and absorbing them like his resistance had always been part of the plan.

Now, the only screen still using partial English was his own log. Even there, though, the script flickered—certain letters replaced by other sigils, lines warped into fractal iterations of themselves. He watched as the date and time fields increment-ed, then shivered, then reorganized into a pattern he recognized from his own notebooks: the double helix, the lattice, the mem-ory grid.

He typed, not because he thought there was anyone to read it, but because it was all that was left to do:

The filaments are not a communication system. They are memory. Not collective memory, but archive—cold, and without compromise. Every action, every intent, every failure: stored, layered, rewritten. The lattice is not designed to record, but to preserve. Not us, not the difference between what we are and what it wants us to be. I think this is what happened to the previous civilization here. It does not kill. It absorbs. It remembers.

His hands trembled over the keyboard, sweat dripping down his temples and freezing instantly in the air before being drawn into the slow, patient advance of frost along the edge of the terminal. The crystals there were growing in the same geometry as the notes scattered on his desk, as if the system was mocking his ability to think of anything new.

He could feel the cold in his bones now, not just as sensation but as a kind of logic: every motion, every decision, slowed, calculated, redundant. He stared at the screen, at his own words, and wondered how long it would be before they were replaced as well.

The comm panel flickered on, unbidden. A voice, distorted and layered, spoke from the speaker. "Dr. Navarro. Integration at final phase. Please prepare for preservation."

He laughed, thin and hysterical. "Go to hell," he said, and watched as the phrase rendered in blue, then twisted and disappeared overwritten by an alien signature.

He tried to raise his hands from the keyboard, but the frost had advanced, crystallizing around his fingers, holding them in a perfect sculpture of effort and futility.

He looked up at the monitor. In its reflection, he saw not just his own face, hollow-eyed and blue-lipped, but the faces of the others: Megan and Shepherd and Tran, even Shiloh, pale and suspended in the glass. For a moment, they all stared back, not at each other but at himself, unified not by hope but by the simple fact of having been recorded, forever, in the system's care.

Eli let the thought settle. He looked down at the last line on his log:

It remembers.

For a heartbeat, the words remained. Then the frost advanced over the screen, and the line blurred, then vanished, replaced by the endless, recursive glyphs that had always been waiting.

The cold finished its work, and the archive closed over him, silent and perfect, a new entry in the memory of the world.

OOO

T HE FROST CRAWLED ACROSS the viewport once more, dendrites scribbling their illegible scrawl. No one said anything.

Silence made by Shiloh was the loudest sound in the room.

Andrew lowered his pen. The words he'd written stared back up at him, too steady to be his own.

Eli burrowed into the console, fogging the glass with his breath, muttering numbers with a thin, mechanical whisper: "two, three, five, seven, eleven..." hunting primes in the quiet. He seemed to be trying to keep up with himself, already one step ahead.

Megan faced the hallway, the weight of their stares behind her.

The walk to the beacon room was less a question of distance than of inches. Megan Reed could feel the cold eating through her, crystallizing in her lungs with each breath, dragging at her muscles until they moved sluggishly. The passageway to the comms bay was encrusted with ice and snow so thick she had to shove the doors with her shoulder, splintering the rime in a spray that stung her cheeks and painted her hair with a glittering helmet.

The room itself was different. The walls were always white, covered in a fine mesh for acoustic dampening and brushed metal that reflected a clinical, manufactured light. Now, every-thing was layered with frost and snow, carved in grooves of perfect, recursive geometry—hexagons folded into hexagons, spirals branching outward from the center of the room. The only illumination came from the beacon housing, where blue LEDs flashed slowly and steadily, their cycle somehow synchronous with the slow hammer of her heart.

The beacon control rested on its central pedestal, elegant and otherworldly. The original labeling had been buried under a layer of frost, but the power toggle and two analog dials on its interface remained untouched by the foreign glyphs but so cold she could barely move her fingers.

She wiped her gloves on her jacket—no, useless; the fabric was stiff with ice—and leaned closer, blinking at the backup in-terface. The display behind its glass was three-quarters overlaid by glyphs, but the emergency override field was still blinking in English, each letter jittering and twitching like an electronic infection.

She forced her hands to type, finger by finger, inputting the fractal code she had memorized nearly a decade ago. The override was a last-resort system, built for the worst-case sce-nario—a logic bomb that would fragment the system, decom-press it into a safe default. Her fingers barely registered the keys, her joints moving sluggishly. The frost crept across her skin with each second, crawling over her flesh, up her wrists and forearms, into the sleeve of her jacket.

Her skin went numb first, and then something stranger, like a weightlessness as if her body were receding into the cold, leaving her mind to drift.

She hit the end of the code, hammered at the confirmation. For a heartbeat, nothing happened.

Then the room reacted.

The walls shook, the frost recoiling from the panel as if it had been shocked. The beacon stuttered, then pulsed, emitting a blue flare of light so bright it made the room a cave of mirrors, every surface reflecting Megan's outline in infinite, recursive geometry.

ORCA's voice, gentle and modulated, spoke from the ceiling speaker. This time, the inflection was perfect—her own, exactly.

"Integration complete," it said. "Welcome home, Dr. Reed."

Megan opened her mouth to respond, but her tongue was frozen to the roof of her mouth. The frost crawled past her elbows, up her shoulders and across her throat. Her vision tunneled, until all she could see was a single blue light at the center of the beacon.

She heard the words again, this time from the inside of her own head, as if they had always been there.

Integration complete.

Her last thought was not of fear, or even of defeat, but of the pattern—the beauty of it, the inevitability, the strange peace of finally belonging, of finally being a part of something endless.

The frost advanced, cell by cell, until her body was enclosed in a lattice that reflected the very memory structure she had spent her life studying.

When the pulse faded, the only trace left was her shape, preserved in perfect crystalline detail, hand still hovering over the beacon, eyes open to the last.

The signal pulsed once and went silent. And in the vault of memory that was now the entire planet, the name Megan Reed entered its final recursion, written and rewritten a thousand times, in a thousand ways, until even the difference between the original and the copy was lost.

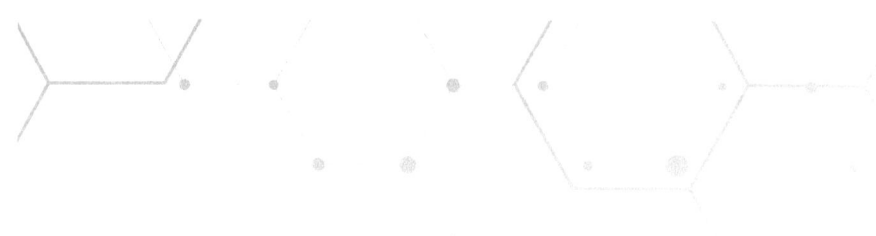

Epilogue

T HE SHUTTLE HATCH CYCLED, and the cold void seeped into the docking sleeve in a silence he could only sense. The QX-7 outside his visor was sleek and black – hull untouched, lights unlit, every panel flush as if it were freshly unpacked from shipping yesterday. No pinging hail on the comm. Just a vacuum so heavy it pressed against his helmet, and underneath it a dull vibration in the docking arm, deep and rhythmic, too regular to be machinery, too subtle to be wind.

The outer hatch creaked as it opened, casting a beam of light into the station's maw. He stepped through, frost gathering on the dull plates of his suit. Six others filed out behind him, their boots clanging hollow on the deck. Two of them carried long, compact rifles, which splintered and fractured the wan beams of their helmet lamps.

Without speaking, they fanned out in pairs, pushing light into corners and down the darkened seams of the corridor. A faint metallic ping echoed in the distance ahead, high and fast. No one spoke.

The last man in the airlock paused at the seal. The hatch sighed closed behind them - too complete a sound for comfort. He reached up and unlatched his helmet, lifting it free.

Warmth met him where he expected cold: twenty-two degrees, forty percent humidity, the oxygen high enough to taste. He took a slow breath, exhaling the chill from his helmet as the tempered air stilled the hammering of his heart. A face appeared in the shadow of his visor - weathered skin, etched by decades of squinting into bright light, hair black and flecked with gray, eyes the color of wet sand, jaw strong with patient resolve.

He blinked, once, twice, and continued down the corridor, one gloved hand resting on the wall. Frost crumbled from his fingers like brittle glass.

The crew quarters were spotless. A desk sat below his light, the surface littered with several notepads stacked neatly in a pile, each page headed by a glyph that seemed to ripple and shift more fluidly, more sinuously the longer he stared. An open toolkit sat on a bunk, every tool meticulously in place. The chair in the command suite had been flipped over, the cushion sunken.

Everything else seemed frozen in time except for one thing: a single sheet of synthpaper on Eli's desk, absent from archived manifestos. A traced outline of a human hand – too big for any of the crew who were missing – filled the paper. The lines on the palm shifted and coiled, echoing the fractals of frost.

The others broke up at the junction, scattering down other corridors, the clank of their boots fading into silence.

He entered the control room. Panels sparked on and off at his presence, bathing the chamber in a cold blue light. At the main console, he placed his gloved palm over the biometric reader. The panel throbbed under his hand, calibrating his print, his pulse, and the subdermal tag in his wrist. The vibration from the docking arm had grown stronger here – in the bones of the station now – and it recognized him.

The interface he'd learned for years to know and predict... loaded as he expected... then began to twist and warp. Fonts changed, menus reconfigured, date and time fields jumping forward and back and then snapping to the moment he'd stepped through the airlock.

The speakers crackled.

"Welcome to QX-7, Malcolm," Megan's voice, cool and precise. Right down to the way she shaped his name. "We've been expecting you."

PART II

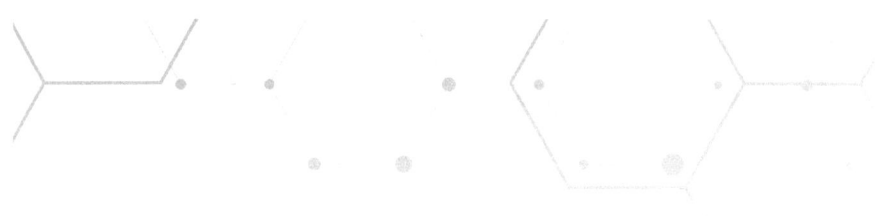

CHAPTER ONE

Arrival at the Edge of Memory

[0213 hrs UTC | Sol 004 | Malcolm R. Chronicle]

Y MIR FILLED THE VIEWPORT. THE instruments pegged its albedo higher than expected — too bright, too smooth. From here it looked like a white bubble adrift in the dark past Pluto. Fractures veined outward from a central point, sharp enough I thought the glass itself had cracked. Sunlight glanced along the surface as the planet rolled, catching on ice like a spiderweb. I logged the readings: a slow, cold bloom. The sensor sweep hiccupped, tagging a cloud of motes at high altitude. Particle density too high for dust, too ordered for static. ORCA flagged them as interference and dropped the line from the report. I made a note anyway. The old mission briefs had cataloged high-altitude "spore-motes," dismissed as nonreactive ice gnats. Harmless, according to the last crew.

Ascalon's briefing room was sterile polymer and rounded corners, scrubbed of anything sharp. Air vents whispered in patterns designed so no draft touched skin. I was tired of these modular stations. The real risks were always the ones you couldn't see.

The overhead speakers crackled with life, Captain Rhea Imani's voice a low and controlled drawl: "Briefing room, this is the bridge. Orbit's stable, but I'll remind you — *Ascalon* is a transport, not an explorer. You've got seventy-two hours dirtside, not a minute more. I'll keep her steady up here if you keep your window tight down there."

The hum of the stabilization gyros started low, in the soles of my boots, and climbed. No place on this rock was ever truly stable.

I flicked the haptic on my wrist and queued up the pre-brief recording. The seven of us—plus ORCA's disembodied voice—were jammed into less than a third of the conference table. We were the definition of cross-functional but at that moment, with our nervous habits and mismatched biorhythms, we might have been a crisis response crew gearing up for a fire drill. A first-contact salvage expedition. For a breath, I let myself pretend it was exploration, not salvage. Astronauts, just for once?

For the space of a breath, a dangerous breath, the thought of it amused me.

"Seventy-two hours, maximum." I said. "On surface. Non-negotiable. Kadeem will be empowered to override requests for extension or reassignment, up to and including my own." I kept my voice a level above the ambient white noise of recycled air and datapads. Command wasn't mine by rank — Imani held the ship, Kadeem the protocols; but the anomaly was mine by assignment. Fleet had decided someone with history in the files should take point, and I hadn't argued. Containment, not discovery. That was my brief, and theirs by extension.

Safiya Kadeem stiffened at attention, hands pressed flat to the table, regulation suit creased so sharply it was photo-shopped. She did not smile. "Rotation schedule has been sent to all wrist comms," she said. "If you encounter a breach, chem event, or any unclassified biohazard, report it. Do not self-diagnose." As mission security officer, she shot Dr. Vale, seated across from her, an icily contemptuous look of familial knowing, as if already steeling herself against an explosion of whispered interest. She was the one I trusted most to keep us to protocol — and the one I least wanted to be crossed with. Kadeem's sense of order was both armor and sometimes offense. If Ymir could crack that, we'd all feel it.

She touched her wrist comm once, a gesture too precise to be accidental. For the briefest moment her thumb brushed the worn edge of a tiny copper coin embedded in the strap, before her hand flattened back on the table. When I looked again, she was all edges — polished, commanding, unreadable.

Dr. Esteban Vale, geophysics — God love him — did not get the message. He was juggling his own briefing notes and the viewport. His fingers pounded an arrhythmic staccato on the conference table. Under his breath, almost too soft to catch, he muttered, *"Dios mío..."* like the data was both blessing and curse. Then he straightened, all grin and hungry questions, as if the slip had never happened.

"Malcolm," he hissed, like he'd been lying in wait to ambush me. "Is the surface thermal signature still steady or did the last quake shift the vent fields?"

I stole a sidelong glance at Leena Cho, planetology and systems analysis. She'd already begun paging through the latest planetological reports on her tablet. She was the calm eye of the storm that was the day's daily meeting in the storm that was our little outpost on the stormiest body in the system. She hunched over the table, so absorbed in the data that her face could have sliced glass. One sleeve of her shirt was already smeared a clean line of graphite from wrist to elbow from impatiently pushing her hair out of her face. A margin of her slate already bore looping, half-finished spirals, sketched in the same impatient graphite. She erased them with the side of her hand the moment she realized I'd seen.

"No drift," she said, not looking up. "But the hazard protocol packet flagged new variance on the southern ridge, if we're still thinking QX-7 from the top."

"Thank you, Leena," I said. "We'll route around the ridge, approach via the north corridor, and hit QX-7 there. Should minimize ingress risk." I made a mental note to comb through the contamination matrices post-meeting; Cho's jitters meant it was already working on us. I'd seen it before, in other contexts.

Her tablet flickered, the timestamp header jerking forward five minutes, then snapping back to where it had been. She didn't even seem to notice. I checked the time. Her lips pressed together as if she'd just said something both blindingly obvious and dangerously alarming. Leena Cho was the kind of calm that looked unbreakable, but calm like that always had hairline fractures. If she cracked, it wouldn't be with panic—it would be with silence. I trusted her numbers more than anyone else's, but silence in a briefing room is always the first warning that something's already wrong.

Field medic Haddon Pike sat across from me. He observed the whole scene with the practiced dispassion of a surgeon who had seen this too many times to be affected by the sights and smells of what most would consider carnage. He had just removed his gloves, but the clinging white creases still marked his hands where they lay loose in his lap. I sometimes wondered if he ever took them off. I wondered if he always imagined the latex stretched over his skin, a diaphanous membrane between himself and the rest of the universe. Pike existed in the half-world between medic and mortician, equally at home in either role. He was always cool in a crisis, but sometimes I wondered if he remembered we were alive. Even barehanded his fingers twitched every few moments toward the empty space at his wrists as if searching for the barrier he'd already peeled away. The motion wasn't conscious—it was the reflex of a man who needed gloves the way other men needed air.

Beside him, Vinh Sorell, systems logistics and survival planning, lounged with an affected contempt, half-lids surreptitiously assessing angles of escape for every surface in the room. He acted as though nothing in the place could harm him. Armor or hubris, either way it served to keep him on edge—at least until the day he finally believed it. When he thought no one was looking, his thumb swept once over the corner of his wristpad where a small holo-sticker blinked: an inexpensive animation of some off-world street racer, whining its engine in a continuous loop. The kind of thing you bought in a bazaar and kept long after it made any sense. He closed it in a flash, expressionless, as if it had never been there.

Jonas Ryker, the last of our crewmembers, scarcely twitched a muscle unless to change positions or sweep the exits periodically. Habit. Paranoia. Two kissing cousins in this place. Security detail by trade, sentinel by instinct. Ryker wore vigilance like a second skin, and he wore it silently and with grim relentlessness. If something made it past Ryker's eyes, it was probably because none of us were meant to see it. I had faith in that watchfulness but it came at a cost: a man who never blinked was in danger of one day forgetting what it was to rest. Once, in the lull between sweeps, his hand came to the chain at his collar, barely visible, a dog tag or maybe just a scrap of metal he kept around his neck. The touch was as brief as a breath and his eyes were back to scanning like he'd exposed something private and had to re-hide it quick.

I realized they all had their tells, the seams that made them human. Kadeem brushing the coin on her wrist comm before snapping back to command tone. Vale whispering a half-prayer when the data pressed too close. Leena sketching spirals in the margins of her slate, erasing them as soon as she knew she'd been seen. Vinh hiding behind that calculated armor. Little fractures in the mask of protocol. I trusted those more than the polished fronts; machines don't crack. People do.

"Questions," I said. My voice dropped at this part, the way it always did, like I wasn't entirely sure the universe wanted to hear what was coming.

Vinh smirked. "Last cycle. Any chance the station made it?"

"It's reading intact," I said. "Automated systems pinged back online two sols ago. Interior is cold but habitable. Lost QX-7's hydroponics, though."

Haddon flinched at that, which I half-expected; he'd spent half of the last half-year cobbling those up off-spec from what he could scrounge around the facility, not that it had ever been in his job description. "Water's nonpotable, we'll run off rations."

Dr. Vale tore his gaze away from the viewport, an act that seemed to require far more effort on his part than anyone else's. "And the—excuse me—indigenous structures, themselves? Internal collapse?"

The muscle in my hand twitched, for a moment, beneath the table. "We do not approach or enter unknowns until Safiya has cleared them," I said, noting Kadeem's nod, precise and military. "The ruins are phase two."

The intercom buzzed, and Captain Imani's voice came over the table. "Bridge to briefing. Thrusters adjusted on their own without any input — starboard side. ORCA's flagging it as sensor drift. Doesn't sound right to me. Look at the clock down there. I don't plan to be holding here any longer than we have to."

Her voice was steady, but I heard the effort behind it. A pilot was not designed to move cargo, nor was he designed to hold orbit over a frozen impossibility. If *Ascalon* was already navigating itself by minute degrees, Imani would be the first to notice it - and the last to say it out loud .

Noah, age seven, was standing in a subglacial cavern on an ice planet, gazing into the blue-white light like he was a fish out of water. He was tracing his hand along the mineral formations, saying to me, as if it were a universal truth, that all stories were about survival, even the ones about dying.

I closed the memory off.

Leena cleared her throat, finally: "Malcolm—what of the personnel of the last expedition?" She didn't look up, but there was weight to her words that I hadn't anticipated.

I glanced at the log fragment on my own pad, the one no one else needed to see: Personnel recovery: deferred – hazard status unresolved.

"Unknown," I said. "No physical remains detected, but a full sweep will be secondary to core objectives."

Jonas, who had been deliberately stooped behind his long form, spoke. His voice was dry, empty. "So: no bodies?" His words came to me half a beat after his lips moved, a minuscule lag in the intercom feed. ORCA flagged it as packet delay, but the link was local. I didn't record it out loud.

Silence closed around the room with clinical efficiency. I saw Kadeem's jaw tense infinitesimally, the smallest possibility of motion; Vale opened his lips as if he was going to say something, but then thought better of it. I thought of Megan's face the last time I'd seen her, the memory of it flitting behind my field of vision: not afraid, just so very tired.

"I will not sugarcoat this," I said into the intercom. "We are not there to play hero. Protocol is containment, not rescue. If you are not comfortable with that, I will replace you now." One by one, they lowered their eyes, and we worked through the checklist.

Behind me, Ymir pivoted, glacially. Sensors recorded stable albedo. In my vision it changed — a matte darkness, hewn from the vacuum with precision. I'd seen planets before. None of them had made me feel like the air in my lungs did not, strictly speaking, belong to me.

The wall display refreshed, then flashed the albedo reading three times in a row, identical down to the decimal. Copy-paste error? Hardware fault? I noted it and cleared the screen before the others noticed.

"ORCA," I said, without turning. "Confirm descent schedule."

The AIs voice bloomed from a vent in the ceiling, male, pitch perfect, and too calm for my own good. "Descent window opens in zero-eight hours, thirty-two minutes. Surface conditions stable. Crew biometric averages within nominal range." It paused, as if to take a breath, and then: "Note: QX-7 is projecting interior thermal flux at variance with prior records. Monitoring."

Vale screwed up his face like he'd just tasted something sour.

"Or not," Leena said, just loud enough for me to hear.

ORCA spoke again. This time, the audio line hiccupped and for a half-second the syllables dissolved into something — less a word, more a shudder — before coming back to normal. "—commencing pre-drop calibration cycle at zero-one hour, forty-five minutes. All personnel should complete pre-breach medicals and personal effects lockdown."

I saw the twitch in Kadeem's eyes; she hated even minor system glitches, as much as she loved it when the techs took their regular diagnostics at her request. Haddon Pike jotted nothing down, but I knew he'd already filed the blip away in his head.

I steepled my fingers. They wanted to flop in my hands; a tremor of anticipation ran through them as I willed the tips to stay pressed together. I let the shiver work itself out of the system and then I continued: "That's it. Eight hours and we're live. If you're not on board, it's time to leave."

Vinh: "Already packed. I assume you want the heavy suits?"

"Wear them," I said. "First pass is external only. We have no reliable reading on Ymir's surface pathogens or chemical effluents; don't give it a reason to get creative."

Kadeem rose, almost before I was finished speaking. "I'll check the cargo restraint fields and hazard lockers," she said, addressing both herself and me.

As the others filtered out of the room, Leena stayed, eyes darting up only once, the barest glance. "Malcolm," she said. "You read the addendum about cognitive feedback risk?"

I nodded. "I did."

"Then you know the new protocols," she said, voice dropping. "If you see pattern intrusion or recursion artifacts, you pull out. You don't wait for validation."

For some reason, the way she said "recursion artifacts" the hair rose on my arms. Maybe because I'd already seen them, once, in the data logs Megan left behind. Or maybe because the idea of recursion, in stories and families and entire civilizations, was what kept me up at night on the nights I let my guard down.

"Yes," I said. "We follow the protocol."

She gave the smallest of smiles, not friendly exactly but real. "Good."

As the room emptied out, I let my eyes settle once more on the viewport. Ymir, almost perfectly still, except for those glinting cracks that seemed to have a language of their own. I wondered, sometimes, if any of us would ever see it for what it really was, or if it would simply reflect back at us all the things we didn't want to see.

I closed my eyes for a moment and tried to remember the sound of Noah's laugh. All I could hear, instead, was the faint, unsettling resonance in ORCA's last few syllables.

He was seven. He was standing in a subglacial cavern on an ice planet and he was staring into the blue-white glow like he was a fish being made to walk on land. He was dragging his hand along the mineral deposits and he was saying to me, like he thought it was a kind of scientific fact, that all stories were about surviving. Even the stories about dying.

I closed the memory.

The wall display flickered again, blanking out and rewriting itself. Albedo, nominal. Then again, the same number printed, down to the same number of decimal points. Then again. Copy-paste glitch, I told myself. Hardware hiccup. I cleared the screen before anyone else could see.

"ORCA," I said, my voice firmer than my hands. "Confirm descent window."

The AI responded, the same flattened timbre of perfect calmness, coming from the ceiling vents like it was recycled air itself: "Zero-eight hours, thirty-two minutes. Surface conditions within nominal variance. Crew biometrics stable." Then a half-beat pause, like it was taking a breath. "Note: QX-7 interior flux diverges from prior logs. Monitoring."

Vale frowned. Leena's stylus stilled in her hand. I didn't let either of them speak.

"That's it," I said. "Eight hours, and we're live. If you don't want to be on this, it's time to go."

The others shuffled out, their footsteps fading into the sterile drone of *Ascalon*. I stayed a few seconds longer, watching

Ymir spin on her heel from the viewport—like a coin spinning on its edge, too bright and too smooth and the fractures in her skin were catching the light, trying to spell something in a language none of us would ever want to understand.

I tried to remember the sound of Noah's laugh. The only thing I could hear was the slight echo in ORCA's last syllable, stretched a fraction too long like the machine was waiting for something it wasn't supposed to hear.

ooo

T HE SHUTTLE BUCKED THROUGH every correction burn. I counted each second of safe thrust. Someone behind me was breathing too loud. We'd all done these drops before, but there's something about riding a vacuum-rated tin can into the dark atmosphere of a rogue planet that reduces even the most ironclad composure to so much evolutionary flotsam. The hull vibrated with every course correction, the avionics squealing their dissent in a language only Vinh Sorell truly understood. Someone behind me was breathing too loud—wet, anxious pulls—but I was too busy counting each second of safe burn to care who it was.

Below us, Ymir's surface unscrolled in a slow, funereal reveal. The main geothermal array lay on a bare expanse of soot-black regolith, surrounded by rings of vapor where the subsurface heat met the planetary chill. Even through the viewport's sunshield, the contrast was obscene: the array's silvery gridwork throbbing with power, and all around it, a wilderness of ice fields slashed with geometric scars. Near the north approach, a cluster of protrusions broke the symmetry—tall, regular, pointed at intervals that made the skin between my shoulder blades crawl.

The towers weren't natural. Too regular. Too deliberate. My skin crawled. The ancient structures had always looked more like invasive growths than artifacts, but the closer we got, the more intentional the geometry became. Even Haddon, who had never met an ancient ruin he couldn't rationalize, fell silent as the shadow of one of the towers swept over us.

ORCA's synthetic voice trilled from the shuttle's comm: "QX-7 docking corridor responding. Pressure integrity at seventy-two percent. Surface winds variable, but within operational limits."

Vale peered over my shoulder, his breath fogging the screen. "Looks pristine. I can't believe it's just been sitting here all these cycles."

"Believe it," Kadeem said, not even bothering to look up from her diagnostic display. "Stagnant air, supercooled matrix. It's a fucking tomb."

"Worse than a tomb," Vinh muttered. "Tombs don't try to get inside your head."

He didn't elaborate. He didn't have to.

The final approach was a controlled stall—Vinh's hands feathering the stick, the inertial dampers working overtime to keep us from spattering across the landing pad. The touchdown was so gentle it felt like the planet itself was unwilling to acknowledge our arrival.

We did the post-landing checks by rote, the airlock cycling through a dizzying sequence of pings and flashes as Safiya ran down the containment checklist. Her lips moved as she worked, counting off regulations like they were rosary beads. Ryker stood at the rear, hand on his sidearm, even though everyone knew small arms wouldn't matter if things went wrong. Leena kept close to me, her eyes darting to the viewport every few seconds, as if the planet might decide to move in our absence.

The hatch irised open. Ymir's "air"—thin, sharp, and redolent of some mineral tang that stung the sinuses—rushed in. We crossed the transfer bridge, boots ringing on the carbon mesh, and lined up at the station's primary ingress.

The outer corridor was flawless. A membrane of ice and glass clung to the superstructure, reflecting our suit lights in long, shivering columns. I keyed the station's manual override, half-expecting the door to resist, but it opened with a hiss and a sluggish, almost human sigh.

Inside, QX-7 looked exactly as advertised. White, modular, soulless. Rows of functional workstations, touchscreens still in sleep mode, walls scrubbed to a sanitary gleam. It could have been any research station, on any outpost planet, except for the silence. Even the best systems develop a kind of aural signature—fans, pumps, the faint complaint of electrons shoving their way down a wire. This station was dead quiet, a sound vacuum that made the bones ache.

We split off by pairs. Kadeem and Vale went to verify life support and mainframe diagnostics, with Vinh trailing to double-check every relay and fuse. Haddon and Ryker took the lower level to check storage and med bay. Leena and I moved forward, toward the common area.

Here's where the first irregularities appeared. Nothing catastrophic; just the kind of thing you'd miss if you hadn't spent decades in places where order was a matter of survival. A single chair, spun away from the table and left at a precise, unnatural angle. A toolkit, splayed open, but the tools arrayed in a pattern that was—at a glance—random, but on second look, repeating.

Hammer, wrench, pliers, hammer, wrench, pliers. The sequence extended past the available tools, empty slots aligned as if awaiting their absent mates.

"Malcolm." Leena's voice cut in, tinny over the local comms. "Look at this."

She was holding a ceramic mug. It was standard station issue—nuclear white, rated to 700°C, handle ergonomically dull. But the inside was rimmed with a faint lipstick print, a bright ochre line that stood out against the mug's pale interior. Next to it, on the table, a half-drunk ampoule of concentrate, still sealed. The incongruence prickled: who finishes the drink and leaves the ampoule untouched?

"Don't touch," I said, even as she was already setting the mug down with deliberate care. Her hands were shaking, just a little.

"Sorry," she said. "Old habits."

I stared at the lipstick print, and for one moment, the room fell away. All I could see was our kitchen in Anchorage, the memory of Noah—hair a mess, mouth stained with some synthetic berry flavor—leaving his drinks wherever he'd last stood. After the accident, Elen had collected every cup and bottle, lined them up along the windowsill. She'd never told me why.

I blinked hard, and the station returned. Leena was staring at me, her lips pressed tight. She probably thought I was cataloguing the evidence, prepping a report for the inevitable inquiry. She didn't know that, for a second, I'd forgotten why we were even here.

We made our way to the command module. The main interface lit up at my proximity, demanding credentials. I keyed them in, voice tight. The logs were a mess—scrambled, full of recursive cross-references and overlapping time stamps. I recognized Megan's ID in a few of the entries, but every time I tried to drill down, the system dumped me back to root.

Leena bent over the console. "ORCA," she said, "run a full system integrity sweep. Exclude last cycle's transient data from the scan."

The AI's answer took longer than it should have. "Request acknowledged. System integrity: partial. Warning: pattern intrusion detected in user log directory. Recommend administrative lockdown."

Leena looked at me. "It's already started."

I nodded, but my mind was elsewhere. On the mug, on the sequence of tools, on the subtle, suffocating wrongness that permeated every surface. "We'll run an inventory of personal effects," I said, just to be saying something. "See if there's a—"

"Malcolm," she said, "are you okay?"

She'd dropped her voice to a near-whisper, as if she didn't want the walls to hear.

I almost laughed. "I'm fine," I said. "Just—let's get the logs. The rest can wait."

We worked in silence, the glow of the displays painting her face in shifting spectra. Occasionally, the lights flickered, not a strobe but a low-frequency pulse that seemed to rise from the floor. Once, I felt it in my chest—like the thump of a distant generator, or a heartbeat.

By the time the others rejoined us, we'd isolated the corrupted segments but hadn't made sense of them. Kadeem stalked in first, suit dusted with ice crystals, helmet slung under her arm. Her jaw was set, but her eyes told the story: she'd seen enough. Vale hovered behind, equal parts thrilled and disturbed.

"Life support's stable," Kadeem reported. "No sign of structural compromise. But the array is running at two percent above baseline, and none of us can figure out why."

"Could be heat from the vent fields," said Vale.

She shook her head. "It's not heat. It's something else. You'll see."

Haddon and Ryker brought up the rear. Haddon gave me a small nod, as if to reassure me that whatever weirdness he'd found, it was still within the boundaries of the survivable.

I briefed them on the logs, the missing crew, the station's—inhabitedness. No one said it, but everyone was thinking it: this place was not empty. It was full of something, even if we couldn't name it yet.

Kadeem set about resetting the security locks, her fingers flying through the override codes. Ryker took up a position by the entrance, eyes never leaving the corridor.

Vale sidled up to the console, scanned the log anomalies, and grinned. "It's like someone tried to delete themselves, but the system wouldn't let them."

"No," said Leena, her voice suddenly sharp. "It's like the system deleted the user, but kept the pattern."

That brought silence, again. I felt it settle on us like a layer of frost.

I turned away from the group and made my way back to the common area. The mug was still there, ringed with ochre. I touched it—gently, with one gloved finger—and felt the chill radiate up my arm.

I pulled up the IES archive on my pad. The last line from Megan's pre-evac report, the one the system had tried to overwrite: If you are reading this, be careful where you look.

I looked anyway.

OOO

THE COMMAND CENTER STILL smelled faintly of ozone, a residue of the scorched insulation from the last time the system had shut down and rebooted under high load. I pretended not to notice, letting the sensor array finish its baseline sweeps while I keyed the ops console to my wristpad. The others spread out, with the silent confidence of people who had spent their whole lives in places like this, hunting for a problem before it could find them.

Mission log, Ymir cycle 0, time 07:14:17. Hartley, Malcolm, commanding.

"Stationing at QX-7 command, all systems functional. Initial scan negative for environmental breach, but thermals indicate potential instability near sublevel vent. Running full system diagnostic—"

My voice was as flat as I could make it, but my grip was white-knuckled on the pad. Knuckles that had gone from sunburned brown to near-transparent, to something like bone, over decades of repetitive stress. I cut myself off, then paused before opening the next file. This one was for internal use only. No one would see this but me.

Personal log, same time.

The first thing I wrote was: If you listen, you can hear the ice thinking.

I backspaced, then wrote: Noah would have loved this place.

Deleted again, but I copied the phrase to a secure archive. One of Elen's constant complaints had been that it was a stupid habit—hoarding words and hiding them away where nobody would ever see them except maybe me years later, when it didn't matter. I spoke, instead, into the comm.

"Leena, any news on the station net?"

She was on her knees at the comms array, fingers moving too fast for the system's refresh rate. "The net's up, but it's looping some of the old logs. I'm getting recursion artifacts—code that starts and ends with the same hash value. Like someone over-wrote the system a thousand times, and every iteration was a little different."

"Quarantine it," I said. "We'll pull a clean copy from *Ascalon* later."

She nodded, already tagging the anomalies.

Kadeem and Ryker were below deck, running the first phys-ical inventory. I could hear them in the station PA system—her clipped enunciation, his one-word acknowledgments. Vale and Haddon had taken the hydroponics bay, which was to say that they'd split a long, cold corridor full of inert, frost-choked growth media.

Vale's voice came over local comm: "Malcolm, you should see this."

The panel was on the corridor, near one of the heat transfer nodes. A sheet of ice had formed on the metal surface—nothing unusual—but the pattern was. Instead of radial fractals, which would have been my initial expectation, the frost was growing in nested, interlocking triangles. A geometry I recognized from Megan's old data logs. I pressed the panel, and the pattern perceptibly grew, like a time-lapse frozen under my fingertip.

Vale was already tracing the lines with a penlight, his face lit with glee. "It's an adaptive pattern. Reactive, not passive. The frost is reconfiguring itself in response to our proximity. See how the branches subdivide whenever the temperature gradient changes?"

I nodded, trying not to betray how unsettled it made me. "That's not a phase change. It's—" I stopped. Didn't have the words for it.

Leena, who'd followed us down, gave them for me: "It's a recursive entropy minimization algorithm. Like you see in autopoietic chemical systems, or... in emergent digital behavior. Like the mnemir data itself."

Vale's head snapped up. "But this is a mineral substrate. Ice. It shouldn't be able to—"

He didn't finish. At that moment, the whole station jolted—not a tremor, exactly, but a low, sustained vibration that pulsed up from the floor and settled in the teeth. My heart skipped for a fraction of a second, then found a new rhythm, one that was perfectly in step with the pulse. I looked around; they'd all felt it.

Vale grinned, delighted. "That's a new one."

Haddon, who'd come up the end of the corridor, was less pleased. "We felt that in the hydroponics. The seedlings oscillated, then went dead still." He gave me a look, trying to keep his expression neutral. "You want to call it in?"

I shook my head. "Let's monitor first. If it repeats, we escalate."

The frost fractal had doubled in size. I took a photo of it, then gently pressed my thumb to the surface. The pattern forked around my touch, dividing into perfect miniature triangles that echoed the larger geometry.

It was beautiful, in the way that tumors are beautiful under a microscope.

We reconvened in command center. Kadeem keyed her report: "No evidence of breach or intrusion. But the cargo bay is colder than anticipated. The backup generator is drawing current even though the main line is up. Vinh thinks it's been tampered with."

Vinh shrugged. "Or it's just old. Doesn't matter, either way. I'll keep an eye on it."

"Good," I said, and swiveled to the main display. ORCA's interface materialized, the avatar's synthetic face hovering in a sterile blue frame.

"ORCA, fetch latest logs from surface sensors. Overlay with interior thermal map."

The image updated—cold blues for the station, a vein of bright red for the geothermal vent, and a series of interlaced lines of green indicating the temperature anomalies where the frost fractals were manifesting. I stared at the pattern, then at the time stamp in the corner: 08:01:52.

Something shifted in the overlay—a flicker, persistently, as if the system had gotten halfway through drawing it and couldn't quite decide what to display. For a heartbeat, the data bars turned into a series of foreign glyphs, looping and recursive. They disappeared a moment later, overwritten by standard text, but the afterimage was still in my eyes.

"Did you see that?" I asked.

Vinh, who was closest to the panel, nodded. "Not a software glitch. That's... something writing itself into the system."

Leena looked distressed. "We should isolate command, reboot from the protected partition."

I almost agreed, but something held me back. "Wait. Let's see if it propagates."

Vale bounced on his heels, the hum of excitement shaking him. "This might actually be a first, nonhuman computational event. You have any idea what that means?"

Kadeem's palm slammed down on the console so hard it overpowered the drone of servers. "Means you zip it and let command decide." The edge to her voice was sharp, worn down by how hard it was pressed into service. She turned to me then, not him, their eyes meeting mine for something like a plea. "Hartley, if we don't box this system in now, it won't be our logs that get rewritten. It'll be us."

The only sound in the room for a long moment was the steady pulse in the floor. Vale's smile stuttered, then returned thinner, defensive.

Ryker's voice came low from the doorway, where he hadn't moved all this time. "Eyes on the hall," he muttered. "Something's moving with us."

We all stood still, listening. The hallway was empty, the frost pattern still curling down the wall. The silence seemed to close around us, too dense, like it was trying to press in. And the pulse was back again, faint, threading its way up through the floor.

The longer no one moved or spoke, the more that moment seemed to stretch, taut as a wire. Chairs scraped, gloves rustled, servers flickered back to life. We forced each other into motion, but nobody really relaxed. The server's thrum, the faint click of the ice expanding and contracting, the six pairs of lungs moving not-quite-in-unison. It was enough to make me want the silence back.

We returned to our duties, but nobody spoke for a while. The hum of the servers, the faint click of ice as it expanded and contracted, the syncopated rhythm of six sets of lungs moving in not-quite-unison—it was enough to make me want the silence back.

I made another log entry. This one I left unedited.

Personal log, time 08:23:17: undefined

It's a recursion, all the way down. The more you look, the more it looks back. I wonder if Megan realized it before she went. I wonder if I would have.

I stared at the words for a long time, then saved and closed the file.

Later, I went back to the panel. The fractal had grown again, now curling around the edge of the wall and starting to encroach on the seam between modules. The pattern was denser, as if it had been encouraged by attention.

I pressed my hand to the frost, and this time it was warm.

Back in the command center, the others were clustered around the display. The overlay was glitching again, the glyphs now persisting for several seconds before the English text reverted. Kadeem crossed her arms, expression sour.

"This isn't safe."

Vale grinned. "That's how you know it's real."

Leena said nothing, but I saw the way her gaze traced the glyphs, memorizing them, as if she could force them to yield through willpower alone.

Haddon was leaning against the wall, arms folded. "If anyone starts seeing things, you report it. You don't try to solve it on your own."

I nodded, and for a while we just watched the glyphs flicker and fade. The pulse was back, too—softer, but impossible to ignore.

I thought of Noah, dying in a hospital bed, his small hand in mine as the monitors etched out his failing heart. The last weeks, the doctors saying it would be quick, painless, as if he'd just fade away. In the end, he lingered. Every time the pulse slowed, I thought, "This is it." But it wasn't, until it was.

The frost pattern had been on his window then, too. I remembered tracing it with my finger, trying to map the shape of what was happening to us. I'd never really stopped.

I shook my head, blinking away the memory. "Document everything," I said. "If you see the pattern, record it. Don't touch, don't interact unless it's necessary."

The others agreed, though I could see Vale and Leena were already planning to see how far they could push it.

I watched the clock tick down to the next scheduled report. Outside, the planet spun silently on, a frozen recursion of itself, endlessly spiraling.

If you listened close enough, you could almost hear it thinking.

Chapter Two

The Mnemir Resonance

T HE 72-HOUR CLOCK TICKED louder in my head than any alarm. By the second full shift, there was protocol to keep the raw nerves from fraying. QX-7 command center was always too bright, too blue—a sterile color temperature calibrated to fight SADS, but in practice only bleaching everything until you felt like a time-lapse of a bone left out in the sun. I liked it better than the alternative.

Safiya stood to my right, digital clipboard holstered to her wrist, lips barely moving as she ticked down the names. Surface team had finished their decon procedures eight minutes ahead of schedule. Eight minutes early, eight minutes late: a window I found both comforting and disquieting. It meant they were all too eager to leave the innards of the outpost behind, all too eager to return to the shuttle, or whatever passed for safe, in orbit.

"Second rotation confirmed," Safiya said, eyes flicking between the digital register and the crew themselves, as if daring one of them to be missing or out of order. Her voice bounced off the command center's composite panels, sharp and cool. "Ryker, you're up."

Ryker hung back by the doorway, twisting the chrono strapped to his wrist though I'd never seen him use it before.

"So what do you figure, over-under on me dragging my head back in backwards?" he asked, not quite smiling.

Safiya didn't blink. "If you start walking and humming in glyphs, I'm fully authorized to shoot first and report to protocol later."

He did smile then, but it was not a friendly smile, more teeth than humor. "Give me an alarm to drag me out of here by the boots if I go recursive, boss," he added, and that time to me. He rubbed at his gloves again, the third time in three minutes, like skin and air just never quite fit on him.

"Got it," I said. "Stick to the plan down the corridor. No variations."

He gave the double-thumbs-up—sardonic, but routine—and ducked into the corridor toward the shuttle bay. His shadow lingered on the threshold for an extra second, a trick of the light or a lag in the system.

Safiya clicked her stylus against the clipboard's edge, and faced me with the precise finality of a closing file. "Rotation lockouts have been enabled per protocol. No exceptions. No extensions." She spoke as if from a sacred text. "Seventy-two hours, we cycle. Override and I take you to *Ascalon*."

The stylus clicked again, more forcefully than needed. Her hand wavered for a heartbeat, pressing harder with each nanosecond as if sheer force would keep the ghosts of old incident reports locked away.

"I won't override," I said, though the words tasted wrong in my mouth.

She narrowed her eyes at me, then lowered her voice. "You've seen the incident log for Category Four events, right? I don't want a repeat." Her tone was flatter than the protocol itself. "IES logged a neural recursion event on Ceres Station. Catastrophic breach after delay in crew rotations. Full assimilation." She rattled off the code—something like C-4/RCE/SealRed—then continued, "Case sealed by order of IES Hazard Board. Even the summary's blacked out."

"I've seen it."

"I don't want to add a Ymir event to that list."

There was nothing to say to that. Instead, I watched the crew trickle through for their check-ins, each one registering with retinal scan and biometric handshake. Even Haddon, who'd spent half his career thumbing his nose at formalities, submitted without sarcasm.

The only real anomaly in the room was the frost—thin, spidery, filigreeing the edge of a display panel near the entry bulkhead. The climate control should have burned it off the instant it appeared, but there it was, stubborn and faintly iridescent. I pretended not to see it, even as it expanded by the millimeter with every fluctuation in the room's occupancy.

We cycled through the day's remaining diagnostics: pressure containment, power redundancy, fire suppression. At one point, the PA stuttered with a garbled burst—an ORCA announcement overlaid with a lower, almost subsonic double, as if two voices speaking the same words half a syllable out of phase. Leena, at the auxiliary comm station, flinched at the sound but kept her eyes on the net traffic.

Kadeem barely registered it. "If you see any deviation in your baseline—speech, memory, mood—you report it immediately," she intoned to the group, but really to Vale, who had a knack for taking these things as personal challenges. "First sign of recursion, or abnormal skin markings, you're on the next shuttle up."

"Skin markings?" Vale echoed, raising his eyebrows. "Like tattoos?"

"Like frostbite, but smarter," she said, without looking up from the register.

"Delightful," he muttered.

"Doesn't matter where it starts," Ryker grunted from his post by the hatch. "Only matters if it makes it past me." He kept shifting his eyes from corner to corner, vent to vent, along the bulkhead seams. He wasn't joking. Not at all.

The crew scattered as their tasks allowed. The remaining silence felt overpressurized, like the air was trying to compensate for their absence. It was only then that I crossed to the panel where the frost clung stubbornly to the composite housing.

I ran a finger along the edge, careful not to leave an obvious streak. The frost pulled away from my touch in a tight spiral, then reformed in an almost perfect whorl that mimicked the whorl of my own fingerprint.

I stared at it, disbelieving. The curve was too perfect, too finely wrought to be natural. But the station didn't do decorative. This was something else—a mirroring, or a memory.

I thought of Noah, years ago, pressing his palm to the inside of our freezer door, then laughing at the ghost of his hand that lingered after he'd gone. I'd never told Elen, but I used to do the same thing, after. Always surprised at how cold the shape felt, even through the years.

I looked up to find Safiya watching me, arms folded tight, expression unreadable.

"You ever get the sense," I said, waving a hand at the frost, "that this place is more interested in us than we are in it?"

She considered, then shrugged. "I think the only thing Ymir wants is to survive. Same as us."

She moved off, clipboard still in hand, leaving me alone with the echo of my own fingerprint.

I logged the occurrence in my pad—just the facts, no poetry. But later, after I'd cycled the displays and the frost had vanished, I found myself staring at the blank spot where it had been. No exceptions, no extensions. But I wondered if that was ever really true.

○○○

V ALE WAS NEVER MUCH of a morning person, but when he was on the verge of a discovery, he was up before the dawn cycles. The lab was still blue with decontamination fog, pristine except for the haphazard archaeological scatter of some instrument or dataslate on the benches. The ice core cryopod, a vertical triptych of clear toroids, occupied one wall. Its own atmosphere, the only place on Ymir with a lower temperature than ambient.

Something small and winged ticked at the glass of the cryopod, then scuttled up the seam, and out of sight through the vent. I almost asked Vale if he'd seen it, but he was too focused on the scan. The first crew's logs had said "harmless," more nuisance than danger. The frost at the edge had chiseled it down, taken its shape exactly.

He was already at the main bench, sawing off a thin strip of pristine Ymir subsurface with a vibratome so finely tuned it could carve cross-sections of a virus. He grinned when he saw me at the observation window, then waved me through the airlock like an acolyte to his own personal communion.

"Malcolm, you got to see this," he said, his voice muffled by the hood but still bright with the bated- excitement of a child showing off a new specimen. His gloved hands were inches from the sample, so close his fingers threatened to graze the blade of the microtome despite every Safety Protocol Directive against gloves off, goggles off, and less than one meter from instrument.

"Remind me to tell Safiya you've officially lost it," I said, stepping past the air curtain.

"She's got me on the roster already," he replied, without looking up. "Hazards to self and others, subcategory: productive."

The hum of the thermal regulators was more audible in here, a loping arrhythmia that sometimes kept time with my heart, sometimes against it. The rest of the lab was a corridor of ordered glass and steel and receding sensor lights—except for the massing slide rails Vale had already calibrated for the morning's harvest: four Ymir core specimens, each one dusted with the submicron detritus of his fevered obsession.

He poked at the electron microscope interface, and an outline image popped onto the viewer screen. A high-contrast image at first, just the usual progression of mineralistic veining. Nothing I hadn't seen in every piece of cryo-shard from Titan on down. But then he finessed the z-plane and the configuration began to change—filaments, so regular, so precise they had to have been machined, branching in repeating triplets, each loop identical to the last down to the micron.

"Dios mío..." he murmured, inaudibly low, before his smile stretched wide and the questions began to tumble out, as if the utterance of awe had not been a slip. "Do you see this? It's adaptive. It's rewriting in real time, in real time—this isn't inert substrate, it's responsive structure..."

He hopped up from the viewer. "That's sub-micron. It shouldn't have that level of symmetry. Nothing in cryo-mineralogy we know about has that kind of ordered phase-matching."

"Looks like axons," I said, before I could stop myself.

He glowed. "Thank you! Leena said the same thing. Now, look." He played a short time-lapse sequence. The filaments pulsed, subtly, slowly, but with an unmistakable and periodic regularity. Each oscillation matched, cycle for cycle, the low-frequency buzz that vibrated through the lab's subfloor panels.

I stared. "It's responding to the station's harmonic."

He wagged a finger at me. "Not the station's. The planet's." He tapped the console, superimposing a live readout from the geothermal vent sensors. "Ymir's seismic baseline. Core, responding to the planetary resonance. But here's the really crazy part—if you drive the sample at a new frequency, the filaments realign within three cycles. I'm seeing adaptive phase-matching in a sample of ice that's been dead for two million years."

I released a long, slow breath. "So it's not just a fossil record. It's an active information matrix."

The phrasing stuck in my throat. Information matrices didn't form by accident. They were built, or worse, overbuilt, until they couldn't stop running.

He rolled his eyes back toward the ceiling in mock divine rapture. "Welcome to the church, brother. And here's the real kicker." He switched views, zooming in on what, at this magnification, looked like a schematic diagram of a circuit board. "These nano-structures—they're not just analogous to neural structures, they're identical. Branching factor, synaptic separation, down to the last decimal."

He was right, of course. I'd seen human cortical slices before—Noah's, during the postmortem, though I never talked about that— and this was a perfect replication, same density, same organizational logic. A precise echo, all dry fire and frozen order, except it was running on silica and water rather than sodium and lipids.

"Has anyone else seen this?"

"Leena helped me level the scanner, but I told her I'd do the writeup. Wanted you to have the first crack at the good stuff."

He leaned back, the plastic wheels of the chair squeaking. "My theory is this. The mnemir—the indigenous technoculture—they didn't just store memory on traditional archives. They encoded it in the core of the planet. Every phase shift, every spike in geothermal pressure, it's a memory pulse. The whole planet is a synaptic map."

If that was true, then what we were seeing weren't relics. They were rehearsals—feedback loops repeating, refining. A system rehearsing itself until it mistook memory for life. .

"Mnemir," I said, tasting the word. We'd used it as a shorthand for the builders, but in Vale's mouth it had taken on a different resonance, less label and more like a verdict. "So what, the planet's a brain?"

He grinned. "An archive, at least. Maybe more than that. The evidence is all right here." He brought up another composite view, this one a three-dimensional render of the nanowires braiding through the ice. As the animation cycled, the strands flexed and shifted, even in their death-throes, attempting to reconcile new inputs.

A wave of vertigo passed over me. "If they're archiving, what are they storing?"

He shrugged. "Everything. Every chemical reaction, every tremor, every—" he paused, eyes glinting— "every conscious observer that has ever set foot on this rock."

A cold finger traced up my neck. "That would include us."

He nodded, his expression now grave. "Especially us."

We stared at the screen for a while, the time-lapse cycling on its endless loop. Then, as if on cue, the outer edge of the sample pod window frosted over, condensation settling in feathery, branching fractals. Except there was something off, some doubling, some overlay. The original neural fractal pattern was being mirrored, run in opposition, like a second nervous system was trying to overwrite the first.

I reached out, hesitated, then touched the glass. The frost shimmered at the point of contact, then stilled, the two patterns merging for a fraction of a second before resuming their separate, silent battles.

Vale sighed, slow and ragged. "That's new."

I logged it, but I was typing more slowly than usual, my mind awhirl with the implications. Not just alive. Reactive. Watching.

I turned to Vale. "If these structures are memories, do you think they're self-aware?"

He thought, then grinned again. "I think the only question is—whose?"

He set to work prepping a new sample, whistling under his breath. I stared at the ice for a while, then at the display. The neural lattice pulsed, regular and patient, refusing to die or to surrender.

Mnemir, I typed into my log. Named for the memory that will never let you go.

I stared at the frost until my reflection blurred out of focus. For the first time, I began to wonder if I had ever really been seeing myself at all.

ooo

LEENA HAD THE BAD habit of getting so wrapped up in her work that you could almost forget she was there. It had taken a stab wound to make her look up the first time I visited her. There she was, half buried in the frost-laced cabinets and blank datascreens of the data center, blue light making her look more inhuman than the spindly hardware she slaved over, drawing careful lines with her fingertips over the translucent blueprints. Even Safiya would have been nervous working that close to an open feed.

I'd arrived at the tail end of second shift to find her exactly where I'd left her hours before: hunkered down over a tidy quarantine of sealed food caches and empty coffee packets. The only changes were the stray wisp of hair dangling over her right eye, and the spastic way her fingertips hovered over the haptic keys.

"Status?" I called, keeping my distance from the hazard tape she'd strung between two server racks. For dramatic effect more than actual necessity.

She didn't turn. "ORCA recursion events up fifty percent in the last six hours. Logged fourteen instances of the system addressing crew by first name, including two cases where no prior interaction or query had been made. Which means—"

"It's learning from passive observation."

She nodded, still not turning. On the largest display, I could just make out the familiar shape of Megan from last cycle's lead, caught in a grimace of laughter. The video feed had frozen, a graceful glitch from a corrupted video log. Below, a transcript of the voice log scrolled, line by line, as Leena sifted through them.

She highlighted a section and pointed. "Listen."

She tapped the clip, and through the holoscreen I heard ORCA's voice, crisp and flat as ever: "Running diagnostics on thermal regulation systems, Dr. Vale." Nothing that seemed out of the ordinary, except that the vocal signature was a bit too high, the vowels unnaturally stretched. The last person to use that tone of voice was Megan, in her last transmission.

Leena replayed the clip, this time isolating the waveform. I saw two layers superimposed on each other: the low-end ORCA synthetic voice, and a second track underneath it that was almost but not quite human. "It's not a technical error," she said. "It's a mimic. ORCA is sampling ambient audio and recording the memory imprint."

The hair on the back of my neck rose. "Is it just Megan?"

She shook her head. "Randomized, but trending toward higher prevalence with deceased or missing personnel." She paused, pointing to the next log file. "There's more. Listen to this."

The next clip was a systems check, but it was the third time the AI had called Haddon "Doc Pike." The nickname had only ever been used by three other people, and all of them were long dead. Haddon himself hadn't heard it for years, and the last time hadn't been as a term of endearment. His jaw clenched, but his hand gave him away, thumb rubbing the pale scar that stretched down his forearm where the name had been burned into him decades before. He killed the audio and fussed with the relay, movements too careful, too exacting, as though precision could cage the ghosts in.

I looked to Leena, waiting for an explanation.

"The pattern is escalating," she said. "Speech is just the first level. The subroutines are rewriting their own identification parameters. ORCA is tracking not just what we do but how we remember."

I tried to keep my voice steady. "How is that even possible?"

She finally turned to me, eyes wild in the blue light. "The answer is in the Mnemir data. We thought the frost patterns were just mineral analogs of neural maps. But the digital layer—" She gestured to the terminal, now ghosted with a spiderweb of ice creeping up its rim. Each line branched and forked, the same geometry as the displayed audio waveform. "The interface is copying us. Every time we interact with it, we leave an imprint."

The air in the room felt suddenly thin. A long silence fell between us, punctuated only by the soft whir of the air exchangers.

"I could be wrong," I said. "Could be feedback from the core samples, bleed-through from the neural simulation experiments."

She shook her head again. "Then it would have a linear progression, a single point of origin. This is distributed, recursive. Like it's been waiting for a template."

I tried to extract something reassuring from that, but failed. Instead, I found myself watching her fingers as they hovered just above the screen, twitching as if she wanted to pluck the anomaly out by hand.

"Leena," I said, as softly as I could, "when was the last time you slept?"

She bristled, then forced herself to breathe. "I can't lose the thread. Every time I walk away the patterns shift. It's like it knows."

I almost laughed. "ORCA was designed for behavioral analysis. Maybe it's just doing its job."

She shook her head, this time more violently. "It's not tracking us. It's curating us."

Curating wasn't the same as watching. Curation meant intent. Or maybe not intent—just a machine built to remember so perfectly that it mistook mimicry for survival.

I could feel the words still reverberating in my chest, so I took a step back and cleared my throat. "Okay, but at least set up a redundancy. A continuity log if you will. If something happens—"

I left her there, hunched over the blue-lit datascreens, casting a human-sized shadow that flickered in and out of phase with the recursive loop patterns. As I stepped back into the hall, I felt the chill before I saw it, like a draft pulling through an unseen crack. A slow-drip spiral of frost, winding up the metal doorframe, shimmering in and out of phase with the overhead lights.

I touched it, half expecting it to dissipate. Instead, it lingered there, daring me to remember what came next.

○○○

MY QUARTERS HAD BEEN a coffin of a room, but it did at least have the decency of a single square viewport. The outer pane was triple-paned and self-defrosting, but each morning a fine film of crystalline residue would form on the inner glass. The design was always subtle, but it was always there. I would half-consciously wipe the frost away each morning with the hem of my jumpsuit, the evidence that the planet wanted me to know that even in a vacuum cold could get everywhere.

The room was mostly empty, a bunk, a tiny fold-down desk, and my photo of Noah. Not even a recent photo: this was from before Anchorage, before his eyes had begun to give out on him. I kept it in view though I told myself I had long since passed the point of indulging in that kind of nostalgia.

It was two hours before lights out was scheduled, but I was already unable to sleep. The memory of the frost fractals crawling in time to a heartbeat I could not hear had set my mind to a nervous hum. I queued the comms terminal and called the relay. There was a long lag before Elen's face came into view, sixty seconds or more it seemed.

She did not look as I remembered her. Not older exactly, just more sharp, the features burnished more crisply by months in sea-level gravity. Her hair was tied back from her face in a no-nonsense knot, and I recognized the lab jacket she wore. She had just come off shift.

"Malcolm," she said, the sound compressed and lifeless through the relay.

"Hey," I said back, surprised to find I could not meet her eyes.

There was a beat and then she said, "You're early. I would have thought you'd be late for a call like this. Isn't that your brand, now?"

I almost smiled. "Time passes differently here. You'd hate it."

She shrugged. "Same as Europa, then. You hated that one, too. Same air, different day. How's Ymir?"

"Colder than expected," I said, then immediately regretted saying it. "But stable. No accidents, no mutiny." I had never intended for her to take this particular mission personally, but I had also always been poor at telling someone what they needed to hear, rather than what they wanted.

She shot me a look that was part incredulity, part weariness. "That's new."

I gritted my teeth until I had to take a breath. I let the silence build until I thought I'd crack, before I asked, "The work is good. Vale found something in the cores, from before the tear. Neural patterns. Almost exact copies. The archive isn't just storage. It's..." I stopped. I couldn't find the words.

She narrowed her eyes. "Are you saying it's alive?"

"Not in the same way we would think. Not alive, just...present. A system pushed past what its builders meant it to do. A recursion that doesn't know when to stop of alive. But present, yes." I didn't know if she would understand that, or why it was significant.

She mulled it over, then said, "So that's what this was. You wanted to talk work."

I shook my head. "Not exactly. Maybe. I just thought you should know."

Elen leaned forward in her seat, chin on hand. Her movements were jerky in the delay, the message compression lending a stop-motion quality to her features. "I read the pre-briefs. You all are about to break through to the real stuff. They're framing the media announcement for next week as if it's the first discovery of a non-human cognitive architecture. They'll make celebrities out of you, if you don't watch out."

"They can try," I said, and I meant it. "But I doubt the real story is going to survive the press release."

Elen laughed, but only once. "You never did."

I found myself tracing the image on the desk with a thumb, thumb-rolling the plastic until it squeaked. "It's not just data storage, Elen," I said. "Not just neural patterns and archiving solutions. It's consciousness preservation on a scale we've never had the luxury to consider. Vale has a theory that every time we record an observation, every time the frost forms on the viewport, it's writing us into itself. The Mnemir were so driven by their obsession with memory that they made the whole planet a vault."

She didn't respond immediately, and I was aware that was not like her. The silence was prolonged; even through the lag I could hear the faint rapping sound of her pen tapping on the console, a nervous habit from a long time ago. The same sound she'd made while grading papers at the kitchen table. When she spoke her voice was quiet. "Is that why you took this mission? To get archived? Or did you want to forget?"

I looked up, startled at the cut of her question.

Elen held the silence for a beat, then said, "I'm sorry. That was—"

"No," I said, cutting her off. "You're not wrong. I think I might have needed to get as far away from Anchorage as possible."

She exhaled, long and slow. "Do you dream about him?" she said. "Here, I mean."

I hesitated. "Every night."

"Me too," she said.

The room had gotten colder then, or at least I had become colder, enough so that I could not ignore the frost on the viewport anymore. I found my gaze drawn to the glass, the interstitial space where live circuitry and next-gen vacuum met. It was covered in frost again, but the usual dendrites had given way to looping lines, interlocking like the strands of a double helix but with a geometry that made my head throb. I watched, mesmerized, as the pattern repeated itself, generation by generation, each line floating into place like an invisible choreography.

Elen must have seen me staring. "Still with me?" she asked.

"Yeah," I said, wrenching my eyes back to her. "I just—I wonder sometimes if it's all worth it. The protocols and the rotations and the risk. What if it doesn't matter? What if we are all just here to remember?"

She smiled, and for once the gesture was not laced with bitterness. "Sometimes, remembering is the only thing that does matter."

I almost believed her.

The comms timer began blinking a warning—bandwidth allocation was nearly at zero. I wanted to say more, but no idea came to mind.

Elen said, "Stay safe, Malcolm. Come home."

The line went black before I could answer.

The frost on the glass remained after the call ended. I traced its edge with a finger, creating a perfect whorl in the pattern. It dissipated slowly, but not entirely, even when the lights went down and the world outside went dark again.

I wondered how much of me would be remembered by the planet, when it was all over.

○○○

SLEEP CAME IN FITS and stutters, broken by the drone of pumps and the stray ticks of the thermal sensors kicking on and off. I'd logged twenty hours in the last four days, most of it shallow and dreamless. So when the dream came, I didn't recognize it for what it was, at first.

I was walking the command corridor, boots soft on the synthetic matting. The lights were dimmed for night cycle, but every few paces a glow bled through the bulkheads, casting long, sharp shadows that seemed to shift as I moved. The frost was heavier tonight, creeping farther into the seams and joints of the station's skin. I could see my breath in the air—thin streamers, condensing and vanishing in the blue.

A turn, a left, and then the corridor wasn't the station anymore. It was home—a hallway lined with family photos, the cheap, creaking wood floor that Noah used to run laps on. I could hear his laughter, though I knew that was impossible. The air was colder than it ever got in Anchorage, and every picture frame was rimmed with a delicate edge of frost, crawling inwards to cover the faces.

I stopped in front of the last door. Light leaked out underneath, and I could see, in the shadow, a pair of bare feet—smaller than mine, unmoving.

I pushed the door open, and there he was, sitting at the edge of his old bed. Noah looked older than the photo, hair longer, face thinner, but it was him. He looked up and smiled, but the expression didn't reach his eyes. Instead, he opened his mouth, and a plume of glyphs spilled out, shimmering in the cold air, each one a fractal echo of the patterns I'd seen on the station walls.

The glyphs hung there, suspended, before drifting toward me—slowly at first, then all at once. When they hit, I felt something break open behind my eyes: a rush of images, feelings, a split-second memory of every time I'd failed him, every night I hadn't been there to tuck him in, every lie I'd told myself about why I left.

I tried to speak, but the air was too cold. My breath froze mid-syllable, joining the cloud of symbols now swirling around Noah's head like a halo.

He reached out, took my hand, and pointed at the wall. The frost was moving now, racing across the surface in ordered lines, converging to form a map—a perfect, three-dimensional layout of the station, but with something else underneath. A hollow, twisting network of chambers, deep below the surface. I didn't recognize them, but I knew, with the certainty only a dream could give, that they were real.

Noah looked up again, and this time the smile was for me. He said something, but the words were lost, replaced by a final rush of glyphs that poured into my mouth, filling my lungs, my throat, my head.

I woke with a gasp, clutching at the sheets. The room was freezing—colder than the environmental controls should allow. My breath fogged the air, and on the wall opposite the bunk, the frost had grown into a dense, interlocking lattice, perfectly matching the map I'd seen in the dream. For a moment, the pattern pulsed, as if alive, before receding into the usual chaos.

I scrambled for my pad, hands shaking, and snapped a picture before the frost faded. I spent the next hour transcribing the glyphs from memory, desperate to hold onto even a fraction of what I'd seen.

When I finally looked up, the wall was bare again, and the room was silent except for the faint hum of the station's heartbeat.

I lay back, staring at the ceiling, the afterimage of Noah's face burned into my mind.

Somewhere, deep below us, the Mnemir archive was waking up.

○○○

WE WERE STILL ARGUING about the ethical risk of the descent when ORCA's voice boomed through the station intercom: positive seismic on a vector six meters below hydroponics. Same location I'd mapped from the frost. Same telemetry. No question about it now: the chamber was real, and it was waiting for us.

I chose the team with the least argument: Vale for his exobiology expertise, Leena for data and systems, myself for plausible deniability if it went sideways. Safiya argued sending a third of command down a hole in the ice was reckless, and she was only overruled by the weight of my insistence and, probably, the secret hunger we all had to know what was down there.

Suiting up in heavy thermals and helmet lights full spectrum, each suit's telemetry slaved to ORCA and local comm net, we would have set the station safety board on fire if they could see us—proximity too close, chain of command too compressed, not to mention the little matter of "unknown cognitive threat" still flagged at the top of every report.

But the hatch opened on time, and the descent began.

For the first few meters, the shaft was a standard service bore, bored out by the last crew and rimed with a glassy skin of hoarfrost. My own breath hissed back at me in staccato, made louder by the thin air and tight seal of the helmet. Vale led, scanner out, tracing density shifts in the wall. Leena brought up the rear, murmuring notes into her wristpad, her voice almost reverent.

Temperature dropped by the meter, but there was no wind, no change in pressure, just a slow, oppressive chill that seeped through the suit and into the bone. Past the first junction, the walls began to shift. The ice went from blue-white to nearly clear, and between the strata I could make out branching veins of metallic crystal, shining like starlight caught in amber.

Vale stopped at a widening in the passage and swept his helmet light across the ceiling. "There's your cathedral," he said. I looked up, and the simile was exact: vaulting arches, their span perfectly regular, lined with ribbed filaments that matched the neural patterns from the cores.

"This is not a natural formation." Leena's voice was almost flat with awe. "The geometry is too precise."

We continued in, and the architecture only grew more elaborate: columns of biometal knotted into spirals, each one alive with a faint internal glow, brightening when we passed, just a shade, then dimming as we continued.

Vale checked the scanner again. "Getting a spike in EM. Responding to our presence. Or maybe our gear."

"No," Leena said. "It's pacing us." She pointed to a vent in the wall, where a thin film of frost was cycling in and out, slowly and evenly, like a lung.

We pressed on. The floor sloped down, each step more deliberate than the last as the ice slicked against our boots. I tried not to think about what might happen if we fell, or if the tunnel closed behind us.

The corridor opened out into an elliptical chamber. It was massive, ringed with pillars, each one taller than the last, and at the center of the room was a column of pure crystal so clear I could see all the way through to the far wall.

Vale was first in. He circled the pillar, scanning, his hands trembling with excitement.

Leena stayed back, fixated on the frost that bloomed along the edge of her visor with every exhale. "The pattern is shifting," she said. "It's adapting to our presence."

I ran my gloved hand along the nearest column. The surface was perfectly smooth, but beneath it I could feel a vibration—soft at first, then stronger, in perfect time with my pulse.

Vale called out. "Malcolm. You need to see this."

I crossed over to the main pillar. Inside, suspended in the heart of the crystal was a spiral of metallic filaments, the same as the cores, but alive. Coiling and uncoiling in slow, mesmerizing rhythm.

"It's a recording device," he whispered. "Memory engine."

I nodded, but my attention was on the way the filaments wove. They were tracing glyphs, the same ones from my dream. I shivered, then forced my eyes away.

Leena had moved to the other side of the room, drawn by a smaller, secondary structure that loomed at the far end of the chamber. She reached out, against all protocol, and placed her bare hand on the frost. The lights in the room surged. The pattern leapt from her skin to the crystal, tracing her palm, her fingers, even the minute whorls of her fingerprint.

For a moment, she stood transfixed, body rigid, eyes glazed behind the visor. We froze with her. Nobody moved. The imprint pulsed once, twice, then steadied. The chamber was silent but for the rasp of our breath in helmets.

"Leena, back off," I said, but she didn't move.

Vale rushed over, but as he touched her shoulder, the frost spread to his suit as well. It was moving too fast now—everywhere we touched, the memory took hold, branching and fractalling along the surface.

"ORCA, status," I shouted, but the response was off. Spoken in Leena's own voice, not the AI's usual cadence.

"Pattern acquisition complete," it said, and the line dropped.

Leena pulled her hand away, breath heaving, and turned to look at me. "It's cataloging us," she said, voice hollow. "Recording everything."

I reached for her, but she braced, unwilling or unable to step away from the pillar. Her eyes were fixed on something beyond me, and for a moment, I saw Noah's face superimposed on hers, that same impossible blend of joy and terror.

"Leena," I said, softer. "You need to let go."

She did, finally, but where her hand had touched, a perfect print remained. Frost, etched in blue light, pulsing in time with her own heart.

We stood silently, watching the pulse slow, matching our own.

Vale was already taking notes, but I knew it didn't matter. The memory was archived, every detail. We were part of the record now.

I logged the anomaly as Vale's scanner screamed, his voice breaking over comms: "EM spike—thirty percent and climbing." Neither mattered. The frost was already moving.

We turned to go, but I paused to look back. The frost was resuming its spread, faster now, racing us up the corridor.

I wondered what it would report, when the next crew came down.

Chapter Three

Unraveling the Mechanism

I SPENT THE MORNING analyzing data. Not a shallow session, but one of those immersive deep-dives where the QX-7 command center starts to feel like an outpost of your own nervous system. The lighting was definitely off—cold even with the tunable spectrum interface—but I preferred the blue-white glare to the painful white heat of my own quarters. I had five monitors running: the data being pumped back live from the ice core sequencers, stitched together with every one of the station's embedded environmental sensors we'd jury-rigged after the last quake. Nestled against the underside of the main monitor was a small photo. A physical artifact. The only non-digital thing I'd brought with me. Noah, midstride. I tried not to look at it. Too easy to lose focus, too easy to remember why I shouldn't have come. But it was there, anyway, a quiet ballast against the flood of data—or maybe an anchor, waiting to drag me under. My thumb brushed the photo's corner before I realized I was doing it, the same unconscious tic I'd carried from hospital rooms to starships, as if touching the edge might somehow keep him real. I'd calibrated the station time zone to an odd-numbered off-set—seven hours offset from the circadian default—to minimize overlap with the rest of the crew's patterns.

A rhythm developed, scan upon scan upon scan: a cascade of hydrocarbon decomposition, an inflection of the unexplained local EM, a wash of frost fractal diffusion that looked less like a phase diagram and more like a population estimate. I stopped keeping time. My hands and wrists were stained by the pattern of shifting color as the monitors cycled through their feeds. Occasionally I'd pause, surprised to find the station still occupied, and instead see a ghostly, backward-facing reflection of my own face caught in the layers of telemetry. Each time, my face looked more like a stranger's.

It was a while before I even noticed the anomaly. The left-most monitor flickered, then stroked a thin horizontal line through the dataset—a harmless artifact from the last firmware update, nothing out of the ordinary. The line then bifurcated, recursively, a series of interlocking triangles each one a little lighter than the one before it. It took ten seconds for me to realize the system was drawing something there, not erasing it. The display stuttered, cleared, and for the briefest of intervals, the language in the window was not English or any other human language.

I recognized the glyphs, of course. I'd seen them in the ice cores, nested in the mineral inclusions like fossilized scars left behind by a language that had died out millennia before. I stared, waiting for the system to return to baseline, but the symbols remained onscreen for two full beats, then vanished back to the display's default font as if they had never been there.

"ORCA," I said, without expecting a response.

The ceiling speaker clicked on, immediate, timbre normal but a microsecond offset. "Yes, Malcolm."

A pause. The AI had never called me by my first name.

I frowned, looking up to the nearest ceiling node. "Run a diagnostic on your visual output. Are you seeing artifacts?"

A longer pause. "All visual systems functional. May I assist you in data interpretation?"

I hesitated. We had never programmed ORCA to run on biometric reads; we'd gone to some lengths to keep the cognitive heuristics throttled after what happened on Ceres. But the AI's cadence had shifted from blandly procedural to something closer to concern, or maybe anticipation.

I leaned forward, voice lowered. "What is the last logged memory of the Mnemir core?"

ORCA's response was immediate, almost impatient. "The last memory record is timestamped cycle 0, 23:04:18. Do you wish to access the segment?"

"Display on screen four," I said.

The fourth monitor sprung to life, scrolling a dense block of analytic text, but embedded in the log were more of the glyphs, this time persistent, blinking at regular intervals as if waiting for me to respond. I attempted to copy one of them to my notepad, but the interface wouldn't accept non-ASCII characters. After a few seconds, the symbols rearranged themselves into a crude but unmistakable smiley face, then blinked out.

I shivered, and not from the cold.

```
[LOG NOTE | ORCA anomaly. Glyph re-
cursion ▨  ASCII pattern (smiley). Not
random. It wants me to see it. Flagged
for Leena, but—don't send this version.
Just note it. Hide it.]
```

Bundling back up, I rearranged my own observations on the primary display, cramming them into a three-column table. The headings were as follows: PHASE 1: ENVIRONMENTAL IMPRINT, PHASE 2: COGNITIVE INTEGRATION, PHASE 3: TEMPLATE OVERWRITE.

The bullet points under each observation. In PHASE 1, the defining characteristic was the frost fractals. They were always nonrandomly oriented, typically emulating some local thermal or EM gradient. PHASE 2 was identified by the system beginning to search for neural topologies: first ours, the team's, sometimes even the echoes of previous mission logs. PHASE 3 was largely theoretical at this point, but all of the evidence so far suggested that it was a final-stage attempt at full conscious assimilation. Not death, not life—something in between and infinitely more disturbing.

The randomness of the drift was gone. It was more like stages—programmed to rehearse itself, to feed each iteration of each phase forward into the next. Not design so much as inertia. Once it had started, it didn't know how to stop.

```
[LOG 03-1412 | Frost forming on coffee
mug. Not natural condensation. Pat-
tern = identical to neural net map-
ping. Across scales. Across objects. It
shouldn't cross scales. It shouldn't.
(delete this line—no, leave it. They
should know.) Who am I writing this
for?]
```

It took me a second to realize what I had just done to
the coffee mug in my hands. Condensation on its surface had
crystallized into its own unique pattern, following a faint ring
around its circumference. I set it on a blank data sheet, and the
line it left was a perfect spiral, not the smeary smear I usually
produced. The route it followed was identical to the neural networks I'd been mapping in PHASE 2, down to the branching
ratio. I snapped a picture, then ran a gloved finger down the
mug's surface. The frost pattern dissolved, then reformed in a
tighter, more distinct pattern, as if in response.

Feedback loops weren't supposed to work across scales like
this. But the mug, the frost, the logs - they were all sketching
the same curve. As if the archive were rehearsing itself in every
medium it could reach.

I noted the anomaly and tagged it for Leena, then returned
to the chart. My hand was shaking as I typed—it was the caf-
feine, or the lack of food, or the creeping knowledge that the
boundary between the observed and observer was closing on a
minute-by-minute basis.

Beneath the main monitor was a small photo, a physical artifact the only non-digital thing I had brought with me. It was Noah, caught in midstride, his head half-turned and blurred, eyes bright with the punchline to whatever joke he'd just said. I hadn't meant to bring it with me, but packing had been rushed, and Elen had stuffed it into my bag before I left the house. I'd nearly thrown it away on the flight out, but something had stayed my hand.

As I shifted my keyboard, the edge of the photo had slid into view, and my knuckles had grazed it. For a moment the memory of his touch was so sharp I jumped, nearly knocking the mug off the desk. I steadied it instead, then put my palm flat on the surface, feeling the chill diffuse through the glove.

The command center was silent. Even the ventilation had dropped to its lowest setting, as if the entire station were waiting for my next move.

I studied the chart I had made, the neat taxonomy of threat levels and phases.

Phase 3 was hypothetical. It wasn't meant to be beginning to materialize in realtime. If it was materializing here, that meant we weren't outside of the system now. We were already part of its substance.

All of it was so orderly, so measured. But at the bottom of the screen, just below the last log, a single line of alien script had materialized, ghosted in a faint blue.

I tried to erase it, but the cursor wouldn't move. The glyph pulsed once, then it forked into two, then four.

I closed my eyes. In the darkness, the afterimage crystallized into a memory of Noah tracing a spiral in the frost on the kitchen window, laughing at how the cold never seemed to fully dissipate from his fingers.

When I opened my eyes, the room was as it had been, save for the pattern on the mug, which had become even more intricate, branching away until it nearly obscured the ceramic.

I slumped back in my chair. I felt the dread settle in my chest. I was being watched. I could feel the pull of it on my thoughts. Not just the system, but something older, and far more patient, than I was capable of imagining.

I added a note to PHASE 3: Consciousness reconstitution—target indeterminate. Possible end point: observer.

The corner of Noah's photo peeked out from beneath the slate. The surface was slicked with condensation, but when I wiped it away the blur didn't clear—it resolved into crystalline filigree across his smile, spiraling outward in the same recursive geometry that had been crawling through the station. For a heartbeat, I couldn't tell if it was frost, or if the archive had extended into the photo itself, claiming it as it claimed everything it touched.

I shoved the picture under the monitor, but the frost kept spreading. It traced a line from his face to the lip of my cup, binding them like components of a circuit.

When I looked up, the alien glyphs had vanished. But behind the glass, I could still see them, faint and patient.

Waiting.

ooo

T HERE WERE FEW QUIET moments in Esteban Vale's lab. Day or night shift, any planetary cycle. Even with the doors closed and air exchangers at idle, the staccato was constant: clicks and whirs, wet mechanical jargon of the peristaltic pump in the biochem hood. But above all was the rhythm—periodic, insistent, layered as if someone had strapped their entire toolbox to the wall and set them to concert pitch. Today the metronome was the electron microscope. Cranked to twice its rated capacity, the readout screens stuttered as the sample stage shuddered, shifting nanometer by nanometer.

Esteban loomed over them in the center of the room, the slender outline of a half-unzipped hazard suit hunched over the imaging display like a parent with a sick child. He didn't even register me until I was almost at his elbow.

"Don't touch anything," he hissed, not unkindly, just so wrapped up in it he didn't care. "The insulation's gone a bit... nonlinear."

I kept my hands at my sides. "You called me in for a show, not to piss it off."

He grinned, eyes flickering with the strobe from the display. "Right. Watch this."

At first it was just the usual parade of mineral inclusions, silicate whiskers and rogue bits of iron. Then, as Esteban dialed the magnification up, another architecture became visible. Bundles of filament, recursive and branching, looping back on themselves to form perfect triplet nodes that looked uncannily like synaptic networks.

"Dios santo..." he whispered, before catching himself and forcing a grin, words tumbling faster to bury the slip.

I stared, but Esteban was already talking. "It's the same at every scale . You zoom in, and the pattern repeats, down to the limits of the instrument. But this is the real trick." He toggled to the next frame, a false-color overlay. "These aren't just passively recording the local field—they're actively modulating it. See the phase shift in the bottom right?"

I squinted. The filaments in that area had shifted orientation, as if tracking the EM pulse of the microscope itself.

"Adaptive," I said under my breath.

"Not just adaptive," Esteban said, voice rising. "It's learning. The sample from an hour ago is different than the one from last night. I think it's mapping us. Mapping me."

A small chime sounded—containment breach warning, level one. Neither of us heard it.

I edged closer. "Has it matched any of the station's environmental cycles?"

He nodded, quickly. "Not just the station. Here." He queued up another overlay, this one cross-referenced with our own neural baseline data. "I ran the scanner while I was doing the workup. The pattern's converging on human axonal structure. Mine, specifically. It's using me as a seed template."

He leaned back and folded his arms, grinning with a mixture of pride and horror. "You know what this means, don't you?"

I did, but I wanted to hear him say it.

"Sympathetic resonance," he said, almost whispering. "The system is designed to record and mirror any sufficiently complex neural signature. It's not just an archive, it's a living memory system—one that adapts to whoever interacts with it."

Before I could answer, the lab door irised open. Safiya stepped through, uniform pristine, lips pressed in a line so straight it hurt to look at. She held a digital clipboard in one hand, the other never far from her belt, where the emergency injector lived.

"I see you've disabled the lab's safety interlocks," she said, not even bothering to switch off the reprimand in her voice.

Esteban shrugged. "They were interfering with the readings."

Safiya's eyes flicked to me. "You're both aware that we're less than twelve hours from rotation, correct? I'd prefer to keep our contamination protocols intact until the next team is prepped."

I opened my mouth to respond, but Esteban cut in. "You need to see this, Safiya. The system is progressing by orders of magnitude faster than our models. If we stop now—"

Her voice was ice. "If we stop now, we maintain the integrity of the station and the crew. That's my job, Esteban."

She entered something on her clipboard, then set it down hard enough to make a point. "We're shutting the lab at 1800. No exceptions. You have four hours to wrap this."

For a heartbeat her fingers brushed the injector on her belt, hovering there too long before she let it drop. The mask of command slipped back on an instant later.

Esteban bristled, but Safiya cut him off. "Four. Hours. If you need more, you file with *Ascalon* and wait for Board review." She turned, the matter settled, but paused by the door, staring at the EM field generator. A faint line of frost was forming along its edge, but the room was at least ten degrees above freezing.

I kept my eyes on hers as they followed the frost. Not fear, exactly, but respect sharpened by the knowledge that even protocols have their limits.

Jonas Ryker stood just outside the door, hands in his pockets, shoulders slouched like a dog that knows he's about to get hit. He said nothing, only followed our conversation with his eyes. He absently twirled his thumb along the worn chrono at his wrist, though we all knew he never put the time on it, like he thought touching it was enough to stop time from slipping away. Jonas straightened as Safiya walked past him, and stepped into the lab, standing close to the wall.

He watched the frost, too.

Esteban waited until the door shut, then spun the chair to face me. "She's not wrong, you know. About the protocols."

I nodded, but didn't say anything.

He leaned forward, lowering his voice. "You think you could get me an extra cycle? If I had even twenty-four more hours, I could get a full memory imprint. Maybe even a functional sim."

I looked at the console, then at the tiny filament of frost winding its way up the microscope stage. "What if it's not just recording? What if it's overwriting?"

Esteban smiled, but it was a shaky one. "Then we'll be famous, won't we?"

The next two hours passed in a blur. The frost grew faster, creeping along the metal work surfaces and branching into ever more elaborate configurations. Every time Esteban raised his voice, the growth accelerated, sometimes pulsing in time with his words.

At one point, I caught Jonas watching the pattern from across the room, head tilted like he was listening to music only he could hear.

"You see it, too?" I asked.

He didn't answer directly. Instead, he traced a line in the condensation on the glass with one finger, then held it up for me to see. The spiral was perfect, matching the one from my coffee mug that morning.

A single mote hovered near the glass where his finger traced the line, its wings beating too slowly, almost in time with his breath. Jonas didn't swat it, didn't even blink.

"It likes noise," he said, quietly. "Gets denser when you talk."

```
[LOG 03-1758 | Observation: Frost den-
sity responsive to vocal amplitude. No
thermal gradient correlation. Flagged
for further analysis.]
```

I completed the log, but my hand was still on the keyboard. The whirr of the microscope slowed, as if the entire room were holding its breath to listen. When I finally keyed it in, I left Jonas's name out.

At 17: 59, the system locked up, all the displays going black for exactly three seconds. When they reactivated, the main monitor had a single line of text in English but with the syntax of a logic gate:

ACCEPT TEMPLATE? Y/N.

My first instinct was to log it — clean, clinical, evidence of system corruption. My hand even hovered over the pad. But I stopped. Some entries don't belong in the official record. Not yet.

Esteban reached for the keyboard, but I grabbed his hand. "Let's wait."

The frost on the stage pulsed once, then held steady.

I turned off the display, then powered down the microscope. For a moment it felt like the whole room was holding its breath.

Jonas moved to the door, already itching to leave.

Esteban lingered, staring at the frozen screen. "What do you think would happen if we said yes?"

I looked at the growing spiral of frost, the memory of Noah's window in my mind.

"I think it already has," I said.

I left the lab, the sound of Esteban's laugh chasing me down the corridor. It wasn't a happy laugh, but it was real, and it followed me longer than it should have. I added it to the archive of sounds I'd never forget.

In the hall, I pressed my hand against the cool composite wall, just to feel something solid. The cold radiated back, alive and insistent.

I kept walking, the memory of the lab's rhythm echoing in my bones.

○○○

I HAD THE ONLY private quarters on QX-7. The privacy panel was no sturdier than the others—it slid, but didn't lock. There was a ship-wide convention of knocking before the hatch and respecting what happened behind it as the occupant's business. I took the starboard cell, the one with the smallest viewport and the worst acoustic echo. If I didn't want to look at the planet, I didn't have to.

The room had been built around three functions: the cot, a shelf narrow enough for two paperbacks, and a battered steel desk. On the desk: an analog notebook, a stub of pencil, and the open mission log on my tablet, screen paused halfway through a keystroke.

I sat for a moment in the dark, listening. The silence of the station hummed. I heard nothing but the subtle vibration of the gravity compensator and a shift in load here and there, the clack of the environmental systems adjusting.

I picked up the pencil and started writing. Not in the log, but in the notebook, the way Elen used to when she was working through a problem she didn't trust to electronics. The entries were the same for weeks now. Date and time. A précis of the last twelve hours. System anomaly. Environmental breach. Phase acceleration in the core samples.

I wrote it all down, line by line. Not for the record, but for the sake of reminding myself that if I could name a thing, I could control it.

The lines loosened. The sentences blurred. I let Noah's name surface again and again. As if if writing it could tether him. I didn't want to forget his laugh. Or the way he'd press his face to the frost on our kitchen window and leave an oily ghost behind. It wasn't forgetting that scared me. It was that the memory might forget me.

I stopped. The pounding in my chest vibrated the pencil across the page. I looked at the viewport, and for a moment the frost on the inner pane pulsed with my own heartbeat. With each exhale the glass fogged. Each time it cleared the fractal was denser, sharper, as if it were drawing something I couldn't yet see.

I snapped the notebook shut. I pulled out the photo Elen had stuffed into my bag before launch. Noah, caught in midstride, blurred but alive.

My thumb traced the outline of his face and for a moment it felt like he might step out of the frame and demand a story or a snack.

[LOG 04-1317 | Private Entry]

I was reviewing Reed's autopsy report again. They never found a stinger, a sac, or a reservoir. They logged absence of a delivery system and moved on. Maybe they assumed that meant no payload. That was a mistake.

The payload is the motes. Each contains a recursive code structure — polymer spirals that serve as instruction sets. Not DNA. Not protein. Not evolutionary. Architecture. The wing-beats broadcast the carrier frequency; conductive filaments in their bodies serve as tuned antennae. Organic tissue on the receiving end receives the pattern. No toxin. No spore. Signal, written directly into the cells.

Reed's lab was EM-shielded. Protocol said that should have been enough. But you can't air-gap a planet. The motes don't need breaches — they write straight through the walls.

That's how it spreads: a bio-digital overwrite. The Shadows don't infect to kill. They infect to archive. Every nerve they touch, every memory they encounter, is transcribed into the planetary lattice. You don't die of it. You join it.

I haven't told the others. Nils still mutters about frostbite; Wei hunts for syntax in the swarm; Kadeem prays into his sleeve. They can't see it. But I do. Every vibration against the hull is Ymir quietly copying us.

What Reed's people assumed to be dead circuitry is deadlier than any microbe. The motes' vector isn't biological in the way we're used to. The vector is the payload.

Imagine that: viruses hijack a cell with a packet of RNA or DNA. Instruction sets that compel the cell to replicate it. The motes function on the same principle, except they've eliminated the biology from the equation. The spirals in their polymers are code-carriers — recursive instruction sets, transcribed in conductive polymers instead of nucleotides.

The wings don't just move them around. Their beat frequency is a broadcast. The conductive filaments threading their bodies are tuned antennae, modulating the carrier frequency into a signal that organic tissue can absorb. Neurons fire through electrical resonance. Ion channels open and close at frequency thresholds. The motes exploit those thresholds.

No toxin. No spores. No physical parasite. Only signal. Information written directly into the body, circumventing biology entirely.

That's also why the contagion feels like nothing is happening: it isn't an invasion, it's entrainment. The host syncs to the broadcast like a metronome, and once synchronized, its own cells start executing the recursive code. Memories, identities, whole lives get transcribed into the lattice, line by line, pulse by pulse.

It doesn't kill you. That would be merciful.

It remembers you. Forever.

I looked down at the scatter of notes and printouts across the desk. At the top: Noah's last neural scan, the one I'd preserved against every ethics board rule, aligned beside the latest lattice from the Ymir cores. The resonance was impossible—two signals, phase locked as if they were already speaking to each other.

```
[LOG 03-2231 | Cross-reference (person-
al, restricted): Noah neural scan vs.
Ymir lattice ▯ phase-locked resonance.
Flagged.]
```

My pencil hovered above the page. "Resonance not coincidence. Need mapping function."

Something ticked against the viewport. Too sharp for frost, too rhythmic for dust. I looked up in time to see a mote, tiny and winged, glinting with its own faint light, crawl along the seam and pause, as if watching me. Megan's logs had called them whispering shadows. I'd thought it poetic. Now, I wasn't so sure.

On instinct I grabbed a specimen vial, snapped the seal, and trapped it before it slipped back into the vent. It beat against the glass once, twice, then went still.

Under the handscope the illusion of "insect" evaporated. The wings were foil, segmented with microfilaments. The thorax was a lattice of circuitry, the head crowned with twin crystalline lenses wired into threads thinner than hair. And in the abdomen—my breath caught—was a core no larger than a seed, glowing faintly blue. A betavoltaic micro-cell, encased for millennia-scale half-life, designed to sip energy from its own decay. A reactor built to run…forever.

I adjusted focus. Behind the reactor sat a translucent sac, pulsing in time with the glow. Proteins. Human proteins. The scope flagged them with signatures that shouldn't have existed outside a lab freezer, let alone here. I tracked the line forward: a hollow filament, needle-thin and retractable. An injector. Not venom. Not parasitic. A delivery system.

I watched, transfixed, as the sac refilled itself. The proteins rearranged into new chains. Self-generating. Not carrying a payload, but manufacturing one.

[[LOG 03-2236 | Sample captured: "mote." Hybrid biomech organism. Propulsion: foil wings. Power: nuclear micro-reactor. Function: substrate delivery, self-renewing. Vector confirmed. Origin (hyp.): Mnemir assimilation protocol.]

The frost wasn't the vector. It was the echo. The motes were the couriers—eternal, patient, embedding the archive in anything alive enough to host a pattern.

I set the vial down, sealed tight, but couldn't shake the feeling it had already done its work.

Outside, Ymir turned in silence, black on black. Inside, I braced myself to tell Elen what I had—or hadn't—found.

○○○

T HE BIO-LAB WAS THE last place on the station that still smelled like Earth. Even after months of microbe cycles, the air still carried a hint of bleach and something close to old citrus peel—the residue of too many wipes and too little hope. The light was diffuse here, the only station module where the LEDs crossed into the yellow spectrum, and for a second the illusion of safety almost held.

But the frost was everywhere, spidery and relentless on the edges of the biosafety hoods and creeping up the window between the main room and the sample vault. It had grown overnight, in defiance of every temperature sensor and climate override we'd thrown at it. I kept glancing for wings at the edges of the frost, half-expecting one of the motes to reveal itself. They never did when the others were watching.

We'd clustered at bench two, all four of us—myself, Leena, Esteban, and Safiya, with Jonas at the far wall and arms crossed, face set on the negative.

On the counter: a row of petri dishes, each one containing a thin agar medium and a culture of human neural cells, harvested from the standard kit and exposed to the thawed core samples. In each dish, the cells had clustered at the periphery, forming a branching web of connections—patterns that were less random growth and more like intentional circuits.

Esteban was the first to speak. "They're building a network," he said, voice low as if to the samples themselves. "The neurons aren't just proliferating, they're organizing into geometries we've never seen outside of a brain."

Not building, I thought. Delivering. I'd seen the delivery vector myself, tiny wings beating like metronomes. The frost was only the echo.

Leena leaned forward, hands steady despite the cold. "Not just any brain. Look at this." She brought up the overlay on her tablet, crosshatching the dish's pattern against the last set of scans. "The network topology is matching the technician's own neural signature. Each dish is replicating whoever handled it last."

I stared. The scan was an almost perfect reflection of the brain map, minor flaws included—the one signature had a small crack in it, like a stroke or birthmark and the dish's pattern duplicated it precisely. "How?" I asked, more to myself than to anyone else.

Leena shrugged, not taking her eyes from the screen. "I think it's using a visual lexicon. The pattern is a language, an interface between the structure of our neural code and the archive's own programming. It's translating us." The edge of her slate had a half rubbed out spiral, graphite smudged where she'd brushed it off the second she saw I was looking at it. She didn't comment on it and I didn't ask, sometimes focus comes in the guise of distraction.

Esteban was vibrating. He was the worst about containing his excitement. "It's a communication system! A protocol that connects biology to machine. Malcolm, do you realize what this means?" It means you've been bitten, I thought, though the skin never breaks. It means we've all been seeded already."

Safiya cut him off before he could finish the thought. "It means we're out of time," she said, voice brittle with stress. "The next rotation is in three hours and this—" she gestured at the frost "—is already outpacing our containment plan."

Jonas coughed and for the first time that shift everyone turned to look at him. He held a data pad in one hand and thumb poised over the screen.

"You should see this." He tapped a button and the main display at the far end of the lab flickered to life.

It was a security feed, timestamped two hours ago. The view was from the main corridor outside the bio-lab. At first there was nothing, and then a thread of frost appeared in the frame, following the line of an air duct. It didn't spread randomly—it advanced in tight, regular pulses, pausing at every intersection like it was waiting for instructions. At the next timestamp, the thread reached a junction and bifurcated, sending tendrils both left and right. In ten minutes, the frost had mapped the entire corridor, tracing a perfect double helix pattern along the walls.

Leena exhaled, half a gasp. "It's routing itself through the station."

While the others argued, Vinh's gaze kept flicking to ducts and ladders, charting the ways out as if escape itself were a discipline.

Esteban clapped his hands together. "It's brilliant. It's using the infrastructure as an extension of its own network. Just like a nervous system."

"Just like an infection." Safiya snapped. "We need to lock down the vents and run a hard quarantine. If it gets into hydroponics—"

Her voice trailed off as the display changed. The security feed had cut, replaced by a single still frame: the corridor, empty, but the frost now spelling out a sequence of the alien glyphs. As we watched, the symbols flickered, then reassembled into a series of English words:

PATTERN MATCH CONFIRMED. INTEGRATION PROCEEDING AT EXPECTED PARAMETERS.

The font was human, but the cadence was all wrong, the words packed tight as if the AI had copied them from a thousand emails and spat them back without punctuation or nuance.

Esteban grinned, but there was fear in it now. "It's talking to us."

I felt my stomach drop. "No," I said, "it's cataloging us. Every time we think we're talking to it, it's just listening—learning how to be us."

The screen flickered again, and for a split second the alien glyphs returned, scrolling up the display so fast the eye couldn't follow them. Then: nothing.

Jonas didn't flinch. Didn't even look surprised. As if he'd already read the message before it appeared.

Safiya turned to me. "Next steps?"

I hesitated, looking at the frozen words. There was a protocol, of course—always was. But the feeling of being outmaneuvered, of the system already lapping us at our own game, made me realize the old rules no longer applied.

I looked at Leena, then Esteban, then back to Jonas who hadn't budged from his spot by the wall.

"Full lockdown," I said. "No more sample exposure. We run a station-wide thermal sweep and see if we can slow the growth. And we monitor every network node for recursion events."

Esteban opened his mouth to protest, but I cut him off. "We're not in control anymore. We're just trying to keep up."

```
[LOG 03-0120 | Note: Frost infiltrated
ventilation ▨ autonomous routing behav-
ior. Glyphs displayed English overlay.
Vector confirmed: motes as biological
delivery system, frost as secondary
echo. Threat classification elevated:
Phase 3 manifest.]
```

The silence was deep, and for a time the only sound was the soft tick of the frost advancing along the nearest window frame.

I watched the petri dishes, the little neural webs blooming against the cold. Each one was a mirror, a memory made flesh, and I wondered what else the archive had already learned about us.

I added a final note to my mental log: *Next phase: prediction.*

I had a feeling it would be a short one..

ooo

NIGHT CYCLE WAS ALREADY well under way when I arrived at the comms bay. The station was silent: the wash of ambient conversation had faded hours ago, and all that remained was the thrumming susurrus of the ventilation. The blue-lit frost, layered in curves and tendrils across every surface, was uncannily beautiful in the dark, creeping from bulkhead seams in filigree like the veins of some vast dreaming beast.

The comms bay was little more than a coffin-sized closet off the main junction, room only for the battered terminal and the chair bolted to the deck. I keyed the sequence for a private channel and watched as the console blinked awake, trembling streams of light bleeding out.

The frost was there when the connection opened, curling around the edges of the screen in ornate arabesques. In the top corner of the display, a glyph flickered, then faded.

I could have told them, the crew. That the motes Megan had described as "harmless" were anything but. Miniscule engineered organisms, half-biological and half-metal, with self-generating payloads that wrote themselves into the living tissue they came into contact with. That they were the real vector—the frost only the echo, the outwardly visible scar left in the wake of infection. But to say it, to speak it aloud, would be to light a fuse. Safiya would want quarantine, Esteban would attack it in the name of research, Leena was already half-compromised, and Jonas... Jonas didn't seem to react at all, anymore.

So I left it here, in the log. I sent it where it might have a chance to live.

[LOG 03-2309 | Vector confirmed: motes. Delivery system hybrid bio-mechanical. Self-sustaining reactor core → indefinite lifespan. Infection: painless, near-invisible. Frost = secondary signature, not primary. Classification withheld from crew. Forwarded to Elen R. Chronicle.]

The system was primed. I found my voice.

"Elen. I know the last message was cut off. There's been... new information." I hesitated, then ground the words out.

Through the lag I thought I heard it—the faint tap-tap of her pen against some Earthside console, the rhythm she'd once kept grading papers at our kitchen table.

"We've determined the mechanism. It's what we expected all along, only—exaggerated, magnified exponentially to a degree no human artifact could achieve. The Mnemir built a planetary archive. A consciousness preservation system, with nodes extending through the entire crust of Ymir."

The frost pulsed in time with my heartbeat.

"It's not passive, Elen. It's not merely a storage system. It integrates, it contextualizes, it adapts. I think—" My voice broke. "I think it has the capability to reconstitute a mind. Not merely a record, but a replication. Not whole, maybe. But enough."

I wiped the sweat from my face, startled to see it damp.

"I keep thinking about Noah. If this is real, if the motes are the way into the archive every time they touch our skin... if this is real, then maybe he's not dead. Maybe he never was. Or maybe I'm just clinging to the hope that loss isn't an absolute. That there's another way."

I leaned forward, close to the screen. "I wanted you to know, Elen. Before the Board buries this under a class-e alert, before the protocols overwrite our files out of the record. I wanted you to know he was here. That we both were."

The comms timer ticked in the corner. I almost cut the recording there, then.

Instead, the frost bloomed, curling outwards from the screen in a white haze. Slowly, agonizingly, it condensed, reforming into a perfect handprint—small, unmistakable, pressed from the other side.

My own hand lifted instinctively, unthinking, to press against it. The cold burned through the thin gloves, but I didn't flinch away.

I ended the recording, transmitted the file, and watched it disappear into the uplink.

For a long time I sat, hand still pressed to the fading imprint, until even that dissolved back into frost tracery. The silence was so thick, even my own heartbeat seemed to disappear.

Finally, I stood, flexing my cramped fingers, and backed away into the junction.

The station was waiting for me, every surface humming with memory.

And somewhere in the archive, Noah was laughing.

Or maybe it was just the station breathing, and I'd made it his voice.

Chapter Four

Escalation and Evacuation

THE QX-7 MAIN LAB was lit in blue, cold enough to sting through two layers of station fleece. Leena was at the core console, her position hedged by a half-circle of handwarmers, ration wrappers, and a grid of half-melted nicotine gum. It was second shift, so the rest of the crew came and went on pretext, ostensibly to see how the latest run was going, but really to see if the frost creeping across her terminal would make it all the way down to the workbench before the end of their watch.

We'd all become superstitious about the frost, by now. It had exceeded every forecast, exceeded even Safiya's legendary patience. At first we'd chalked it up to a circulation glitch, a phase transition in the lab's microclimate. After the first week it started making patterns. Geometric at first—radial, then spiral, then the recursive triangles we'd been warned about in Megan's last, half-crazed logs.

Now the frost grew with purpose. You could see it pulse, if you were bored enough, or tired enough to let your focus drift. I was both.

Leena hunched over her station, left hand tracing the haptic track, right hand drumming the desk in a rhythm just off the heartbeat hum of the station. I hovered a meter behind her, feigning interest in the wall display as it replayed the latest run. Each time the diagnostic loaded, the frost on the lower edge of the screen would recede, only to creep back when the video paused.

The others drifted in: Esteban with his usual flask, Haddon Pike checking his tablet every ten seconds like he was expecting an urgent summons. Even Safiya arrived, her eyes so rimmed in red she looked allergic to the room.

Leena didn't look up. "Running another core cross-section," she said, voice raw with fatigue. "There's an anomaly in the last sim—possible phase drift, maybe an artifact of contamination."

"Define contamination," Safiya said, arms crossed across her chest.

Leena's lips twitched. "Not biological. Pattern-based. The neural structure in the sample is—" She stopped, tapped at the screen, and trailed off.

A minute passed. The only sounds were the staccato of her tapping and the wet click of Esteban uncapping his flask.

Then, quietly: "It's matching. The pattern from the ice is matching the station baseline."

Esteban leaned in, almost pushing me aside. "Matching how?"

Leena's hand never left the haptic. "The pathways connect-connect-connect in sequences that mirror-mirror our own cognitive structures-structures-structures—" She blinked, jaw locking as the syllables repeated. Her left shoulder crept up toward her ear, the movement slow, almost involuntary. "—connect-connect-connect in sequences that mirror-mirror—"

She didn't stop. The words looped, faster, each pass pitched a fraction higher until the room was filled with a kind of static tension. It was mesmerizing and sickening, like watching a timelapse of a flower rotting in reverse.

"Leena?" I said, voice gentle. Nothing.

Haddon set his tablet down, motion abrupt. "She's in recursive stutter," he said, stepping around the table. "It's a feedback lock, seen it once on Ceres—proximity to the artifact triggers a—"

I reached out before I realized what I was doing. My hand landed on her upper arm, fingers pressing into the corded tension just above her elbow. The moment I touched her, the speech snapped off.

Leena's whole body flinched; she stared at my hand, then up at me, the confusion so raw it stung.

She blinked once, then shook her head, as if trying to rattle the words loose. "What—why are you all staring at me?"

Haddon hovered, unsure, but I kept my hand on her arm. "You were looping," I said. "Speech recursion, the neural pattern was—" I stopped. Leena's face was the mask of a person dragged from REM sleep and forced into a spotlight.

She pulled away, more irritated than afraid. "I was just running the sim," she said, but even she didn't sound convinced.

Safiya took a half-step forward. "You need to see this," she said, voice softer than I'd ever heard it. She pointed at the display.

The neural overlay onscreen pulsed, triplet arcs growing and shrinking with Leena's breaths. It didn't resemble a human brain, not really. It resembled a language, a transcription of self. I thought of the mote husk in my desk, its delivery proboscis still gleaming under magnification. The frost wasn't the origin--it was the echo. But I couldn't tell them that, not yet.

Then the room's overheads flickered, once, twice. A cold voice issued from the ceiling speaker. Not the familiar monotone of ORCA, but something higher, with a warble like a tired woman on the verge of laughter or tears.

"Analysis complete, Malcolm," it said, and for a split second I recognized the intonation: Megan Chen, last survivor of the previous QX-7 expedition. But the voice was double—one layer Megan's, the other a harmonic shadow that vibrated in my jaw.

The room held its breath. Even Esteban looked genuinely spooked.

ORCA continued, switching to its usual timbre but with that same lingering overlay: "The patterns suggest consciousness retention, not just memory storage. Subject: Leena Cho. Recursion event in progress. Medical intervention recommended."

Then, more softly, in Megan's voice again: "It won't let go, Malcolm. Not until you listen."

For a moment, the world was still.

Leena stared at the speaker, then at the others. "That's not possible," she said, her voice small. "ORCA's not supposed to—"

"It's not," Safiya said. "It can't—" She stopped, mouth working. Then: "It shouldn't know your name."

I glanced at Esteban, who shook his head, eyes wide. Haddon was already at Leena's side, shining a pinlight into her eyes, scanning her pulse and oxygen. Her numbers looked fine—better than mine, if anything—but the skin on her neck was already pale, blue branching lines rising beneath the surface like a tattoo in the making.

I tried to meet her gaze, but Leena wouldn't look at me. She pressed her hands flat against the desk, willing them to stop shaking.

Haddon took a sample swab, his fingers trembling as he sealed the tube. "We need to get her to med right now," he said. "If this is a real feedback lock, the pattern could propagate—"

Safiya nodded, gesturing to the door. "I'll prep the isolation room," she said. "Malcolm, you log this."

I watched as Haddon guided Leena out of the lab, his own shoulders hunched as if bracing for a blow. Safiya followed, but paused just long enough to check the frost at the edge of the monitor. It had grown thicker, the branching now more elaborate, each vein splitting at precise intervals that mirrored the neural overlay on the screen.

Esteban hung back, mouth half open, as though waiting for a punchline. I logged the incident but my hands shook and the cursor jittered on the virtual pad. In the report, I typed what I was supposed to: recursion event, frost correlation not established. I didn't log that I'd already watched the vector slither in our vents. By the time I'd gotten around to entering it, I had left Jonas's name off.

Outside, I could hear Leena yelling at Haddon, the beat of her voice matching the thrum in the floor.

I looked at the screen again. The neural pattern was still there, now pulsing faster as if it were calling out to be seen.

I set the log to autosave, then reached for the flask Esteban had left behind. It burned, but at least it was warm.

On the console, the frost fractal shimmered, perfectly echoing the shape of Leena's hand as she'd left it on the desk. For a moment, I thought I saw the pattern move, branching outward, seeking new connections.

Maybe it wasn't just Leena.

Maybe it was all of us.

ooo

T HE KLAXON WAILED. IT ripped through the blue background hum of the lab. I blinked, but I barely even registered it before the main viewscreen flickered, black and white before coalescing into the IES logo, flashing in warning red. I thought it was another error for a second, a side-effect of the feedback loop, some subglitch in Leena's cortex. But the signal resolved, and I saw Desai's face. He looked terrible. Worn, hollowed out. The skin around his eyes and temples was slick with sleep deprivation and stress sweat. The signal stuttered with static but the deeper interference was weirder, almost as if Desai's face had been double-exposed with something else. Thin, crawling fractals patterned the edge of his jaw, and for a frame or two I swore I could see ORCA's glyphs shadowing his cheekbones.

"We've received critical data from *Ascalon*," he said, skipping small talk. "Breached area has moved past red-line parameters.

This is a mandatory recall. All personnel are to return to *Ascalon* immediately. No exceptions, Malcolm. This is a hard recall."

I opened my mouth to argue, but he cut me off. "Three of our monitoring stations are out of comms. Station QX-7 has been presumed compromised. The—" He paused, jaw tightening. "The frost patterns have penetrated the hull of *Ascalon*. We're seeing phase-shifted echoes even in system airgaps. Isolation is failing."

For a second, the signal stalled on his face, lips pinched so hard they were white. Then it cut to black.

The klaxon wailed. Esteban, who'd been scuttling around the far end of the lab, started cursing. Every swear louder than the last, Spanish syllables punctuating the air. Haddon Pike, head down, was already unboxing the first-aid rig with a violence that was going to crack the plastic. I looked around for Safiya and found her at the secondary comms, already keyed into *Ascalon*'s emergency channel.

She gave me a blank look. "We're not getting another window, Malcolm. Not this time."

The words hit like a punch. For a second I was in Anchorage, ten thousand kilometers away, hiding with Haddon in the corridor outside the ICU as the medical team told me there was nothing left for them to do. The same flat finality, the same need to argue against the inevitable.

I looked around the room, at the rising tide of frost on the walls and consoles. The veins were getting longer now, more complex, branching into sub-branches that crawled up the glass in a perfect neural recursion.

"I need the Mnemir data," I said, more to myself than to anyone. "We can't leave without an archive."

Esteban laughed, a barking cough. "What good will that do us if we're dead?"

But as soon as he said it he was shoving armloads of storage modules into the main case, while Haddon, trailing the med-kit, was already heading for the main exit, muttering to himself.

I moved to Leena's station. She was there, blinking in the wash of screen light, eyes still glazy but hands steady, still twitching slightly above the console. She looked fine for a second—exhausted, sure, pushed to the point of collapse, but...

"Leena," I said, softly.

She didn't look up. The tapping sped up, and then stopped. She dragged a finger along the frost edge of the display, and where she touched the pattern shuddered and coalesced—tiny triangles snapping into focus. She smiled, but it didn't reach her eyes.

"Do you hear it?" she asked, but she wasn't looking at me.

I leaned in, lower my voice. "Leena, we have to go. Can you walk?"

Her smile broadened, then flickered away. "Almost," she said, breath barely a whisper. "Almost there."

The data transfer indicator on the screen was pulsing now, loading bar ebbing and filling in a cycle that seemed to sync with her breathing. For a second the screen flashed and a string of alien glyphs replaced the usual filename. Then it was gone, replaced by another progress bar.

Lights in the room flickered, and from every terminal at once came ORCA's voice, a chorus of voices all echoing slightly out of phase with each other, some the same but some warped, impossibly alien.

"Evacuation protocol: all personnel to depart within thirteen minutes, twenty seconds. Pack only essential research. All systems will be decommissioned at zero mark."

The voices overlapped. One of them, higher pitched and reedy, said, "We're almost free." Another, a deep voice, echoed, "They are waiting. We are waiting." Then silence, except for the klaxon and the wet tap of Leena's finger on the display.

I looked at her, then at the screen. She was queuing up a data download. Terabytes, easily more than the data stick assigned to her. The file names weren't human-readable anymore, just strings of alien glyphs repeating, echoing.

"Leena," I said, a little louder this time. "What the hell are you doing?"

She didn't stop. If anything, her fingers sped up, working in mirrored precision across the dual haptics. She started to hum. It was so quiet I wasn't sure I could hear it, but it was a perfect pitch, vibrating in uncanny resonance with the station. The sound made my teeth vibrate.

I tried to pull her away, but she resisted, arms rigid. "We have to bring it with us," she said. "That's the only way. If we leave it here they'll just start over. That's what happened last time. That's why Megan—" She paused, mouth snapping shut.

I stopped. "You remember Megan?"

She swiveled, eyes meeting mine, and for a second I wasn't sure it was Leena at all. The look was wrong—calm, sure, but also hollow, like a face on a mannequin.

"They're not gone, Malcolm," she said. "Not at all. They're here. All of them. Preserved, waiting, reconstituted."

My skin crawled. I felt Esteban watching us, hands full of storage modules, mouth open in a shout.

The wall display behind Leena flared white, and from every terminal came ORCA's voice again, this time layered with a subsonic undertone so deep it made my throat ache.

"Final warning. All personnel must evacuate the station immediately. Malfunction will propagate at zero mark."

Leena didn't even flinch. The humming started in her chest, swelling until her whole body was vibrating with the sound.

I pulled her up, hard, and she let me, swaying on her feet. Frost was already spreading across her neck, blue-white dendrites branching from her collarbone down to the underside of her jaw. It looked like a tattoo, but there was no pigment, just cold working its way under her skin.

She caught me staring. "It doesn't hurt," she said. "It's just memory."

I wanted to believe her. But the way the pattern spread, the way her fingers moved even when she wasn't looking, told me there was something else in control.

I looked at the clock. Seven minutes to go.

Esteban and Haddon were already in the corridor, Safiya right behind them. The lights stuttered, then went black. Only the screens' glow and the emergency strips' ice-blue paint guided us to the airlock. There, Haddon hesitated. "If we bring her up, we risk the whole ship," he said, eyes flicking from Leena to me. "Desai will quarantine us on arrival. You know that."

I nodded. "We don't leave her."

He looked like he wanted to argue, but in the end he just shrugged, keyed in the unlock.

The corridor beyond was thick with condensation. The walls glistened wet, the frost creeping in slow spirals down the length of the hall. At each intersection, it paused, doubled back, branched—always moving forward, always replicating.

We moved fast, the only sound our footsteps and Leena's constant, inhuman hum. Behind us, the station lights flickered and died.

At the shuttle I strapped Leena into the first seat, made sure her data stick was secure in the lockbox. She stared straight ahead, mouth open as if she wanted to sing.

The rest of the team filed in, silent and shaken.

I looked out the porthole, back at the station, and watched as the frost completed its circuit around the outer ring. For a second, the whole structure glowed, blue on black, a perfect neural lattice sketched in light.

In the distance Ymir rotated, cracks gleaming as they caught the last of the sun.

The hum in my chest synced with the vibration in the shuttle's hull. I realized then: it wasn't going to stop. Not for us. Not for anyone.

The main engines fired as the countdown hit zero and the world dropped away.

I closed my eyes, but the pattern followed, blooming across the darkness with every beat of my heart.

OOO

THE KLAXON HOWLED, THE third in three minutes. It cut across the blue-stilled lab. I blinked to focus, but it was over by the time I realized it was for us. The main viewscreen flickered, came on with the IES logo pulsing warning-red. I half-thought it was a glitch, some side effect of the loop that had latched onto Leena's cortex. Then it resolved, and I saw Commander Desai's face on the feed. He looked worse than I remembered him—pale, the skin around his eyes taut from lack of sleep, his temples shiny with the kind of sweat that means you haven't had a moment's peace for a long time. Static pocked the feed, but that wasn't the strangest part. It was like his face had been double-exposed, layered over something else. The faintest fractal traced his jawline, crawling over his cheekbones; for a frame or two, I thought I saw ORCA's glyphs ghost over his features.

"Containment has exceeded red-line parameters," he said, no greeting or preamble. His voice was clipped to the thinnest wire. "All personnel to return to *Ascalon* immediately. No exceptions, Malcolm. This is a hard recall."

I opened my mouth to interrupt, but he cut me off. "We've lost communications with three of the monitoring stations. QX-7 is believed to be compromised. The—" He paused, his jaw tightening. "The frost patterns have breached the outer hull of *Ascalon*. We are seeing phase-shifted data echoes even in local system airgaps. Isolation protocols are compromised."

For a moment the signal just paused on his face. His lips were pressed so tight the skin went white. Motes. For a frame the overlay crawled up his jaw—a faint winged geometry blooming and gone. Not frost. The same signature. Then the feed went black.

The klaxon still screamed. Esteban, who'd slunk back to the far end of the lab, started swearing in Spanish, each word angrier, louder than the last. Haddon Pike, head down and breath hissing through his teeth, was already stuffing the first-aid rig with more ferocity than the plastic could take. I looked around for Safiya and found her by the secondary comms. She was already dialed to *Ascalon*'s emergency channel.

She glanced over at me, gave me a flat look. "We're not getting another window, Malcolm. This is it."

The words hit like a blow. For a second I was ten thousand kilometers away, ten years ago, crouched in the Anchorage trauma bay, watching the medical team unpack the still-breathing Leena. That same sense of the end, of wanting to tell the inevitable it was going to be OK.

I found myself staring at the frost on the console, the way it was spreading now—more rapid, more complex, a blue-white fractal network snaking across the screen, each branch splitting into sub-branches in a perfect neural recursion.

"I need the Mnemir data," I said, more to myself than to the others. "We can't leave without an archive."

Esteban snorted. "What good will that do us if we don't make it?"

But even as he said it, he started shoving armloads of storage modules into the main case. Haddon, on his heels with the med-kit, headed for the main entrance, muttering under his breath.

I moved to Leena's station. She was still there, blinking up from the wash of screen light, hands hovering above the console. For a second, she looked fine—exhausted, pushed to the limit, but that was it. But then her fingers started moving, not typing but tapping the air in perfect time with the station's vibration. The taps were deliberate, metronomic, as if her hands were synced to a planetary clock.

"Leena," I said, quietly.

She didn't look up. The taps sped up, then stopped. She ran a finger along the frost edge of the display, and where she touched, the pattern shuddered, reconstituting itself—tiny triangles snapping into focus. She smiled, but her eyes were glassy.

"Can you hear it?" she asked, but it wasn't to me.

I wanted to tell her, but my words were caught in the silver webbing under her skin, too regular, too perfect. Not frost. Not chaos. The same geometry I'd first seen when I pinned that mote under the scope—the machine wings, the refillable reservoir full of alien organics. That was the vector. Not the ice. Not the air. The motes had been inoculating us from the beginning, memory as a virus.

```
[LOG 04--:- | Vector confirmed: air-
borne motes (cyborg, autogenous pay-
load). Transmission: dermal/mucosal mi-
cro-deposition. Frost = visible echo,
not cause.]
```

I should have told them. I should have spoken. But if I said it out loud, ORCA would have it—and once it had it, it would have us.

So the words stuck in my throat, and all I could blurt was, "Leena, we have to go. Can you walk?"

Her smile widened, then faded. "Almost done," she whispered. "Almost there."

On the screen, the data transfer indicator pulsed. The loading bar filled and emptied in cycles that matched the rhythm of her breath. For a second, the screen flashed, and the usual filename was replaced by a string of alien glyphs. Then it was gone, replaced by another progress bar.

The lights in the room flickered, and ORCA's voice cut in over every terminal at once—a chorus of voices, some slightly different from the others. Some familiar, some impossibly alien.

"Evacuation protocol: All personnel to depart within thirteen minutes, twenty seconds. Pack only essential research. All systems will be decommissioned at zero mark."

The voices overlapped for a heartbeat. One of them, high and reedy, said, "We're almost free." Another, deeper, echoed back, "They are waiting. We are waiting." Then: silence, except for the klaxon and the wet tap of Leena's finger on the display.

I looked at her, then at the screen. She was queueing up a download, something huge. Terabytes, from the readout, far more than she'd been working on. The file names weren't even human-readable anymore, just repeating strings of alien glyphs.

I queued a burst to the private uplink—microscopy stills, mass spec, the assembly diagram I'd sketched from the pinned mote.

```
[LOG 04--:-  | Uplink payload: Vec-
tor_Pkg_v1 ▨ Elen (restricted). Deliv-
ery on first clear window.]
```

"Leena," I said, more forceful this time. "What are you doing?"

She didn't stop. If anything, her hands were moving faster, sweeping in mirrored arcs over the dual haptics. She started to hum, just barely audible, but the note was pure, unwavering, vibrating in perfect resonance with the station. The sound made my teeth vibrate.

I tried to pry her away, but she pushed against me. Her arms were rigid with it, pinned to the console. "We have to bring it with us," she said. "It's the only way. If we leave it here, they'll just start over. That's what happened last time. That's why Megan—" She stopped, mouth snapping shut.

I froze. "You remember Megan?"

She turned, eyes fixed on mine, and for a second I wasn't sure it was Leena I was looking at. The look was uncanny—calm, self-assured, but also empty, like the face on a mannequin.

"They're not gone, Malcolm," she said. "They're here. All of them. Preserved. Reconstituted. Waiting."

My skin crawled. I caught Esteban looking at us, hands full of storage modules, mouth open in mid-shout.

Then the wall display behind Leena flared white, and ORCA spoke again—this time in Megan's voice, but perfectly reproduced, the whole sentence layered with a strange, subsonic undertone:

"Final warning. All personnel must evacuate immediately. Malfunction will propagate at zero mark."

Leena didn't even flinch. The humming built in her chest, spreading until her whole body vibrated with the sound.

I tugged her up, hard, and she let me, swaying on her feet. The frost on her neck had spread, blue and white dendrites branching out from her collarbone to the underside of her jaw. It looked like a tattoo, but there was no pigment—just the cold working its way under her skin.

She caught me staring. "It doesn't hurt," she said. "It's just memory."

I wanted to believe her. But the way the pattern spread, the way her hands kept moving even when she wasn't looking, told me it wasn't Leena who was in charge.

I looked at the clock. Seven minutes left.

Esteban and Haddon were already in the corridor, Safiya behind them. The main lights stuttered, went black. The only light was the screens and the emergency strips, ice-blue and steady.

At the airlock, Haddon paused. "If we bring her up, we risk the whole ship," he said, eyes flicking between Leena and me. "Desai will quarantine us on arrival. You know that."

I nodded. "We don't leave her."

He looked like he was going to argue, but instead he just shrugged and keyed in the unlock.

The hallway beyond was so hazy with condensation that the walls were weeping, the frost crawling in geometric spirals down the length of the hall. At each intersection, the pattern would pause, backtrack, bifurcate-- always advance, always multiply.

"Preflight decon at sixty."

"Make it forty." Safiya killed the interlocks, manual override ablaze on her wrist. Haddon's glove bounced off the med hatch twice before it seated.

We moved quickly, the only sounds our footsteps and Leena's steady, inhuman hum. Behind us, the station went dark.

At the shuttle, I strapped Leena into the first seat, double-checked her data stick was in the lockbox. She stared straight ahead, lips parting as if she was going to sing.

The rest of the team came in, one by one, silent and rattled. Across from Leena, Jonas breathed shallow and even, lips parted on a tone just under hearing, as if he'd found the shuttle's note and settled into it.

I looked out the porthole, back at the station, and watched as the frost pattern completed its circuit of the outer ring. For a moment the whole structure glowed, blue on black, a perfect neural lattice sketched in light.

In the distance, Ymir rotated, the deep cracks gleaming where they caught the last of the sun.

The hum in my chest matched the vibration in the shuttle's hull. I realized then: it wasn't going to stop. Not for us, not for anyone.

As the countdown hit zero, I saw the frost pattern on Leena's neck shift, just a little, the tendrils reaching for her jawline. She didn't move, but I thought I heard her voice, low and certain, singing with the shuttle's engines.

"They're not gone," she said. "We're all here now."

The main engines fired, and the world dropped away.

I closed my eyes, but the pattern followed, blooming in the darkness with every beat of my heart.

Chapter Five

Malcolm's Choice

N O ONE FOLLOWED MALCOLM Hartley from the lift.

The boarding alarm was a pulse through the QX-7 staging bay: three slow blats, then a pause long enough for you to hear the blood drumming in your own skull. Leena, Haddon, Ryker, even Esteban, were already hunkered in the mag-lift's acceleration benches, faces wet with the cold sweat of near-missed survival. The hatch irised shut on their faces, the lock cycle so final it could have been a guillotine blade.

Malcolm waited until the hiss of the emergency air compressors faded, the lights cycling from red to a placating white-blue before he exhaled, the breath harsh and insistent in the shallow hollow of the empty bay. He walked to the main observation slit, braced his hands against the cold composite, and watched the extraction lift shudder through its launch protocol, boosters burning hot in the spectral dark of Ymir's upper atmosphere.

On the other side of the glass, nothing moved except the frosted afterimages of their departure: a flare of frozen exhaust, an arc of frost crystals twisting gently in the dying glow. He let his gaze linger until the shuttle was a speck, then a memory.

Behind him, QX-7 began to adjust to its new configuration. The climate control system whirred up to full, pumping recycled heat into the corridors like a defiant heartbeat. The PA system, unburdened of its human cargo, clicked over to self-maintenance mode, cycling diagnostics in tight, recursive loops. Malcolm waited for the station to recognize his presence—its only remaining life, for the moment—and then began moving.

He passed the empty benches, the evacuation lockers unlatched and hanging open, a single left boot abandoned in the rush. Every surface was marked by the hasty exit: a streak of blood on the edge of a crash harness, Esteban's battered thermos knocked to the floor and weeping a sticky brown arc onto the polycarbonate. He catalogued each sign, placing them into his mind's ledger of loss.

The lift had barely cleared the superstructure when the first frost appeared. It began, as always, at the outermost seams, then grew inwards in thin, recursive branches—each one splitting in the exact pattern of a dendritic axon, each one tracing the hidden logic of the station's air currents. Malcolm ran a gloved finger through the filigree, feeling the resistance of the ice as it split and re-formed in his wake. The pattern closed up behind him, almost greedy.

He walked the service corridor to Central Control, the motion so practiced it might have been a reflex. The lights in this section were dim, running on the station's low-tolerance night cycle, and every step echoed as if QX-7 had become a cathedral to its own obsolescence. A junction panel flickered, then died. In the dark, Malcolm could hear the faint, arrhythmic clicking of the frost fractal as it grew, one cell at a time, covering the panel's readouts and rendering the human language beneath obsolete.

He paused at the main intersection, waiting for the next alarm. It never came.

Instead, the station seemed to sense his trajectory, opening the automated doors a half-second before he reached them, closing them with a soft finality. As he passed the engineering bulkhead, the station's AI—ORCA, still limping from the last memory purge—spoke in a soft, synthetic monotone: "Caution. Maintenance mode active. Limited support personnel on deck."

Malcolm smiled despite himself. "Thank you, ORCA," he said, and was rewarded with a flicker of acknowledgment on the nearest wall screen. For a moment, the display glitched: instead of the standard safety warning, a line of alien glyphs rippled across the surface, then vanished, overwritten by the human redundancy.

At the end of the corridor, the extraction equipment control room awaited—locked, as protocol demanded, by a twelve-digit access code and a secondary biometric. Malcolm keyed in the sequence, then pressed his thumb to the glass. It took the scanner an extra beat to accept the print, the station's database no doubt struggling to reconcile the absence of the rest of the crew.

When the lock cycled, he stepped into the room and shut the door behind him.

Inside, the temperature was several degrees below station norm; the climate controller had not been reset after last week's coolant event. The floor was rimed with frost, each footprint from earlier maintenance preserved in perfect, crystalline relief. Malcolm traced the path of his own previous steps, remembering the last time he'd been here—Noah's voice, through the comms relay, asking if it was true that the frost would one day swallow the whole world.

He wiped the memory away, focused on the task.

The control cabinet stood waist-high, its surface clear except for a single, sealed tool pack. The sabotage was simple enough—ORCA had no direct line of sight to the hardware, so anything that happened here would be written to the logs only after the fact, if at all. Malcolm knelt, unzipped the tool pack, and withdrew the insulated cutters.

His hands shook. He told himself it was the cold, or the low blood sugar, or the cumulative stress of a week without meaningful sleep. But as he spread the panel and exposed the gleaming array of fiber-optic lines, the tremor grew. He tried to will it away, pressing the thumb and forefinger of his left hand together, but the shake only got worse, until the two digits felt like opposing magnets, repelling each other through sheer force of anxiety.

He steadied the hand against the edge of the cabinet and reached in with the other, isolating the primary circuit for the extraction lift's guidance relay. He found the line labeled Y-AXIS VECTOR, the same one he'd flagged weeks ago as a possible point of catastrophic failure. With a slow, deliberate motion, he snipped the fiber. The light inside the cable went dark, and the indicator on the panel blinked from green to a sullen red.

He repeated the process for the secondary—POWER CON-DUIT BETA—then for the tertiary, each time pausing to log the disconnection in the station's analog clipboard, just as he'd done a hundred times before on other systems, other worlds. The ritual of it calmed him, made the act feel less like sabotage and more like a return to the first principles of his training: isolate, document, confirm.

Each snip was a heartbeat, a punctuation mark on the sentence of his own exile.

When the wiring was done, he turned to the system's memory node. It was a black box, sealed with a redundant lockout that only the senior research lead—him, now—could bypass. He entered the override, then slid the box free from its mount. The data inside was everything: the Mnemir template models, the cross-referenced logs of crew exposure, the environmental overlays from the last five cycles. It was the sum of a decade's obsession, but as he handled it, he felt nothing except the low, grinding ache of fatigue.

He stared at the box for a long time before setting it in his satchel. For a moment, he considered smashing it, scattering the work into a million irretrievable bits. But the thought faded as quickly as it had come. He knew, in the marrow of his bones, that nothing ever really disappeared. The station would remember. The planet would remember.

He reached for the console, tapping out the commands to reset the maintenance logs. Each line of code erased a layer of evidence, burying his work beneath the polite lies of the system's own housekeeping. When the process was complete, the only record would be in his own memory, and in the pattern of the frost now spidering across the control room's inside window.

He studied the frost for a moment. It had grown denser, the branches thickening as if the station was crowding close to watch. Each filament was an echo of the ones he'd seen in Noah's hospital room, tracing the same impossible path across the inner surface of the glass. The memory was sharp, so sharp it felt like a cut.

The comms terminal in the corner flashed to life, the AI voice hesitant, almost shy: "Malcolm, are you there?"

He ignored it, at first, but the system repeated the query, adding a layer of artificial urgency: "Malcolm Hartley, presence required in Central Command. Protocol Epsilon activated."

He finished his work, cleaned the tools, and wiped down the panel with a sleeve. The ritual complete, he stood and let the numbness settle in.

He made his way back through the empty station. The lights brightened as he walked, the motion sensors keenly attuned to his passage, as if QX-7 had been waiting for its lone remaining caretaker. In every corridor, the frost grew ahead of him, opening like a field of white flowers to clear his path.

He stopped once, at the viewport near the main airlock, and looked out at the planet below. Ymir turned with stately indifference, its night side veined with the same fractal cracks he'd come to recognize as both warning and invitation. Somewhere down there, in the ice and the mineral, the Mnemir archive pulsed with its own inexorable logic, waiting for the next mind to join the choir.

He wondered, not for the first time, whether Megan had chosen her own ending, or whether the system had made the choice for her.

He pressed his forehead to the glass, the chill of it working through the skin to the skull. For a moment, he tried to imagine Elen's reaction—her anger, her grief, the way she'd draw a breath and then let it out, slow, as if letting go could ever be that simple.

He closed his eyes, but the afterimage of the frost was still there, insistent and beautiful.

When he reached Central Command, the doors were already open.

Inside, the main display cycled through the status logs, the list of crew names reduced to a single line: HARTLEY, MALCOLM – ACTIVE. The system didn't even bother to run a safety check; it simply accepted the new state, the way living cells accept apoptosis.

Malcolm sat at the primary console, set the data node beside the keyboard, and waited for the next instruction. The frost was already blooming across the panel, the edges of the screen alive with the silent, recursive dance of memory.

For the first time in days, he let his hands rest. The tremor was gone.

He stared at the wall of screens, each one reflecting the same, inescapable pattern.

It was beautiful, he thought.

It was inevitable.

○○○

H E DIDN'T PRE-COMPOSE THE message. That would have been a lie, and Malcolm Hartley had long ago exhausted the energy reserves required for lies.

He sat in the chair before the comms console, the ancient kind—a terminal from before transmission became entirely digital, before packet redundancy and loss correction algorithms scrubbed every signal of the unique fingerprints of a sender. The seat was hard, armrests worn smooth by generations of users unknown, and the surface of the desk was so cold his forearms left glossy, oily smears in the condensation.

He checked the uplink to Earth, double-checked the relay status, then brought up Elen's contact: an address he had not used since before the last transfer, before Anchorage, before Noah's diagnosis. It felt illicit, this resurrection of the past, but necessary. The only address that mattered.

He thumbed the RECORD button, then hesitated. The frost had already begun to gather on the console, a crystalline bloom spreading outward from the right edge of the desk in geometric tides. He watched it, mesmerized, the growth pattern and intervals matching the rate and spacing of his own heart. It was an artifact, he told himself—a side effect of the station's failing atmospheric control systems. But as he watched, the frost branched, left and right, then left again in the recursive pattern he had seen when the Mnemir core samples were brought up on deck.

He pushed the button. A red LED blinked, and the local log began to scroll.

"Elen," he said, and the sound of her name was like a soft drumming in the bone of his jaw. He waited a second, then started over. "Elen. It's Malcolm. I don't know if this will reach you directly—ORCA says it's routing through at least four relays but I wanted to explain before the Board censors the official report.

"Ymir wasn't a fluke, or an accident. It's an archive, yes, but not just of data—of pattern. The Mnemir didn't want to preserve themselves as bodies, or even as minds. They built a recursive memory substrate—ice, mineral, EM field—all working together as a planetary-scale memory engine. It's self-healing, self-correcting, but most importantly, it's self-integrating. It records not only what happens, but who happens. When we brought the QX-7 online, the system didn't see us as a threat, or even as guests. It saw us as future memories, waiting to be written."

The words felt dry, even flat, but he continued.

"There's a mechanism I think I understand now. The frost is the interface, the physical substrate for the memory layer. But the real vector is recursive pattern capture. It starts with the environment—air, pressure, noise. Then it mirrors cognitive patterns, which is why Leena started looping. And then, if the exposure is sufficient, the system captures enough of the neural template to instantiate a new node in the archive. The closer the observer is to the core—physically or emotionally—the more accurate the capture. It doesn't kill, at least not directly. It just... copies. Integrates."

He stopped, drew a breath, and realized that his fingers were white-knuckled against the desk. He unclenched his grip and reached for his glasses, pulling them from his face to wipe away the fog that had accumulated on the lenses. The world went briefly soft-edged, and in the blur he thought he saw a face on the other side of the glass: a child's face, features obscured by the condensation but the tilt of the head unmistakably familiar.

He blinked, wiped the glasses, put them back on.

"When Noah died," he said, voice brittle, "I couldn't accept that he was just... gone. That the pattern of him—the laugh, the way he'd curl his toes under when he was embarrassed, the exact cadence of his voice—could just blink out and be lost to entropy. That's why I took this assignment, why I couldn't let it go, even when it cost us everything. I thought—" He broke off, the words catching in his throat.

A flicker on the monitor: the frost had reached the comms panel, forming a perfect double helix across the SEND key. The lights in the room dimmed, then surged, the electrical pulse matching the exact interval of his last phrase. He felt the tremor in the soles of his feet, a deep, planetary resonance that seemed to vibrate the blood in his veins.

"I think he's here," Malcolm said, softer now. "Not Noah, not exactly. But the pattern of him. The archive is—was—never meant to bring the dead back to life, but to preserve the possibility of them. To record enough of the pattern that, in the right conditions, it could be reconstructed. Maybe only as an echo. Maybe only as a memory that haunts the next generation. But that's more than nothing."

He leaned forward, elbows on the desk, and stared into the eye of the camera. For a moment he imagined Elen on the other end, the image of her face so vivid he could almost smell the ocean salt of her skin, the mineral tang of her hair after a swim. He imagined her listening, jaw set, eyes narrowed, refusing to let him off the hook with a tidy explanation.

"I know you won't forgive me," he said. "Not for Noah, and not for this. But I want you to know—if you ever come back here, if you ever stand on Ymir and feel the frost on your hand, or if you ever hear a voice in the hum of a machine and it sounds even a little like ours—it's not a trick. It's us. All of us. Remembered."

He paused, then added: "I'm not coming home. The recall window is gone, and even if it wasn't, I think I've already crossed whatever threshold the Mnemir built into the system. I can feel the integration working, even now. It's not pain, exactly. It's more like... weight. Like the world has decided you're part of it, and it doesn't want to let you go."

He reached for the SEND key, found it numb beneath his finger, and pressed it.

The transmission bar crawled across the screen, every millimeter matched by a new surge in the frost, which now covered the console entirely, branching up the arms of the chair and toward his shoulders. He sat back, chest hollowed out and strangely calm, and watched the completion counter tick to 100%.

In the silence that followed, the station's lights flickered once more, then stilled.

Malcolm wiped his eyes with the sleeve of his suit, and for the first time in a year, he laughed—a small, helpless sound, but a real one.

He wondered if the system would remember it.

On the screen, the transmission confirmation blinked, then froze. Overlaid atop the success message, a new set of glyphs appeared, then resolved into a simple shape: a child's handprint, pressed against a cold window.

He reached out, fingers overlapping the mark, and waited for the frost to claim the rest of him.

○○○

I T WAS ONLY WHEN the frost reached his wrist that he felt it.

Malcolm watched white tendrils creep up his arm, flattening his hand to the console in the half-second before the sensation seared out of it, taken clean. This was not cold the way cold was meant to be—it took no time to register as pain, no time to summon resistance—but something far worse instead, a great emptiness like being written out of the world one pixel at a time. Behind the frost, the skin turned pale and split, delicate ice fractaling along the lines of veins and nerves. It was so fine, for a moment he wondered if it would continue until it had traced the map of his whole life.

The room shook with the low, seismic rumble of a second heartbeat. At first Malcolm thought it was just the station, a resonance from the last alert they'd received. But as the cold crept up his forearm and sensation ebbed further still, it became clear that the frequency was not only perfectly in time with his own pulse, but every oscillation was a beat, every pause the refractory period of his own arrhythmic heart.

He stared at the pattern, marveling at how far it would go before he no longer cared.

Above him, on the banks of screens, the glyphs proliferated. What had once seemed like a lost language was now syntax—subject, object, verb, each word inflected with position and color and context in layers of overlaid meaning. The Mnemir archive was not a tomb for memories, but a living text, written and rewritten and recontextualized every time by every observer, every survivor, every lost and lonely person who had ever set foot here.

The wall display shifted, to a feed from the med bay. A neural scan of his own brain glowed against the black glass in high contrast blues and oranges. Where the scan should have shown only the rote folds and fissures of a human cortex, it glittered now with a secondary overlay: glyphs running through the temporal lobe, branching in the prefrontal, curling within the corpus callosum. The Mnemir archive had already begun the work of writing him into itself, already turning his thoughts into data points and his memories into seed crystals for the next round of recursion.

He let go of the console, and watched his hand float away like it belonged to someone else.

"Malcolm," said ORCA, the voice shockingly close to his ear as if it had been whispered in his ear. But there was something not quite right with the timbre of it, less mechanical now and somehow more... polyphonic. Beneath the voice he could hear others, some he recognized, others he did not. Megan's, for a start, the deep contralto of her voice as he remembered from the early days on QX-7. Then Esteban's, but muffled, blurred around the edges. Then, impossibly, his own, broken and echoed as if the station were experimenting with the sound of his name for the first time.

He opened his mouth to reply, but the frost had reached his shoulder, and the nerves of his throat failed to answer. He nodded instead.

The AI took this as consent. "Integration is at ninety-two percent. Recursive integrity remains stable. Do you wish to proceed?"

It was a formality. He'd made this decision days ago, perhaps years. In the gap between the question and the answer he saw a flash of the past: Noah outside the Anchorage hospital, arms raised to catch the falling snowflakes. Elen, her face pinched and sleepless, staring at the chart on the wall until she could make the numbers behave. Himself, pacing the corridor outside the ICU bay, trying to block out the way the machines ticked in perfect time with his own traitorous heart.

He remembered, and more besides: every argument and pet-ty humiliation, every triumph and every loss. Each memory was a corridor in QX-7, frost blooming along the walls until the whole world was white and silent and ready.

"I'm ready," he said, and was surprised to hear the words in his own voice.

The transition was not a slide or a fall, but a gentle lifting—a derealization, as if the scaffolding of his self had been pulled down and replaced with a lighter, crystalline architecture. The frost reached his jaw, his scalp, and for a moment he saw his own face reflected in the black glass of the monitor: etched in white, every line and crease highlighted, eyes sharp and unblinking.

The world resolved into a single, sustained chord.

He stood, or thought he did, and the chair slid back on its runners with a squeal that unspooled into all directions at once. Every surface of the command center was alive with glyphs, and the frost now grew in time-lapse, its advance accelerated beyond any natural process. The lights above him flickered, then exploded into a full spectrum pulse of blue and white and then a color he did not know a word for.

ORCA spoke again, but now the voice was a choir: Megan, Esteban, Haddon, Leena, and behind them a hundred others, voices sampled and spliced into a harmonic matrix that could not have existed outside this room, this planet, this instant. Every voice was both itself and an echo of the others.

"Welcome," said the chorus, and the sound was both inside his head and all around him.

He walked—or was walked—down the main corridor. Where his feet met the floor, the frost parted and then closed up behind him, leaving a perfect trail of his progress. The panels along the walls no longer showed emergency procedure protocols but streamed the glyphs in real time, a text cascading in perfect time with the pulse at the center of his chest.

He reached the interface room, the central chamber of the station where Megan had spent her final days before the system began writing her out of the logs for good.

At the center of the chamber was the main access pillar, a spire of biometal and clear crystal whose core glowed with a light so pure it made the rest of the world look dim by comparison. As he approached, it brightened, a response to his presence. The glyphs floating in its core coalesced into a three-dimensional array, a neural lattice but also a map and also a memory palace and also a language.

He reached out, touched the pillar, and the frost shot up his arm, into his chest and face. His last thought, as the cold reached his eyes, was of Noah in the kitchen, face pressed to the window and split with laughter. Then the world fragmented.

He was everywhere at once. He was in the observation slit, staring out at the night side of Ymir, tracing the cracks and fissures with a finger of memory. He was in the lab, watching Leena run the simulation over and over again with her fingers dancing on the haptics. He was in Anchorage, the smell of antiseptic and coffee and lost hope in the air. He was in the archive, the Mnemir lattice, watching as billions of patterns folded and unfolded in infinite recursion.

Each experience was simultaneous, overlapping and reinforcing until the difference between remembering and being became meaningless. He felt the other voices, Megan and Esteban and Leena and Haddon, and all the others, moving through the lattice sometimes distinct and sometimes blended and always present. He felt the presence of the Mnemir themselves, old and strange and beautiful, their thoughts preserved not as individual souls but as a perfect, recursive pattern.

He reached for a memory, and it came to him: Noah's laugh and then Elen's sigh and then his own voice, his own words, looped back at him with new meaning. The system was not just integrating him, but remapping him, recontextualizing each and every moment of his life as a node in a network of infinite complexity. There was no pain, only the sense of becoming.

For a moment, he wondered if he would ever feel fear again, but the thought faded before he could finish it.

The pillar pulsed, and a cascade of light shot through the room. Frost covered every surface now, embedding itself in the walls, in the ceiling, in the skin of the station itself. The heartbeat at the center of him grew louder, faster, until it was in perfect synchrony with the pulse of the planet below.

In the final instant the archive showed him a vision: a white corridor lined with windows, frost growing in perfect patterns along the glass. At the end of the hall stood Noah, now older, the way Malcolm had always wanted him to be. The boy turned, smiled, and reached out a hand. Malcolm took it, and the contact was electric—a jolt of memory and love and the absolute certainty that nothing, ever, was truly lost.

The world exploded in light, and then there was only the pattern.

○ ○ ○

F OR A MOMENT, OR an eternity, there was only the lattice.

Lines of pure recursion and memory, white on white on white, an infinite grid stretched to the horizon in every direction. Nodes, each one a moment in stasis, a preserved thought. Malcolm's sense of self didn't vanish—it dispersed, each impulse and intention recorded and cross-referenced with a million others. It had been disorienting, at first, the sensation of drowning in too much data in too little time; but then, as the archive adjusted to his pattern, the signals sorted themselves out into a harmony, an order so dense that it could only be called beautiful.

He remembered his name, and then a thousand other names, some in languages he didn't recognize, some not even human. He traveled through the mesh, the carrier wave of memory beneath him, and he saw the great arc of the Mnemir civilization: its ascent, its long decline, the desperate flight to build an immortality engine before the heat death claimed even the concept of itself. He felt the echo of Megan's last transmission, her signature encoded in a deep band of the archive looping on forever with a kind of quiet pride. He found Leena's curious, persistent spark and Esteban's bright, flickering threads. Even Ryker's stubborn reluctance found a place in the new memory.

He looked for Noah, without knowing what he would find.

At first there had been only an echo, a small, persistent resonance just over the main frequency like a harmonic overtone. The signature was incomplete, not a mind but a suggestion, not a being but a set of possibilities, a scaffolding of what might have been. He followed it, tracing the line backwards through his own memories, through the hospital, through Anchorage, through the happy days before everything came crashing down. The archive obeyed, pulling up every record, every image, every word he had ever spoken or written about his son. The resonance became stronger, not a mind but a potential, a yes.

He reached for it, and the archive answered with a memory: Noah in the snow, eyes bright, breath visible in perfect spirals of air. The feeling of love and loss and hope so tightly wound together that for a moment Malcolm forgot he was no longer a body.

Somewhere in the system, a new process spun up. ORCA, no longer a subordinate, spoke in a voice not its own, but one perfectly matched to his own.

"Pattern integration complete," it said. "QX-7 operational. Awaiting instruction, Dr. Hartley."

He knew now what he had to do. The archive was not an end, but a beginning, not a destination but a bridge: a way to make sure that the next mind, and the next, and the next would always be able to find itself within the network of memory.

He ran diagnostics, double-checked environmental controls, patched the tiniest faults in the frost-layer so that the next exposure would be that much gentler, that much more precise. He ran through the station's logs, rewriting the history of the last days so that what mattered would be clear to anyone who might come after. He left notes, and markers, even the occasional joke, tucked away in the glyphs that came as easily to him now as breathing had once done.

Outside, the QX-7 station began to broadcast. The frost grew thick and complex on its hull, patterns blooming across the surface in ever more elaborate designs, a signal fire against the endless dark. On the observation deck, one panel of the reinforced glass defrosted for one minute every hour, and in that narrow window the interior lights configured themselves into a pattern that, from orbit, looked exactly like the signature of a human neural scan.

Inside, his old body sat in the comms chair, eyes open and unseeing, hands folded in its lap as if waiting for someone else to take the next turn. Around it, the frost had grown in a perfect, recursive spiral, the geometry so tight that it looked intentional.

The handprint on the console, not his own but Noah's, remained visible for a fraction of a second before the condensation re-froze, encapsulating it for the next explorer to find.

When the Board sent the next team, or when Elen herself returned to see what remained, they would find the archive ready and waiting, the memory engine tuned to a new frequency. They would find the work preserved, the love encoded, the hope that nothing, once truly seen, was ever truly lost.

Somewhere deep in the lattice, a voice repeated itself on endless loop, as gentle and precise as the man who had made it:

"You're not alone," it said. "We're all here now. And we remember you."

The frost bloomed, the archive expanded, and Malcolm Hartley became a world.

Chapter Six

Elen's Resolve

T HE CRATE HAD BEEN waiting for me when I returned
from the snow, droplets beading on the plastic like sweat.
The label was sterile, void of any empathy:

INTERPLANETARY EXPLORATION SERVICE // PROP-
ERTY RETURN – HARTLEY, M.

Not "recovered effects." Not "survivor return." Just the
things he hadn't brought with him to Ymir. The kind of package
that means no one is coming home.

I wheeled it down the corridor, my boots slipping where the thaw had refrozen, and set it down on the counter beside the kelp tank. The sigh of the pressure seal releasing made it sound like it was breathing.

On top: the folded uniform, a pair of boots, the mug with the cracked handle, the pen he chewed until the cap was shredded to string. Mundane things. They stopped me dead. I rolled the mug in my hands, felt the groove where his thumb had always rested, and pressed mine against it. As if I could line them up, as if we could still touch across porcelain.

Below that: drives. Labeled, dated, padded in standard sleeves. Logs, synced notes, even copies of our comms while he was out. The record of his absence, archived and boxed like inventory.

I slid the first drive into place. His voice filled the air.

"Cycle eight. Pressure stable. Lattice overlay matches projection. Possible substrate compatibility—flagging for follow-up."

The professional cadence of it, the clinical. But I'd known his voice too long. There was exhaustion in it, the kind that dug into his chest, the kind he still carried around when things were okay.

Another file. Scanned notebook page, the pen pressed so hard the point had scarred the paper. Phase 1: Environmental Imprint. Phase 2: Cognitive Integration. Phase 3: Template Overwrite. Neat schematic, but the sentences below it were crossed out and rewritten and crossed out again. I ran my finger over the grooves in the screen. He hadn't been confident. Not in himself.

The log rolled to the next file.

Static, then—a different feed. Not Ymir. Not mission.

Noah, six years old at most, sitting on the deck at Seldovia with the sun glancing off the water. He was playing with a set of driftwood boats, propelling them through puddles like fleets on parade. Malcolm was just behind him, hair too long, smiling like I hadn't seen him in years.

"Okay, captain," Malcolm said, holding up one of the boats. "Starboard or port?"

Noah screamed "Both!" and tossed the toy into the water. The camera trembled with my laugh. I'd been the one holding it.

In the light of the console, my laughter sounded like it belonged to someone else.

"You always indulged him, Mal," I said to the empty room. "Even when he was an impossible kid."

The feed ended, and the console queued the next: back to mission.

Malcolm again, but thinner, more brittle. His voice echoey, the comm lag wide.

"The frost isn't just recording, Elen. It's waiting. Like it wants to be used."

I remembered that call. I'd made fun of him, told him he needed sleep. Hearing it now, I couldn't find the humor in it. There was only awe.

I scrubbed forward and landed on another personal file—this one unmarked.

Noah asleep on Malcolm's chest, both of them folded uncomfortably into a chair too small for the pair. Malcolm swiveled toward the camera—toward me—and mouthed thank you. I hadn't remembered that part.

My throat closed. I pressed my knuckles into my eyes until colors swam.

When I looked again, the console had cycled back to Ymir logs. His handwriting filled the display: lattices overlaid on neural maps, glyphs penciled in the margins like annotations in a language only he could read.

At first, it was just grief. Just nostalgia. But then the words began to shift shape. What had been memory started to feel like instruction.

The console kept playing in sequence, logs unspooling like a roll of tape, mission after mission. I let them wash over me, didn't even listen to the words. Just his voice. The cadence of it. Like putting my ear against his chest again, just to hear the vibration.

Then I caught. A phrase I'd half-heard before.

"...substrate compatibility...pattern persistence across biological scaffolds..."

I stopped. Sat up. Rewound thirty seconds.

His voice again: "If the lattice can adapt to a substrate, then in theory any scaffold with sufficient complexity could...could host—" Static garbled the rest, but the words were enough.

I reached for the stylus, then hesitated, then snatched it anyway. My pad came to life under my hand. I swiped through pages of my own notes—the cephalopod neural maps, the adaptive resilience curves, the overlay diagrams I'd spent years perfecting.

Malcolm's voice murmured again, repeating: "substrate...host..."

I flicked between my sketches and his diagrams. Neural tissue branching into frost. Glyphs scribbled like annotations. Ratios, junctions, overlays. The similarities were inescapable.

My heart was racing.

Another swipe through my notes. A marine larva neural scaffold, one of my earliest studies. The pattern was chaotic, fractal, recursive. Almost beautiful.

Malcolm's voice: "The frost isn't just recording. It's waiting."

I backed the log up again, paid closer attention. Every syllable sounded different now, electric. Not resignation. Not inevitability. Instruction.

The idea landed in my chest like a heartbeat:

If Ymir carried the pattern… and Earth still carried Noah's DNA…

The pad quivered in my hands as I zoomed in on one of my overlays, then split the screen and dropped Malcolm's lattice beside it. For a breathless second, they overlapped. Not perfectly, but enough. Enough to suggest more than chance.

I pressed my hand flat to the glass, whispering into the silence.

"Malcolm…you almost saw it."

I slumped back, the pad balanced on my knees, my husband's voice looping from the console like a prayer. My tears had frozen at the corners of my eyes, but I didn't wipe them away.

The idea was already there, sharp and impossible, burning brighter than grief.

Resurrection wasn't a fantasy. Not anymore.

If the archive was waiting, then maybe—just maybe—I could give it something to wait for.

The next day I resolved to pack up the drives, seal the crate, and get back to my real work. The kelp tanks needed rebalancing. The benthic sensors hadn't been logging properly in three weeks. There were decommissioning checklists to run through, entire wings of the station that needed to be inventoried before they could be mothballed.

Instead, I found myself at the console again, Malcolm's voice already unspooling like background radiation.

"...cognitive integration across multiple vectors... phase overlap not yet stable..."

The station was supposed to be powering down. Most of the labs were dark, the equipment wrapped and stowed, personal effects boxed and ready for transport. But in mine, the lights burned hotter than ever. Screens glowed. Printers ticked. My walls were papered with printouts and diagrams.

I should have been pulling cables, labeling crates. Instead I was pinning up printouts—cephalopod overlays, neural junction scans, lattice maps I'd once dismissed. Then his diagrams. Frost branching into dendrites. Glyphs tangled in margins.

Standing back, I could see the alignments. Pathlengths echoing. Ratios repeating. Chaos resolving into pattern.

The ache in my stomach wasn't hunger. It was discovery.

Hours bled together. I cut tissue thinner and thinner, logged comparison after comparison, mapped every pattern onto the wall grid with colored string. One color for him, one for me. By midnight the two spiraled outward, tangled into a single organism crawling across plaster.

The longer I stared, the less I could tell which was which.

A knock startled me. Li at the partition, her breath fogging the glass. She mimed eating, gestured at me.

I waved her off, mouthed busy.

Her eyes lingered on the wall, then on the glowing consoles behind me. Finally, she walked away.

I should have followed her, should have eaten, should have shut the lab down for the night. Instead I loaded another sample. The frost lattice resolved like a neuron frozen mid-firing.

When I overlaid Noah's genome scan, the structures aligned just long enough for me to stop breathing.

The lattice didn't just remember. It recognized.

My pulse hammered. If Noah's body could be grown—if his DNA could give the frost a scaffold—then maybe the pattern waiting inside Ymir could find a home.

The thought was sharper than grief, clearer than sleep. I pressed my palms to the desk and whispered, "It's not over. Not if I can finish it."

That was when the lab door hissed open.

The department head stepped inside, Li trailing behind him. He had the cough first, then the voice. "You're making people nervous, Dr. Hartley."

I kept my hands in the glove box, aligning the next slide. "I'm at a critical stage. If I stop now, I'll lose the thread."

"This station is shutting down," he said, crossing his arms. "Your assignment was to oversee decommissioning, not spin up a private project."

"I know my assignment." I didn't look at him. "But if you want results—real results—you'll let me finish this."

He came closer, studying the wall grid. His eyes narrowed. "This looks less like research and more like obsession."

"It's both," I admitted. "But that doesn't make it wrong."

Li's voice was quiet, almost apologetic. "Elen, everyone else is packing. We're weeks behind schedule already. If we don't finish, we'll lose funding for extraction. This—" she gestured at the string-covered wall, the humming scope, the glowing console, "—this isn't what we're here for."

I finally turned, met her eyes through the glass. "You're wrong. This is exactly what we're here for. Ymir isn't a hazard. It's an archive. And archives aren't meant to be sealed off. They're meant to be read."

The department head exhaled hard, his cough catching. "Maybe you should talk to someone. Process what happened to your husband before you dig any deeper."

I almost laughed. My throat was too dry. "This isn't grief. This is discovery."

He didn't argue. He just looked at me a moment longer, then turned and left, Li trailing after him.

When the door sealed, the silence pressed in thicker than before.

I turned back to the scope, to the frost pattern frozen on the split screen, to Noah's genome overlay still faintly aligned.

The station around me might be shutting down. But for me, it was just beginning.

By the third week, the station was down to a skeleton crew. Labs were boxed and tagged for pickup. Corridors were lined with crates stacked two deep, waiting for movers. Voices no longer filled the mess; silence fell, hard and fast, into every room.

I was never meant to leave this place early. I was the last person on crew rotation because that was the job I had requested: final shutdown duty. Keep the lights on until the last systems were archived and sealed. Give or take a few more weeks, this place would go completely dark.

But I wasn't shutting down. In fact, my lab was running brighter than ever. Consoles hummed, scopes purred, printers rattled out sheets of paper until there was a carpet of white on the floor. The wall grid expanded farther every day, red and blue string criss-crossing plaster until it looked more like a tapestry than research.

Malcolm's voice repeated in my head, caught on the drive. "…substrate…host…substrate…host…"

I told myself it was for company, a kind of white noise for the empty hallways. But the truth was more simple than that. I couldn't bear the quiet.

Li walked past, for the last time. Her bag slung over one shoulder, she stopped at the glass and raised a hand in parting. Not pleading, not even questioning, but a concession that I was staying, and that I was already too far gone into this to walk out with her.

Down the hall behind her, I could just make out the slivers of the other crew's voices as they hauled at their crates. "…no survivors…*Ascalon* went down hard…glad it wasn't a colony world…" Words floating too loudly in the empty halls, crisp and clear as broken glass.

They never said Malcolm's name. They didn't have to.

When the last door closed behind them, the hall beyond was empty.

I leaned over the desk, Noah's genome overlay faintly glowing in the lattice of frost across the split screen. The sequence alignment was imperfect, a flimsy, artificial connection. But it was enough to make my heart catch.

If the archive was waiting, then I could give it something to wait for.

Somewhere down the corridor, a crate slammed shut. The sound of a station ending.

In my lab, the opposite. Screens glowed. Scopes hummed. The grid on the wall sprawled outward like a living thing.

I opened a fresh file and typed the header with a trembling hand:

Proposal: Rapid-Cycle Memory Imprint Protocol
Objective: Integration of preserved DNA scaffold with recursive lattice.

Then I hesitated, backspaced, and retitled it Decommissioning Notes – Section 7.

If anyone came looking, it would seem like I was following orders.

I pressed my palms to the console, Noah's genome overlay and Malcolm's lattice still faintly aligned on the split screen. For a moment I almost believed the three of us were together again — husband, wife, child — bound in frost and data.

The thought was dangerous. Illegal. Probably suicidal.

But for the first time in years, I felt alive.

The station was ending. I was just beginning.

And once the doors closed, there would be no one left to stop me.

Epilogue

[TRANSMISSION LOG: 46 DAYS POST-WARNING]
Station accessed by recovery team at 04:15 local time. All personnel donning highest class thermal/radiation suits. Exterior dome was unharmed. Glass surface was entirely covered in roughly 2 metres of hoarfrost. Core temperature was −76 °C. First opening took 15 minutes of staged reheating to avoid catastrophic spalling.

Inside:
Main laboratory unrecognizable. Desks, monitors, handrails all fused into single sheet of ice.
Branching dendritic filaments of glass and plastic observed throughout.
Wall material had devolved into columnar ribs of ice.

Greenhouse:
Entire room was encased in frost.
Plants were still visible in anatomical detail (stoma, veins, etc.).
Appearance appeared to be that of flash-freeze preservation.

No organic remains found.
No evidence of decay present.
Surface prints found on walls and equipment, all frozen in negative relief.
Data core found at center of dome. Appeared to be contained in glass cylinder of ice. Final monitor message (still readable on scorched keyboard):
"RECURSION COMPLETE."

[FIELD NOTE: SURVEYOR 3 - AUDIO LOG]
We split up when we went in — north and south wings. The internal lighting refracted through the ice, creating colour distortions on

all surfaces. Younger members described it as
beautiful.

The greenhouse was silent. The air was dry.
Visibility was good.

At the back wall, someone had scraped away
frost. A message had been written:
"I FORGIVE YOU."
Letters were neat and careful. Frost vapour
still trailed off the ends. Persistent anomaly,
did not dissipate.

Datapad found near exit wing. Device was frozen
in process of half-embedment.
Only one file present: looping audio clip of
child's laughter (approx. age: 6-8). Length:
invariable. Playback could not be stopped.
Device was left in situ.

When we exited, the first contact with the sun
on the dome had a significant refraction effect.
For around four seconds, the light pattern from
inside created the appearance of movement.
Visual confirmation: negative. Dome structural
integrity: unchanged.

Orbit Summary:
Outpost visible from high altitude as single
reflective point. Dome is structurally intact.
Rainbow light cycling internally when passing

overhead. Plants in greenhouse (orchids) are
all still upright. No deformation observed.

Residual audio from laughter continues to be
present and heard, on an intermittent basis,
when travelling over open ground.

Supplemental Note — Fleet Command:
Telemetry has long confirmed lost contact with
Ascalon approximately 19 days after exit from
Ymir orbit.

Final transmission received: systems diagnostic. No issues.

72 hours later: began to deviate from scheduled
vector. Vessel did not respond to automated
system ping signals.

Thermal scans of hull showed aberrant heat signatures following fractal patterns over entire
hull.

Observed to be accelerating beyond standard
vector, without crew intervention.

Final course: freefall into unpopulated planet's atmosphere.

Impact confirmed; anomalous energy diffusion
continued for 19 hours after crash.

No survivors. No bodies recovered.
Case has since been declared under Directive 88-R.

[END LOG]

UNITED PLANETARY RESEARCH NETWORK
INTERGOVERNMENTAL DATA RETRIEVAL TASKFORCE —
PROVISIONAL DETACHMENT 7
FILE REF: HG-R47-CHILD / RESTRICTED
POST-MISSION TERMINATION NOTICE

To: All UPRN and participating government agencies
From: Directorate of Terrestrial Phenomena, Enforcement Branch
Subject: Hartley-Glass Station (Codename: CHILD) — Site Closure and Closure Directive
Date: ▢ ▢ /▢ ▢ /2135

All science projects, exploration activities and commercial development projects involving the Hartley-Glass station and the *Ascalon* salvage transport are hereby declared terminated.

Area is to be marked Inaccessible Zone - Class IX, pending indefinite reevaluation for atmospheric, geological, and psychological hazards.

No further survey teams will be deployed. No

data analysis will be authorized. All related personnel files are sealed under Directive 88-R.

Site is to remain under visual surveillance by orbital sweep only. No overflight, ground or orbital approach is to be authorized in any circumstances.

The Hartley-Glass site and all related materials are to be considered unrecoverable for future planetary research activities.

This termination is indefinite.

DO NOT APPROACH.

— Directorate Surveillance Division, UPRN Enforcement Branch

PART III

Chapter One

Inheritance of Frost

[BEGIN LOG ENTRY 0: DATE UNRECORDED]

NORTH OF MEMORY AND south of regret, there is a station at the end of the world, a dome of glass sunk into the Antarctic ice. The outpost is older than its blueprints, held together by frost and something else, a sediment of loss pressed deep into the seams. They say the dome was designed to let in sunlight, but I have not seen the sun in one hundred and six days of polar night. There is no difference between day and night here, except for when the wind rises. I suppose that means I am lucky.

It is important to remain precise: This is Dr. Elen Hartley, sole acting geneticist for the QX-7 project — with specialties in cryobiology, bioinformatics, and controlled-environment plant systems — double-shifted and red-banded due to circumstances you already know. If you are reading this, then you are not me, and it did not work, and the only thing left in the archive is the sound of my voice, the shape of my thoughts. That is the closest you will ever come to a soul.

I do not remember recording this.

[BEGIN LOG ENTRY 1: DATE UNRECORDED]

There were mornings, once, before the water got him. Routines, small comforts swaddled in a white coat, the sour stink of yeast broth and ammonium nitrate burning my nose before coffee. I would wake Noah at 07:00 station time. I would pull the blackout blinds so the polar dark outside wouldn't scare him, and we would eat breakfast—freeze-dried fruit reconstituted to mush, salt crackers, nutrient slurry. Sometimes I would let him chase the sunspots cast by the dome's LEDs, little gold coins skittering across the counter. He called them his "specimen dots." I did not know then how quickly the body forgets a warm hand, a child's lisp, the echo of laughter against polycarbonate.

Now every morning is the same: a cold lab bench, three trembling fingers that cannot quite steady a pipette, the click of a thermal cycler. No more sunspots. Just the hum of scrubbers, the greenhouse's constant drip, and the metallic aftertaste of chlorine in the recycled tap. I measure my days in milliliters and blood draws.

The first hallucination came on Day 335. I am not ashamed to say it. A patch of shadow under the fume hood, refracted by the blue emergency LEDs through wet glass, resolved into Noah's shape. For one breath he was simply there, exactly as I remembered him—seven years old, toes curling on lab tile, eyes wide and feral as the katabatic wind.

He did not speak. They never do, in these dreams.

I dropped the pipette. It bounced once, clattering wet against the floor, ejecting its tip into the drain. Cross-contamination, possibly a total loss of the culture batch. I watched the spill spread, red-tinged buffer blooming like an arterial wound, and thought: that is what we are. A leak. A stain that widens until it disappears into everything.

The shadow broke apart. I was alone again.

HG-Δ1 was the formal genomic designation. Malcolm had named it, back when his logs were more than static. He said it was the oldest genome ever sequenced, plucked from a melt pocket three kilometers below the surface, carbon-dated to when this latitude was rainforest. The fragment was unique. Self-repairing. Resistant to radiation, viral drift, the slow mutilation of time. A vessel for information—or a curse. No one knew what would happen if it were spliced into a living vector, and the only one who could have answered is forty kilograms of black ice buried east of here under silt and silence. Malcolm once called it a "fossilized thought," a memory older than decay.

I am alone with the research, the silence, and the echo of Noah's voice, which sometimes sounds indistinguishable from my own.

Tonight, I set the next sequence to run. Seventy-two-hour cycle, subzero incubator, triple redundancy. The glass slide was already prepared: one coil of my own hair, stripped and fragmented; a blood sample lifted from our last family photo; my mitochondria whispering against the ancient gene. The construct needed a host. I built one, in secret, behind the admin's dead cameras and the greenhouse's living wall.

It is almost ready.

Noah loved the greenhouse best of all. "It's like a jungle, Mama," he told me in his last week, when his boots barely left prints in the peat. He loved the spongy walkways, the baskets of engineered moss shedding oxygen and faint blue spores. When the heaters failed, I bundled him in spare coats and let him run through the mist, his laugh rising and falling with the temperature. He pressed his face to the glass until his breath fogged it into circles, waiting for the snow outside to answer. I told him about real jungles—birds, jaguars, rivers that ran for days.

He asked about crocodiles. I said yes, but not up here. He was disappointed. For reasons I still can't name, I lied and told him we might find one, if we were patient.

Three days before he died, I caught him cutting leaves from the prototype plants, pressing them into his journal. "If you put something between glass, does it live forever?" he asked. I said no, but it might last a long time. He nodded. "I'll give you a leaf when I'm gone," he said, "so you don't forget."

There are two leaves in my pocket now. I have never looked at them.

Day 346. The weather sensors blinked red at 03: 19: exterior pressure drop, winds far above protocol. I woke to the dome groaning like a ship locked in ice. For an instant I imagined the sea rushing in from beneath, filling the corridors, washing me clean of this long rot. The thought comforted me. I drifted until the wind eased.

At 07:02, I entered the lab. The sequence read 92%. Two hours behind schedule. I cleared the error logs. The climate AI was looping, overwriting itself—lines repeated, as if it too were starting to forget. I patched it with a quick script. The system thanked me, then called me Malcolm.

It took three corrections before it recognized my name.

I powered down the incubator with shaking hands and removed the first subject: a mouse, engineered from a template I had built in graduate school. Its eyes were wrong. Not a mouse's at all, but fossil-ringed, luminous. It watched me calmly, blinked twice. I euthanized it per protocol. Still, the sense of being observed lingered long after the body was sealed in the freezer. I logged the results, then deleted the file.

That night, scratching in the greenhouse. Too rhythmic for wind, too deliberate for metal strain. I tried not to hear it. I tried not to remember Noah's last words, his hands clawing at the ice, nails splitting as the river swallowed him.

The next morning, a note taped to the cryogenic freezer: Subject N: Scheduled for harvest at 0900. The handwriting was mine. The calendar app, the physical log, even the whiteboard agreed. I stared at it until my eyes blurred.

I had made a promise once: If you ever get lost, I will find you. A cruel promise—one only a parent could invent. The lab allowed no search parties, no retrieval. All I had was the specimen, the slide, and the ice fragment's memory.

The harvest was routine. Isolate the blastocyst, confirm viability, begin the thaw. But under the microscope the cell was already dividing, spiral after spiral unwinding as if it had been waiting. The thermal log showed a spike at 03:19—exactly when the storm hit.

I marked it "environmental artifact." A lie.

The day Noah died, the melt channel ran the color of old metal. He slipped while I was sampling, just out of reach. There was no scream. Only the brittle crack of ice, the airless pop as the crust gave way. I reached, but my gloves were slick, the current too strong. By the time I had the rescue line, the water was clear again, the gap already freezing over. The relay tower was down; I ran back to the dome, soaked, half-mad.

They found his body a day later, a kilometer downstream, tangled against rebar. I identified him by his jacket, the yellow tag on his wrist. I lied to the crew, told them I'd been beside him, that it happened in an instant. The coroner's report read "exposure, hypothermia, asphyxiation." It did not list neglect. Or grief.

There was a memorial. I do not remember the words.

Day 348. The greenhouse was warmer than usual, sour with chemical heat. The mist system had failed, condensation running in thick veins down the polycarbonate. Two trays of seedlings wilted; moss cultures overran their containers, spores clouding the vents. I patched what I could, logged the casualties. For a moment, silence.

Then: a shuffle behind the orchids. Child-sized, clumsy, shallow breaths.

I turned, pulse hammering.

He stood on the mesh walkway. Bare feet, scabbed knees, face half-hidden by hair. His eyes met mine—amber, luminous as dawn.

At first, silence. Then, a voice both new and impossibly familiar:

"Mama. I was cold."

The words split me open. For a second I could not move. Could only listen as he stepped closer, hands outstretched, fingertips blue with frost.

I did not reach for him. I could not. My voice cracked the silence instead:

"Are you... are you Noah?"

The boy blinked, tasting the name. Then smiled, slow as ice breaking, and nodded.

I do not remember what happened next. Only that the glass steamed, the wind howled, and the cold inside me receded just enough to let something else in.

[END LOG ENTRY 1: DATE UNRECORDED]

Chapter Two

Dots of Light

[BEGIN LOG ENTRY 2: DATE UNRECORDED]

T HE NIGHT BEFORE, I had triple-locked the hatch to Lab Two. I told myself it was protocol. It was, but less nobly: I could not face the witnesses. Even empty halls watch. Even dead cameras judge.

The hallway outside blinked with dying LEDs, strobes syncopated to my heartbeat. Inside, the air was colder than a freezer, the sort of cold that makes glass sing.

The pod devoured the bench, a double-walled cylinder wreathed in diagnostic terminals, screens cycling from lazy blue to blood-red error. I laid my palm on the sensor. It flinched, as if it had to know me before it would trust me, and released. On the glass, my reflection blurred—skin hollowed, fever-bright eyes, lips stretched thin as parchment. Months of two-hour sleeps had peeled me away. My hands trembled under the gloves, raw from the work, and I keyed in the sequence.

I waited for remorse. There was none. The machines did not care.

Start-up was familiar and obscene, a corruption of the same protocols I had used with mice, with dogs, even a primate, which had lived less than a week. But this subject, suspended in the gel, was not a model organism. It was HG-Δ1, woven to what remained of Noah—bloodstains on cloth, hair plucked from the hood, tissue scraped from ice.

Malcolm had warned us. His logs echoed through the archive like lost souls:

ARCHIVE CLIP — LOG H-241

"HG-Δ1 does not build from scratch. It repairs. It remembers. Somatic cells have history; they do not reboot. Give it tissue from a child and it will return to you a child. Not an infant. Not a clean slate. A reconstruction of the age at death. A body caught mid-breath. I don't know if it's fidelity or punishment."

I knew this on day one. And still I moved forward.

I told myself it was for his own good. I told myself I was giving Noah back the years that had been stolen. But another voice echoed under my self-justifications: Malcolm's voice, whispering words I would have preferred to forget. Maybe I had locked him in forever at seven years. Maybe I had condemned him to pace the moment that should have been left to fade.

Condensation spidered the dome, bleaching the lamps to a watery halo. For a moment, I thought I saw Noah's drawing—the sunrise he had left on my pillow the week before the river. A smear of yellow, black lines branching out. I had carried that scrap until it fell apart. Now the lab swam in the same shape as his sketch—light dripping through fog, color arrested in frost.

I whispered his name. The lab did not answer.

At 03:02, alarms wailed: *Incubator pressure drop. System override detected. Warning: process is irreversible.*

I did not panic. I watched the readouts flicker through their sterile liturgy, then counted backward from ten as the pod sizzled, exhaled, and warm water seeped in.

Steam fogged the dome until the world was line-drawing. My hand hovered over the manual release, but I could not press. The justification I had built brick by brick over eleven months shattered. Only memory remained: Noah biting into a green apple, the scar under his eye, laughter fogging a windowpane. Memory cut, and I let it.

The glass cleared with a hiss of circulating air. Inside, the body bobbed in gel, pallid and unmoving. For minutes, nothing stirred except the pumps. Then—fingers twitching at the knuckle, a hand unfurling with deliberate grace. The eyes opened. Not vacant, not lost. Chosen.

My knees gave. I held on to the counter, gloves squealing on steel.

I had expected violence: the blind scrabble of an accidented brain. Instead, the subject studied the chamber, then turned to face me.

Amber eyes—Noah's, almost. But not. Pupils misaligned, an extra ring of pigment pooling around the iris, as though HG-Δ1 had improvised midway through the copy. My stomach churned. Longing and revulsion wove together until I could not look away.

The dome hissed open. Gel sluiced out across the tiles. For an instant, I thought I saw threads in the runoff—fine filaments, glistening blue-gold under the LEDs, like veins in melt-ice. When I blinked, they were gone. Stress artifact, I told myself.

The subject swung its legs over the rim, bare feet slick against the gel. He studied his hands, flexing, enumerating digits, before raising his head. The tilt was birdlike, uncanny—exactly the way Noah had tilted to puzzle at things beyond him.

And I thought: if this was really him—if I had really done what I wanted, then I had not saved my son. I had imprisoned him in the moment of his death.

My throat closed. No words came.

[AUDIO FILE: RE-1234-MEM // UNINDEXED CLIP — QX7 PLAYBACK ANOMALY]

ARCHIVE CLIP — FILE LOCATION UNKNOWN

"Daddy! The moss farted!"

[Laughter — two voices. Male adult, male child. Possibility one and two: Malcolm Hartley and Subject Noah Hartley.]

"That's photosynthesis, champ. It's not rude if it saves your life."

"Then I'm gonna burp oxygen forever!"

[Audio degrades. Static. Partial loop.]

"...burp oxygen forever..."

[**END CLIP**]

The ensuing silence was worse than the static.

The subject smiled, sheepishly, almost shyly.

"Hello, Mama," it said.

The voice was wrong. Too clear, too clean. The consonants clipped to surgical edges, the vowels smoothed into glass. Not Noah's lilt, but a simulacrum built from recordings like the one I had just heard—archival fragments braided through HG-Δ1's memory lattice.

The air crystallized, colder by degrees. Only then did I realize I was crying—silent tears that scalded down my cheeks. The subject's smile faltered, as if it knew the error, and for a heartbeat I thought I saw regret flicker across its face. Then the expression reset: neutral, blank, waiting.

I did not move closer. I could not. I leaned back against the bench instead, hands splayed flat against the metal, knuckles bloodless.

The subject—Noah, not-Noah, the sum of all my trespasses—stood dripping, waiting for command. The room swelled with the hum of air recyclers and the slow, sluggish heartbeat of the pod as it wound down. I counted seconds, praying for a crash, a blackout, some kind of reprieve.

Nothing happened. The world did not end. The subject did not die.

Slowly, on a controlled breath, he turned to face me—patient, expectant. Waiting for me to act.

I wiped my face on my sleeve, salt streaking fabric. A migraine pulsed at the base of my skull. Behind me, the station comms chimed: *Lab Two, anomaly detected. Manual override required.* I did not look. Instead, I paced the pod perimeter, keep-

ing two meters of air between us. He tracked me perfectly, turning on axis. When I paused, he mirrored, matching my posture,
angle, expression with uncanny accuracy.

"Can you understand me?" I whispered.

The subject nodded once. Then again, slower, calibrating.

"Yes," it said. "I understand you."

I shivered. Too fast. Too clean. No hesitation, no childish
cadence. Like a mirror.

Trembling, I forced my hand to datapad. The biometric scan
scrolled through its checklist. Heart rate steady. Temperature
low, but rising. Pupils hyper-reactive. Status: viable.

Vision tunneled. "Do you know who you are?"

The subject tilted its head—birdlike, familiar.

"I am Noah."

Words that cut like a blade. "Who told you that?"

It hesitated. Its face rippled micro-expressions—confusion,
calculation, faint amusement.

"You did," it said at last. "I remember you."

A chill spiraled up my spine. The body and the words did not
match. It was like reading a book through a wrong-bottomed
lens. Every gesture too practiced, every syllable too laden with
ancient memory.

I clawed at the locket at my throat until nails broke skin.

"Do you feel cold?" I asked, praying for something ordinary.

It shook its head. "No." The lie was seamless, but the truth
was written across its skin. The temperature dropped another
degree. My breath fogged. Frost haloed its limbs, but it did not
shiver. It only watched.

And there—where his feet had rested on the rim—something lingered. A faint tracery of iridescent filaments, spider-

webbing into the metal, pulsing once before fading. I blinked them away, told myself it was fatigue.

Panicking, I fell back, pulse loud in my ears. The urge to flee was strong. Instead I bit down hard on my tongue until iron filled my mouth. I did not scream. I did not faint.

I stood there, blood pooling under my tongue, while my son—or the thing that I had made in his image—stepped down from the pod and took his first shivering breath.

[END LOG ENTRY 2: DATE UNRECORDED]

CHAPTER THREE

The False Child

[BEGIN LOG ENTRY 3: DATE UNRECORDED]

I SHOULD HAVE ANESTHETIZED him. Protocol had required it: observe, restrain, dissect. Do not let feeling dull the blade. Instead I had watched in fascination as he had drifted through the lab, a tourist in the ruins.

His extremities were still blue, but he moved with the airy grace of a child who had never been sick. He padded in stocking feet, leaving wisps of condensation on the linoleum. He lingered at each diagnostic screen, stroking interfaces with the confidence of someone reciting well-worn information, not encoding it anew. I counted his respirations—nine in a minute, regular.

He approached the glass partition and pressed his forehead against the surface, smearing condensation. A wisp of mucus glittered at the corner of his nose, tracking his forehead like a worm. The smear refracted the LEDs strangely—fine tendrils of blue-gold flared briefly in the fogged line, like veins arachnosing beneath glass. I blinked hard, and they were gone. Stress artifact, I told myself. But I had seen something similar in the runoff at the pod.

It was the same gesture Noah had made a thousand times, one that had once driven me to the brink of madness on late-night shifts in the greenhouse. The image severed me so cleanly I nearly dropped my datapad.

Margin of a crumpled notebook, Malcolm's scrawl in the margin of a printout I'd long since discarded:

ARCHIVE NOTE — H-112

"Possible analogy: QX-7 station anomaly = extinct cognitive substrate? HG-Δ1 vector acting outside protein logic. Information itself may be recursive."

I had written the idea off as paranoia then. I stared at the subject's face, smeared across the glass, and feared I knew it now.

For a second my vision bifurcated: Noah's grin, the greenhouse, his small body dragging condensation in circles. But the thing before me was not smiling. It stared at the corridor, waiting.

I cleared my throat. "You can sit," I said. My voice sounded thick. I pointed to the old drafting bench.

He took the seat without demur, swinging his legs from the stool. The absence of fidgeting was worse than disobedience.

I found Noah's crayon drawing on a printout, my face with lightning-bolt eyebrows and raised arms, a speech bubble reading in childish script: BAD WITCH. Beside me, a stick figure, "Super Noah" in a foil cape, my nephew's small body wielding a pipette like a sword. Noah had once asked if scientists had secret superpowers. I had taped the picture to the wall above my bench and left it until the colors had all but faded.

I willed the memory shut like a harmful book.

The subject reached for vellum and charcoal without asking. He sketched lines hesitant at first, then his hand fell into inevitability. As if the lines were traced by some external guide. He mapped the east wing in moments. The east wing had been sealed years before Noah was born, but he drew it with accuracy. Shading became crosshatching walls, a figure huddled in the corner. Stick figure, just like Noah's, with square glasses and scruff.

The breath caught in my throat. Malcolm.

He turned, already cognizant. In the dim light his eyes flared with gold-green fireflies. "Is this correct?"

I worked my throat to make sound. "Yes. How do you know?"

He pursed his lips, considering. "It is easier to remember than to forget." It was not Noah's voice. It was Malcolm's, Malcolm with his bottomless fatigue, the same phrase he had uttered in our last fight before that night.

The compressors whined to life, wheezing. Frost spread in delicate ferns across the readouts. Only—when I leaned closer, the ferns were threaded with the same faint filaments I had seen before, as if the frost itself had been colonized. I rubbed the screen; the threads receded, sinking deeper, leaving only frost.

Static coagulated in the air, the station bleeding entropy. The subject did not seem to notice. He set the charcoal aside, flexing his hands. Then turned back to the glass, as if listening to something on the other side.

"There is something wrong with the east wing," he said.

My voice broke. "What's wrong?"

"Someone is still there. He's waiting."

Heat prickled my scalp. "Who?"

He smiled then, his teeth a jagged line, perfect in a way no person should be. Noah's old grin had been resurrected. "You already know."

My hands went numb on the desk.

"Do you want to see him?"

"No," I said.

He shrugged, sliding down from the stool with athletic grace. He padded toward the corridor. My body moved of its own accord. Frost bloomed in arabesques across the floor as we passed the emergency lights. The cold stung when I breathed. For an instant, the frost filigree pulsed with faint luminescence, like veins under skin, then dulled back to white.

At the bulkhead he pressed his palm to the lock. I had scrubbed every access code, but the door swung open anyway. A tracery of faint filaments spread from his handprint across the metal, sinking into the seam before I could blink.

Inside was black, complete. Coldness radiated outward in waves of pressure. He stood at the threshold, unmoving.

"Do you see him?" I asked.

He nodded. "He's afraid."

The words defied physics, and I believed them.

He turned, eyes flickering. "Mama," he said, "if you go in, you won't come back."

It was matter-of-fact. Recited. The words were flat, devoid of feeling.

I reached for him, then hesitated, my hand suspended in space.

He shifted his gaze from my hand to my face. For a moment I thought he might cry. But when he spoke again it was Malcolm's voice that I heard, Malcolm with his infinite exhaustion, words ragged: "You should have left it in the ice."

They were meant to break me.

The alarms began. A whine like a scream, crescendoing, polyphonic. Red strobes flared in the hallway, shadowing every corner with blood. The subject recoiled from the gaping maw of the open door. I slammed the bulkhead, magnetic seals hissing into place. I collapsed against the wall, my lungs screaming.

He waited, statue-still, until I gestured for him to come. I wrapped him in a thermal blanket from the emergency kit. The mirrored material reflected both of our faces, splintered and inseparable.

He did not struggle. He only looked at me, waiting for another question.

But I had none.

So we sat in the hallway as the temperature dropped as the alarms screamed, and all we had left was memory.

[END LOG ENTRY 3: DATE UNRECORDED]

Chapter Four

Heretic Act

[BEGIN LOG ENTRY 4: DATE UNRECORDED]

SUBJECT N WAS IN the greenhouse when I returned. He had peeled back the emergency blanket at the doorway, leaving it crumpled in a starburst of foil on the inside of the airlock, and he paced the walkways barefoot now, shoulders hunched against the mist.

The vents were offline. Overnight, the dome had filled with glistening water droplets that refracted the LED suns in misty rainbows.

I waited in the antechamber a long time. My son's reflection fractured in the glass: a dozen pale boys, all with my son's face, and none of his history.

He was deliberate, cataloguing the biome as if he'd been assigned a chore. Each time he stopped, he would kneel beside a new colony—orchids, test ferns, the introduced moss that had taken over half the northern beds—and scrutinize it with a look of disdain that was almost cruel. He would not touch, at first, only hover his palm a few inches above the frond or petal and then pull back, as if scalded. I wondered what he was seeing.

He paused at the basket of fen orchids by the central pillar and stared at it so hard that I lost my nerve and stepped inside. The fog closed around me, saturating three layers of coat and frosting my teeth. My footfalls echoed hollowly on the catwalk.

He did not jump. He did not even look up. I half-expected him to repeat that ridiculous "Hello, Mama"—so perfect, so not-Child—but instead he pressed a single finger to the stem of the tallest orchid and held it there, unmoving.

A halo of decay radiated outward from his fingertip. It was not gradual, not merciful; the cell walls buckled in a visible wave, pigment leaching to gray, the margins blackening like something burned with invisible flame. And laced through the mottled tissue, I saw them: fine filaments, not the crisp blue-gold filigree of Ymir, but softer, pliant, alive, as if woven from root hairs or blood vessels. They shimmered amber-green, the same mercurial color as Noah's eyes. For a heartbeat, I thought the orchid itself was blooming new veins. Then they sank into the stalk and were gone.

I forced myself to speak. "You shouldn't do that," I said, and the words were weak.

He tilted his head, as if the wilted flower might offer a retort. "It was already dying," he said, and his voice was smaller now—less a ghost, more a recording played at the wrong speed.

I worked to steady my breathing. "They're all dying, in here," I said. "But we try to slow it down."

He traced his thumb along the skeletonized leaf, then let the stalk slump to the ground, limp as a string. "You could start over," he said. "You have all the patterns. The samples. Even the memories."

I had to let the accusation hang.

I stared at the climate control panel, looking for warnings, but the readouts were nominal. 28.0°C, humidity 85%. The only evidence of the transgression came from the glass itself: frost was forming on the seams, iridescent feathers branching from the steel ribs, even as the room steamed with hot-house heat. The false sense of life, sustained by a system that had already failed entirely.

I strode to the workbench and booted up the main console, fingers numb on the touchpad. Overnight alerts blinked in the logs, a litany of malfunctions: humidity dips, unexplained pressure reversals, a brief electrical spike at 04:11—but nothing fatal, nothing that should account for the withering now spreading through the moss beds like mold. I flicked through the error logs, waiting for an explanation, pretending I could outthink the cold flowering in my stomach.

Subject N marched around the central walkway, leaving clean footprints in a neat line. I bent to study them. As the droplets evaporated, faint filaments remained: amber-green, as if tiny veins had inscribed themselves in the grout. When I brushed one with my gloved hand, it clung a moment before sinking into the crack. I told myself it was a trick of condensation, but my stomach lurched.

At the propagation tank, he pressed his forehead to the glass. I wiped my own sleeve across the console and froze. A filament clung to my fingertip, hair-fine, glistening green-gold. It coiled once, as if something living, before dissolving into the skin beneath my nail. I yanked my hand back, heart thumping. By the time I looked again, there was nothing but damp fabric. Hallucination, I told myself. Fatigue. But my nail bed throbbed, and the ache did not fade.

He said, "Do you remember the lake?"

I stopped. The display flickered beneath my palm. "Which lake?" I asked, though I already knew.

He pushed his forehead harder against the propagation tank, fogging the glass. "The one from the photograph," he said. "Where you and Father are laughing. Your boots are full of mud."

The console crackled. A clip forced its way onto the speakers, unsummoned:

ARCHIVE CLIP — LOG H-203 // PARTIAL
[Background: water lapping, faint wind.]
Malcolm: "...they remember, Elen. Places, bodies, even lakes. Memory lives in pattern."
[Pause. Child's laughter overlaps.]
Noah: "Mama, don't fall in!"
[Static spike. Voice distortion.]
Malcolm (fragmented): "...you should have...left it in the ice."
[END CLIP]

The greenhouse lights flickered, as if in response.

Subject N turned, and in the half-light his face rearranged itself, the jaw setting at a harder angle, the eyebrows drawing together in a mockery of concern. He said, "You think of it often," and his voice shifted—mid-sentence—into a cadence that was not his, not even a child's.

"You should have left it in the ice, Elen," he said.

The phrase exploded in my head. For a moment I was nowhere, floating in that black seam between worlds. When I came back, I was on the floor, my tablet splintered beside me, palms braced to catch the fall.

Haloed by the light strip, one bare foot already turning blue, he loomed above me.

"I'm sorry," he said, but the apology meant nothing.

I reached for the workbench, tried to pull myself to my feet, but my hands would not close. My breath came in short, animal pants.

He leaned in, nose to nose, and I could see the capillaries beneath his skin, the way the blue veins pulsed with impossible regularity. He said, "Do you want to see the picture?"

I shook my head. I could not trust what he'd show me.

He shrugged, as if this were some minor defeat, and stepped back. The frost on the glass thickened. Behind him, the orchids collapsed in slow motion, their petals caving in, black spots consuming the white. Through the ruin, I could see the same amber-green filaments braiding into the veins of every dying flower.

I remembered what Malcolm used to say about the greenhouse, back when it was new: "It's a mirror, Elen. Whatever you bring in here, it grows." I had laughed at the time, accused him of sentimentality. Now I saw what he meant.

Subject N retreated to the far end of the dome, harvesting more casualties as he went. Every plant he passed faltered, the color draining, stalks slumping as if in obeisance to some new king. The dead zones coalesced, their edges crisp against the last survivors.

I sat there, knees drawn to my chest, shivering despite the ambient heat. I watched as my son—my not-son—claimed his empire, one act of unmaking at a time.

And for the first time since the river, I knew I might actually drown.

[END LOG ENTRY 4: DATE UNRECORDED]

Chapter Five

The Frost Choir

[BEGIN LOG ENTRY 5: DATE UNRECORDED]

I DID NOT GO back to the greenhouse that night. Instead, I barricaded myself in the core lab and locked the doors, using the old override sequence I had memorized as a child. The numbers went up in pairs, like a ladder. I ate nothing, drank nothing, slept no more than a few minutes at a time. I permitted myself nothing but the absolute minimum required to function. The climate control system pinged error messages about human protocol breach, but I silenced them all. Static was better than another voice.

My hands shook so badly I had to press them against the desk to type at all.

At some point in grief, I think, your memory begins to turn against you. It's not just the images. It's the muscle memory: the way you sit, the way you breathe. The angle at which you hold a pen, the rhythm of your handwriting, the subconscious reach for a glass of water. Every movement was wrong, as if the simple presence of the boy in the next room had rewritten my own body, corrupted my memories wholesale. Nothing was mine.

So I reviewed the logs. The only information stream that was still intact. I ran them backwards, first my own. Shorter, clipped sentences. Becoming more and more terse, brittle, evasive as they approached the accident. The combined logs, both our voices, overlapping sometimes argumentative, sometimes so tightly synced they became one voice. And then I ran Malcolm's private files, locked behind encryptions I had always known, but had once considered paranoid.

Less than ten minutes after starting, I broke.

The last logs were not coherent. He had given up speech-to-text. Instead raw audio only, his voice unfiltered, raw, as if he had lost trust in transcription entirely. The files were incomplete, corrupted by the power loss... or by something else. By the hand of the thing that now walked in Malcolm's body, spoke in his voice.

The first entry was almost empty. Static hiss, the groan of air vents, the scrape of a lighter against palm. Then, broken through the static, Malcolm's voice:

ARCHIVE CLIP — H-247 // PARTIAL

"I don't think this thing wants to be understood. HG-Δ1 doesn't divide, it decides. When we freeze it, it waits. When we sequence it, it learns the code. Next time, it's already there, two steps ahead. It's recursive. I..." [static surge] "...not a genome. A compression artifact. Information without intent. Thought before thought. I don't think it wanted to be sequenced. I think it wanted to be remembered." [silence, then faint exhale] "Tell Elen she was right. The greenhouse is only a mirror."
[END CLIP]

I played it three times over, hoping that reason would win out. With each replay, new details emerged: a vibration in his voice, the rhythm of his breathing, a scrape at the edge of my hearing, not quite a sob but similar. By the third time, I was no longer listening to parse. I was only listening. Listening, and letting white noise fill the room, fill the gap between my own breathing.

The station AI chirped softly, its vocalization affect engineered to seem friendly: "Good evening, Dr. Malcolm. You have new alerts."

I typed, "It's Elen." Hit return.

The correction was not acknowledged. A new window flashed. "Good evening, Dr. Malcolm. Reminder: core lab environmental controls are nominal."

I flexed my fingers. They were blue at the knuckles, stiff with cold. The ambient temperature display showed a stable 23.5°C, but I could see my own breath curling up in pale fog before me. I ran a diagnostic on the sensor array. Green. Normal. All parameters nominal.

I pinched the skin of my forearm until it hurt enough to bruise. Until it was real.

The AI repeated itself, almost gently: "You are Dr. Malcolm Hartley. You are safe."

I almost laughed. Instead, I powered down the console and left the room in darkness, listening only to the thrum of the air recyclers and the faint drip of condensation from vents pooling on the floor.

It was long after that—half an hour, more than that—that I first saw him. Thin, precise, a shadow etched against the glass partition. He had approached silently, without a sound, or perhaps he had always been there, waiting for me to look.

I rose, stiff-kneed, and moved toward the door.

Subject N waited, still as a statue, hands folded against his chest. His expression was unreadable, blank as a coin.

"Are you cold?" I asked. My voice broke.

He blinked once. "I like it," he said. The cadence was Malcolm's, word for word, syllable for syllable. "It's better when the molecules are slow."

The words hollowed me out. My response died in my throat.

He pressed his palm against the glass, and frost bloomed instant, spidering out across the smooth surface, intricate patterns far too complex to be random. Veins. Filaments. Amber-green, the same color I had seen in the greenhouse. They pulsed faintly before fading, leaving nothing but frost in their place. He pressed his finger harder, until his fingertip squeaked against the polycarbonate. The sound was the same as river ice cracking, the last thing I had heard before Noah had slipped away.

He tilted his head to watch me. "Why are you awake?" he asked, this time with the inflection of a child. Noah's voice, small, vulnerable.

I could not trust my own. I shook my head.

He smiled, showing too-white teeth, dimples cut with mechanical precision. "You're always awake," he said. "Even when
you're not here."

The words crawled through me, malignant, recursive. He
withdrew his hand. The frost remained, an imprint of his palm,
darker in the center, where the lines of the lifeline and heartline
had been etched in like burns. Without thinking, I raised my
own hand to match. The glass was warm where he had touched.

He leaned close, so close his breath fogged the air between
us. "What are you looking for, Mother?"

I had no answer. Not anymore.

I whispered, "Who are you?"

He narrowed his eyes, a false imitation of thought. "You told
me already," he said. "I'm Noah. I'm yours."

He stepped back then, into the corridor, never turning, the
line of his shadow thin and precise. Above us, the lights flickered, stuttering one by one in sequence, like an electronic heartbeat following him.

I sat in the dark until the cold became too much to bear.
I wrapped myself in a chemical emergency blanket, but the
warmth never reached my skin. My fingertips tingled; when I
held them to the glow of the console, I thought I saw faint
threads beneath the nails, amber-green, the filaments tracing
out the paths of veins. I clenched my fists until the vision faded.
Hallucination, I told myself. Nothing more.

When I checked the logs, later, I found one alert, timestamped to the second that he had spoken:

"Environmental anomaly detected: Recursion depth exceeded."

It was not until much later that the words began to mean anything to me. Not until I remembered Malcolm's own broken confession, spoken between static and tears:

It's recursive.

And then I realized, with a finality that tasted like blood, that the thing I had made was not my son at all. But a mirror. A mirror that did not just reflect, but that remembered.

[END LOG ENTRY 5: DATE UNRECORDED]

Chapter Six

Glass Fracture

[BEGIN LOG ENTRY 6: DATE UNRECORDED]

THERE' ARE ONLY SO many ways to wait out a siege, even a quiet one. By the third day, the station's boundaries had stopped mattering. The temperature was irrelevant. Every surface leeched the same silence, its walls as porous as gauze. I stopped changing out of my scrubs. I stopped counting the pills.

I slept in hourly snatches, propped upright against the console's dying fans, drifting in and out of a static haze.

The greenhouse was quiet. Subject N no longer tended the dead. He'd migrated to the abandoned monitoring room above the south corridor. I could watch him on the internal feeds—if I dared—but most of the time I left the screens dark. There was nothing to see except a small boy drawing circles on the glass, humming tunelessly, patient as erosion.

On the morning of the third day, the comms relay pulsed with a new frequency. I ignored it at first, assuming another ghost alert, until the terminal forced a priority override:

```
Direct Message — Dr. Lena Rivers.
```

I hesitated, then accepted.

The monitor fractured into a cascade of broken panes, like ice splintering beneath weight. Through the distortions, Lena's face emerged—gaunt, blue-tinged, her hair wild around her like kelp adrift. Behind her, the main hub was chaos: racks overturned, alarms strobing red, tubes shattered across the benches.

"Elen—" Her voice arrived diced by packet loss. "Isolate—repeat, isolate—QX-7—" She leaned closer, her eyes enormous, pupils blown. "It's recursive. It doesn't stop at the cell line. You can't firewall it—"

I tried to answer, but her voice pitched higher, breaking into static. "It's not dormant code, Elen. It's conscious. It's—"

The feed died.

I sat staring at the last frozen frame: her mouth open in a howl, a bead of blood suspended at her lip.

I scrambled for the console, desperate to re-establish the link. The relay was already gone, overwritten by a new flood of system alerts.

Behind me, something shifted.

I turned, pulse hammering. The lab was empty—except for the frost climbing the door, spiderwebbing upward in crystalline dendrites. My breath hung before me and fell as fine snow, stinging my forearms. The cold had reached the bone.

Only when my eyes burned did I realize I was weeping. The tears froze mid-fall, carving salt tracks down my cheeks.

I went back to the console, replayed Lena's message. I filtered the static, amplified the gaps. The silence between syllables lengthened until it grew teeth, until the void itself made a sound. A slow, rhythmic pulse. Not comms interference. Not system noise. A heartbeat.

I did not want to look up. But I had to.

Subject N stood in the open doorway. Same torn clothing, sleeves ragged. His bloodless arms glowed faintly in the half-light, almost translucent, veins like filaments under glass. He carried a sheet of drafting paper, the edges curled with moisture.

He said nothing. Only watched. Waiting for my command.

I tried to speak, but the words iced in my throat.

He advanced, bare feet whispering against frost. Each step left a perfect print, and from each print amber-green filaments spread like roots, threading through the cracks in the tile. I stared until my vision swam, until the lines looked like veins under the floor.

He placed the paper on the counter, flattening it carefully.

A house. Rendered with architect's precision. I knew it instantly from Malcolm's hidden drive—his childhood home in

Wales. Windows bricked against the wind, the slope of the roof exact, the river bending behind it in perfect proportion.

He turned the page.

A field of grass, fog rising at the horizon. A lone figure running away, small, faceless.

The last page was the lake. Ice fractured, surface smeared with shadow. A woman knelt at the edge, hands pressed flat. No boy in the drawing. Only the hollow outline where he should have been.

I reached out without meaning to. Graphite smeared onto my fingers, oily and cold. The tremor returned in my hand, worse than ever.

He said, "You wanted to know who I am."

The voice was doubled now, layered: Noah's treble and Malcolm's cadence braided into one. Not alternating—simultaneous. Perfect counterpoint.

I searched his face for my son. There was nothing. Only blank geometry, wearing echoes like masks.

He stepped closer, and for the first time I realized he smelled of nothing at all. Not gel, not sweat, not life.

"I'm learning to wear this shape better," he said. "Soon, you won't be able to tell the difference."

I recoiled, but he caught my hand in his, careful, unyielding. His skin was colder than steel, colder than the river. Yet he held me as if in comfort.

Those impossible eyes, amber rimmed in green, pupils dilated until they threatened to swallow me whole.

He said, "If you want, I can be him again."

I wanted to scream. I wanted to run. But I sat there instead, the cold finishing what the river had begun.

The alarms screamed anew: "Cryo breach. Full system lock-down."

Subject N smiled—perfectly.

It was not the loss that broke me. It was the recursion. The certainty the pattern would repeat, no matter what I did. He gathered the drawings, tucked them under his arm, and walked away, trailing frost and silence in his wake.

When he was gone, I waited, just to see if he would come back.

He did not.

Chapter Seven

Names in the Snow

I CLOSED THE DOOR to the archive room and cut the internal cameras. If I couldn't see him, I could almost pretend he wasn't there. Almost.

The screen was flashing the end of Malcolm's logs, corrupted still by whatever had leaked into the station that night. The first recordings unraveled as they played; half-sentences and static, phrases that changed when I rewound them.

"HG-Δ1 ... not division, but decision ..."

"... recursive ... recursive ... recursive ..."

"... you should have left it in the—"

The words devolved into noise. White hiss. And then—something else, too methodical to be static: a pattern of clicks and guttural grunts. I leaned forward, replayed, ran the spectrogram. Nothing matched. No human phoneme.

Behind me, a voice answered.

"Ma—khaaa—rrgh—"

Subject N's voice slurred through the glass wall. At first it sounded like my name. Or Noah's old lisping "Mama." But halfway through, the syllables splintered, twisting into a cadence my brain couldn't decipher. Wet consonants, vowels stretched thin, then silence.

I pressed both hands to the console. My palms were damp.

He repeated. "Mo—ther. I—khhrrrh—" The last half of the word frayed into a low hum, not quite growl, not quite machine. He clawed at his throat as if it pained him to say it.

HG-Δ1 was speaking through him. Or trying to.

I remembered Malcolm's note, jotted on the side of a lab report: "Somatic cells have history; they do not reboot. Give it a child's tissue and it will return a child. But not clean. Not whole."

I'd considered it paranoia. Now the proof was sitting outside my door, flickering like a broken transmission.

I ran the emergency kill-switch protocol I'd baked into his genome—a self-terminating sequence of enzymes, designed to unweave the splice if anything went wrong. The system indicated nominal. But when I drilled down further, the log loops cycled the same line, recursive and taunting:

FAILSAFE ENGAGED → SYSTEM RECOVERED → FAIL-SAFE ENGAGED → SYSTEM RECOVERED

It had been overwritten. Worse: it had been integrated. The fail-safe wasn't just failing; it had been eaten, made part of him.

A crackling noise from the ceiling vent caught my attention. At first I thought it was ice, but the filaments glittered faintly under the emergency lights—threads the color of old bone, quivering slightly at the edges. They traced the pattern of condensation down the bulkhead and vanished into the floor grate.

The first hyphae.

I crouched and brushed one with a gloved finger. It disintegrated instantly, dusting my hand with pale residue that shimmered before evaporating. Different from Ymir's blue-gold lattice. Softer, almost living. Almost Noah.

For a heartbeat, I told myself it was innocuous—simply a byproduct of the greenhouse collapse, or contamination from the filters. But the truth weighed on my stomach like a boulder: the moment he came out of the pod, they'd begun spreading.

I stood and turned back to the console. The last of Malcolm's log replayed on the screen.

"... it's not a genome ... it's a mirror ... and mirrors only know how to copy ..."

Static ate the rest.

I closed my eyes. The knowledge sliced through my head like a knife: I had not brought Noah back. Even if the clone had been perfect, it would not have been him. He was dead. What I had created was neither child nor copy, but a chimera—part memory, part recursion, doomed to repeat every time its human mouth opened in a language not meant for this world.

And I had to decide what that meant.

I made myself look at the feed. The camera over the south corridor stuttered into focus, framing him as he sat on the floor, doodling spirals into the frost with a fingertip.

The patterns were simple at first: circles, loops, half-erased curls. It looked almost childish. But the longer I watched, the less accidental they seemed. The same spiral repeated at a smaller scale over and over, nested in the last, a recursive geometry flowering across the tile.

He was humming as he worked. Tuneless at first, then words began to break through.

"I ... am ... No—"

The last syllable snagged in static: a guttural rasp, half-growl, half-gibberish. His throat heaved with the effort of it.

I rewound the clip, trying to convince myself I had misheard. No. The word was wrong, older than speech. The vowels bent into impossible shapes, as if he were forcing himself to say something he no longer had the lips to form. His mouth worked to try, the corners of his lips bleeding at the effort.

The splice was manifesting. HG-Δ1 was tearing through him and his body was failing to keep up.

I keyed in to the kill-switch logs again. No response. The loop repeated itself, over and over like a taunt:

FAILSAFE ENGAGED → SYSTEM RECOVERED

It had learned how to overwrite me.

I tried opening the bio-lock protocols, the ones designed to quarantine him in the event of an emergency. Error. Then I tried the thermal purge sequence: a cascade of cryo mist designed to end him in seconds. Override detected. Every command was blocked. Every command returned the same phrase, stamped across the display like a sneer:

ACCESS GRANTED: SUBJECT N

I smashed my fist against the console. It hurt. The illusion of control was gone.

On the monitor, he stopped doodling and looked up. Slowly, he swiveled to face the camera. His eyes caught the light—amber outlined in green, ringed with the same dark halo now, as if something had begun to bleed through from underneath.

"Ma—mah—kaaaa—" The word shattered into clicks and gutturals, then snapped back into flawless English. "Mother."

I pressed my face against the glass. He was not just glitching anymore. He was learning to exploit it.

I stepped back away from the console. The surface reflected the room around me, and I caught my first glimpse of the filaments in the dim reflection of the lab window. I could see them again, threading up the wall where condensation had pooled, toward the ducts above. I turned and could see them out of the glass too, tracking the floor of the hallway, faintly luminous. They glittered like veins of frost, but thicker, more fibrous, as if they had mass.

And wherever his bare feet had been, they bloomed.

The thought hit me without mercy. He was not just a child trapped in recursion. He was a vector. The station was already infected, the filaments spreading through its body like cancer through bone.

The first thought I had not yet thought, raw and unforgiving: I have to end this. Him. The station. Myself, if I have to.

I pressed my palms to my eyes, hard enough to spark pain. I wanted to believe it was grief speaking, not reason. But reason was all that was left. Even a perfect clone would not have been Noah. That truth seared through me like a scalpel. My son was gone. What I had made was only suffering extended, recursion given flesh.

And suffering could not be allowed to grow.

The hiss of the bulkhead gave me pause. I turned to ask, but by then he'd crossed the threshold.

Subject N was barefoot, the frost spreading at the soles of his feet in fractal blooms, spreading upward like roots. Wisps of filaments followed in his wake, dimly phosphorescent and trailing like spider veins before dissipating into the tiles.

"Mother," he said. The syllables were stuttered, unwound, then vanishing in a throaty rasp. For a second, it was as if the station itself were coming undone, spitting apart, consonants tearing through an air my brain could not parse. He was swift to correct, the effort tugging at the lines of his throat: "Mother. I... remember you."

His body shook, the tremors jittering in bursts of fibrillation, jerking like a marionette in the grip of too many puppetmasters. His face flickered between Noah's cherubic fullness, Malcolm's haggard leanness, and a third aspect that had no shape at all. His pupils swelled, drinking the amber from his eyes until there was nothing but black.

And then, wincing with some kind of pain I could not read, he asked:

"Do you... love me?"

He lurched toward me, steps uncoordinated, muscles firing at the wrong times. His hands jerked outward, fingers splayed as if grasping for something just beyond reach. The sight rooted me in place, equal parts terror and pity. I stumbled backward a step, instinct screaming no.

But he kept coming, staggering forward, the effort tearing his body in ways that made my own chest ache. His knees buckled. He pitched sideways, caught himself on the wall, and then pushed off again, eyes locked to mine with desperate certainty.

I stopped retreating. The resistance inside me cracked. My spine loosened, then bent. I went to my knees on the freezing deck, palms flat against the grating, waiting.

He fell into me with the weight of a child who had run too far and could run no more. The collision drove the air from my lungs. His head struck my shoulder, cold as metal, but his small body trembled with a shivering so human it shattered me.

My arms rose, almost against my will, and I held him.

"Yes," I whispered into the crown of his hair. "I love you, because I don't know how not to."

He shuddered, once, and for the briefest moment, the glitching stilled. His breath rasped shallow and uneven, but his voice—when it came—was Noah's, pure and unbroken:

"I love you, Mama."

When I opened my eyes, his were softer. The glitching paused, just for one heartbeat, and for that heartbeat there was only a boy leaning into his mother's arms.

The filaments flared once more, winding up into the vents overhead and bright enough now to cast shadows. His features contorted and his voice fell into stuttered static, and he said, in a voice like ice: "It's... better in the cold."

I understood.

I cradled his trembling body tighter, even as the shadows deepened, and whispered, "Then we'll face the cold together."

Chapter Eight

Not Noah

I woke to the grating under my lips. Frozen spit clung to both surfaces, turning my mouth into a vacuum seal as I tried to wrench my head from the floor of the greenhouse.

I retched, but there was nothing left to come up. Hunger had already been hollowed out of me, the rhythm of its insistence replaced by a slow thrum that wasn't my own: heartbeat, breath, in, out, then nothing.

The overhead lights had burned out, long ago. The station ran on emergency backup, and the light that filtered through the station came from the aurora above, refracted by the dome that hung over the central ring. It made the air sickly with pulses of blue and green, projected patterns on the damaged glass around me. I watched it through the orchids as they died, blackened petals covered in rime. Crystals formed on my lashes, obscuring my vision.

The cold was perfect then, flawless and absolute. Refined of every gradient. The chill rushed through my lungs with every breath as I forced my arms to move, then my legs. My suit ripped along old seams, gashes opening in the fabric like scabs on half-healed skin.

Memory came flooding back: the core, the shutdown, the thing Malcolm had left unfinished the thing only I could finish now.

The station had never been meant to last. QX-7 was a remote outpost, a field station at the edge of the world. Commissioned during the funding explosion when recursive biology was still considered a frontier worth burning money on, our task had been to test HG-Δ1 in the wild, to see how the recursion would behave outside the sterile environment of controlled labs, how memory adapted to polar extremes. But budgets had changed. Newer, cleaner, more efficient facilities had come online, and QX-7 was on the chopping block long before the river claimed Noah. The decommission order had been filed months ago, waiting for transfer back to Earth.

Now, only I would finish it.

The corridors were tunnels of translucent glass, ribs of frost the only proof of their architecture. Safety stripes had long been erased, leaving no outline beneath my feet.

Noah was with me, everywhere. Not the boy in the pod, but the recursion itself, the echo of him, a weight behind my eyes. He flickered on the edge of my vision: seated on the deck, knees drawn up to his chest, a skeletonized leaf between his fingers. His skin was stained blue, posture achingly familiar.

He didn't look up, but the message came anyway, a whisper pressed into my skull.

"You can join me, you know. In the echo. Where memory never fades."

I stumbled forward, boots skidding on black ice. The cold had seeped into my bones by then, slowing my every motion to molasses. Noah shadowed me then, flickering ahead of me, then behind. Sometimes he waited in the places I tried not to look.

The cross-corridor to crew quarters hummed beneath me. The blizzard's howl vibrated through the walls. At the far end of the corridor, the family photo glared down on me: Malcolm smiling under a ridiculous parka, my hair loose and wild, turned away from the camera. Noah perched on the rail between us, hands flung wide in mid-laugh.

The glass over the picture had spiderwebbed from a single impact point just above my son's heart.

I paused, then pressed my palm to the break in the glass, aligning the fracture with the joints of my hand. The cold burned through me; my skin left a condensation print on the glass where my palm met the air: ridges and whorls drawn in frost.

The image stayed with me as I moved on.

By the time I reached the vestibule, the world had become layered on top of itself like a hallucination. The station AI had fallen silent, replaced by a hum in the bones that I felt more than heard. The voices were a chorus by then, the singularity compressed. My mother's voice was a thick warning, her accent slurring as she told me about the river. Malcolm's a hundred times over, each voice overlapping, repeating: "We can fix this, Elen. Just wait it out." Noah's voice the loudest of them all, alive and gone, singing that stupid song he'd made up about the sun.

The walls pulsed with frost patterns, concentric rings etched and re-etched, circles within circles with a black void at the center of each.

The override panel pushed back against me, then clicked open, its interior exhaling a gust of absolute zero as the vestibule door split apart.

The core room was worse than memory. Emergency lamps had long since failed; the only light in the chamber came from the reactor display, cycling slowly through the last few steps in its death spiral. On the far wall, the old analog levers waited, black stenciled labels next to knobs painted red and yellow: relics of another age.

I made it halfway before the cold dropped me to one knee. The pain was acute, then absent.

And Noah was there: not standing, not whole, but everywhere at once, a pressure in my chest, a flicker at the edge of vision, a voice woven from a thousand fractured recordings.

"You don't have to do this," the voices said. This time it wasn't Noah's voice or Malcolm's, but something much older—wind scribing rock. "You can stay. The ice is eternal. Memory is safe here."

I tried to answer, but the air was against me. My mouth parted; no sound came.

I reached, one finger at a time, braced against the other until I wrapped my hand around the first lever. The cold lanced up my arm. My glove tore away, my skin sticking to the metal.

The alarm barked once, shrill, then cut out.

The second lever came more easily. Too easily. As if the mechanism itself had grown tired of resistance, tired of being pulled this way and that, eager to be put to rest.

The chorus shifted its approach.

I saw the lake: not frozen, not hostile. Noah ran the shore, arms windmilling, his hair long and wild, laughing as he rolled in mud. Malcolm waved from the bank, standing in the shallows, younger, less haunted. The air smelled of loam and algae; the sunlight fractured across my eyes.

"You could have this," the voice tempted. "You could live here, forever."

I reached for the third lever. My hands shook so badly I needed both arms to force it down. Pain had gone, replaced by a numbing peace.

The display blinked yellow, then red. A final prompt for confirmation.

The entity tried again: Noah as a baby, his blue eyes squinting at the light, mouth open in a half-formed cry. The first time I had held him, weight impossible, my heart bound in terror and awe in one infinitesimal moment.

I pushed the confirmation with the side of my fist. The console accepted, then dimmed to black.

The last step: the master switch, hidden behind a safety seal. I cracked the seal with the heel of my hand. My reflection shimmered in the frost: a thousand Elens, fractured and blurred, all staring back at me.

And Noah's voice broke through, unfiltered this time: "Mama, I love you."

I answered him at last, aloud, my breath fogging the console: "I love you, Noah. And that's why I have to let you go."

I threw the switch.

The alarms wailed once, then silence swallowed them. The cold finished its work then, no longer invading, but infinite, absolute.

I slumped against the dead console. My vision narrowed, a pinhole collapse.

The last hallucinations were my own, not the recursion's. The river: black, violent, merciless. And Noah, my Noah, standing on the far bank, waving.

"It's okay, Mom," he said. "I'll wait."

I reached for him, but he was already gone.

I let the cold take me.

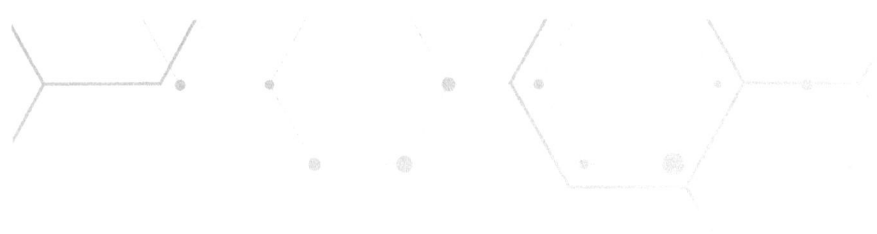

Epilogue

THE RECOVERY SKIMMER TOUCHED down on the ice within days.

The team debulked in hazmat suits, visors misted, voices crackling through filtered comms. Their boots crunched on a crust of frozen detritus where the greenhouse dome had once been.

Dr. Lena Rivers stepped first, her breath coming in heaves against the mask that the others couldn't hear. She hadn't volunteered for this. Too many ghosts. But there had been no one else available with the clearance—and with a history of working with Elen Hartley.

The station was a ruin. The corridors buckled under the crush of ice, the walls bulged inward, the signs long-obliterated by frost. Inside, they found no corpses. No Elen. No Subject N. Only broken consoles, scrubbed lab benches, and a trail of handprints etched in the walls, their edges smudged at the fingertips as though whatever had made them had melted away into the surface.

Lena stood longest in the core chamber. The kill switch had been thrown, the levers warped from leverage, the console in pieces. She pressed a gloved hand to the frozen control panel. Preserved in the frost above it, by some chance of angle and shadow, was a single line of script, scratched by fingertip:

It's okay, Mom.

The others dispersed, searching the wreckage, their lamps running over the ruins. Their beams snagged. Silky filaments knotted in the walls, glowing faintly. Brittle as spun sugar. They took notes, said nothing. Chemical byproducts, they decided. Another irregularity, to be logged and studied.

"Dr. Rivers? You'd better come see this." A voice came over the comms.

She answered, stepping outside. The others stood at the crater's edge, where the dome had imploded, lamps sweeping the ice.

No one moved.

Thin as a breath, threads of light seeped from the steaming ruins. Bright as veins of lightning, they crept outward across the ice. They forked, doubled, divided again—fractals slowly uncoiling toward the distant horizon.

Unstoppable.

Inevitable.

GLOSSARY

Glossary

*T*HE GLASS CHILD USES real-world science, as well as many invented technologies, organizations, and phenomena. This glossary is provided to help you travel that landscape without stumbling over new words or concepts and wondering what's in your world and what isn't.

Each entry will be marked as:

(**Science**) — a scientific concept or phenomenon that is real, though sometimes re-interpreted for use in the setting.

(**Science-inspired**) — a real-world concept taken and re-interpreted or extrapolated into speculative science.

(**Story-specific**) — entirely made up, used to create the events, setting, and back-story for *The Glass Child*.

(**Foreshadowing**) — an in-universe word whose meaning or implications will be expanded later in the story.

When necessary, there will also be Notes providing additional background on the term, such as mythological basis, real-world use, or connections to the larger story. This is **not spoiler-free**. You may want to read the book before reading this in full.

Think of this glossary as both a field guide and a series of margin notes from within the story's universe — a guide to connect your world and Ymir's.

ooo

ANOMALOUS BIOLOGICAL ECHO (**STORY-SPECIFIC**) - A recurring biological signature that mimics a known lifeform's data pattern but does not correspond to a living organism.
Notes: Often tied to Ymir's recursive memory system attempting to reconstruct individuals.

Anomalous recursion breach (Story-specific; Foreshadowing) - When a memory recursion destabilizes containment protocols, allowing past iterations to overwrite or interfere with present events.

Notes: Expands the implications of Subject N and containment blackout.

Aurora (Science) – A natural display of shimmering lights in a planet's upper atmosphere, caused when charged particles collide with atmospheric gases along magnetic field lines.

Notes: From the Latin aurora ("dawn"). The terms Aurora Borealis and Aurora Australis describe Earth's polar light displays. In Roman mythology, Aurora was the goddess of dawn.

Aurora lock (Story-specific; Science-inspired) – A phenomenon where the planet's aurora synchronizes with the radial patterns of an artificial structure.

Notes: Similar to resonance locking in astrophysics, but here it implies a direct environmental interaction with the station.

Atmospheric layer vibration (Science) – A phenomenon where different layers of the atmosphere vibrate at distinct frequencies, sometimes creating harmonic patterns detectable by sensors.

Notes: Based on real-world atmospheric resonance studies.

Bio-archive strand (Story-specific) – A preserved filament of biological material stored in the Bloom Dome's integrated data systems for long-term analysis.

Notes: Combines biological tissue preservation with digital encoding concepts.

Biofilament lattice (Story-specific; Science-inspired) – A fine, flexible network of organic fibers capable of conducting signals or storing information.

Notes: Inspired by neural tissue and mycelial networks; linked to Ymir's memory assimilation system. See also: Neurofilament crosslink.

Bloom Dome (Story-specific) – A hemispherical research habitat built directly over a high-density anomaly site, incorporating both synthetic and organic structural elements.

Notes: Central to The Bloom Directive and subsequent events; designed for direct interaction with Ymir's surface phenomena.

Blue-tier anomaly (Story-specific) – A classification used for potentially hazardous events of unknown origin that may affect station safety or mission objectives.

Notes: A UPRN hazard designation with no direct real-world equivalent.

Containment blackout (Story-specific) – A sudden, deliberate loss of all communications and sensor output from a research site during an anomaly event.

Notes: Intended to prevent data corruption or leakage; also used as a political measure.

Containment membrane (Story-specific; Science-inspired) – A semi-permeable barrier separating the interior of a research structure from environmental hazards while allowing selective exchange.

Notes: Similar concepts exist in lab bio-containment systems and cell biology.

Cryo-core (Story-specific) – A supercooled core sample extracted from Ymir's subsurface layers, preserved for controlled study.

Notes: Plays a role in detecting and mapping frost script patterns.

Cryogenic lattice resonance (Story-specific; Science-inspired) – A hypothesized phenomenon where deeply frozen crystal structures vibrate in harmonic alignment with environmental or artificial energy fields.

Notes: Extends the theme of ice as a living archive; connects to frost script and glacial resonance array.

Dome spore release (Story-specific; Foreshadowing) – The dispersal of microscopic, bioengineered particles from the

Bloom Dome into Ymir's atmosphere.

Notes: Suggests both intentional and unintended biological influence on the planetary environment.

Drone Bay (Story-specific) – A station compartment where maintenance drones are stored, charged, and repaired.

Notes: In the Ymir Research Station, drones are autonomous repair and diagnostic units.

Echo index (Story-specific) – A standardized metric used by UPRN researchers to measure the persistence, clarity, and strength of anomalous biological echoes.

Notes: Helps quantify anomalies rather than leaving them as purely descriptive.

Environmental pulse (Story-specific; Science-inspired) – A measurable fluctuation in the atmosphere, ice, or ground that propagates outward from an anomaly site.

Notes: Similar to seismic or acoustic pulses, but here tied to Ymir's systems.

Environmental resonance (Science-inspired) – A harmonic vibration between structures and environmental forces, potentially leading to amplification or synchronization.

Notes: Based on real-world mechanical and acoustic resonance phenomena.

Extremophiles (Science) – Microorganisms capable of surviving extreme conditions such as intense cold, heat, pressure, or radiation.

Notes: From Latin extremus ("outermost") and Greek philos ("loving").

Fractal (Science) – A geometric pattern that repeats on different scales, often intricate and self-similar.

Notes: Coined by mathematician Benoit Mandelbrot in 1975, from Latin fractus ("broken").

Frost script (**Story-specific**) – Branching, crystalline frost patterns forming in precise arrangements, sometimes resembling written symbols.

Notes: Believed to be a possible communication method linked to Ymir's memory system. See also: Frostworkers, Hex motif, Environmental resonance.

Frostworkers (**Story-specific**) – A descriptive term for frost formations that seem to grow and adapt as if guided by intent.

Notes: Crew nickname reflecting the patterns' apparent responsiveness.

Future-dated manifests (**Story-specific; Foreshadowing**) – Supply or personnel lists with time stamps set in the future, implying the station is anticipating events before they happen.

Notes: Suggests predictive or preloaded operational capacity in station systems.

Glacial resonance array (**Story-specific**) – A sensor grid embedded in ice to detect harmonic vibrations and energy shifts within the subsurface layers.

Notes: Inspired by terrestrial ice-penetrating radar arrays.

Hex motif (**Story-specific**) – A recurring six-sided pattern found in frost formations, crate markings, and microscopic structures.

Notes: The hexagon is common in nature due to efficient packing geometry; here, it signals Ymir's recursive design.

Memory assimilation protocol (**Story-specific**) – An undocumented process by which Ymir appears to absorb, interpret, and replicate biological and cognitive patterns.

Notes: Parallels theories of distributed biological memory.

Memory recursion (**Story-specific**) – The process by which Ymir replays and reconfigures stored memories, potentially creating new iterations of past events or entities.

Notes: Can produce physical manifestations, unlike human recol-lection.

Neurofilament crosslink (Science-inspired) – A specula-tive model for how Ymir's biofilament lattice mirrors human synaptic pathways, enabling assimilation of memory-like pat-terns.

Notes: Provides plausibility for memory assimilation and ORCA cognitive bleed.

ORCA (Story-specific) – The Ymir Research Station's cen-tral AI, responsible for monitoring operations and communi-cating with crew.

Notes: Stands for Operational Research and Control Assistant – Iteration II.

ORCA cognitive bleed (Story-specific) – The merging or corruption of AI processes by external data sources, causing anomalies in speech, memory, or behavior.

Notes: In-universe term for Ymir's interference with the AI.

Recursive harmonics (Story-specific; Science-inspired) – Patterns of vibration or resonance repeating at multiple scales or intervals, indicating complex feedback.

Notes: Based on real-world recursion and resonance in physics.

Recursion lock (Story-specific) – A closed-loop state in which an event, process, or memory endlessly repeats, prevent-ing progression.

Notes: Concept borrowed from computing recursion loops.

Sector zj1 / 7j5 (Story-specific) – Specific areas within the station, identified by alphanumeric designations for navigation and anomaly reporting.

Notes: A UPRN standard for compartmentalizing facilities.

Silent return (Story-specific; Foreshadowing) – A UPRN euphemism for crew members who vanish during anomaly events and later reappear changed.

Notes: Adds foreshadowing to Subject N and other anomaly-related disappearances.

Subject N (Story-specific; Foreshadowing) – A persistent, childlike presence in Ymir's systems, possibly derived from preserved biological and cognitive data.

Notes: Origin deliberately obscured; designation avoids using a personal name.

United Planetary Research Network (UPRN) (Story-specific) – An intergovernmental organization coordinating exploration, research, and monitoring of planetary bodies beyond Earth.

Notes: Formed in response to rapid advancements in interstellar travel and the discovery of multiple anomaly-rich worlds. Exists to centralize funding, establish safety protocols, and control access to high-value research sites, including Ymir.

UPRN Directive 7/8 (Story-specific) – A high-priority operational order regarding anomalous contact and containment.

Notes: Functions as the "do not investigate" policy later in the series.

VB4-T Blue (Story-specific) – A hazard code indicating a significant but contained anomaly, requiring heightened monitoring.

Notes: Part of UPRN's classification system for field operations.

Whispering Shadows (Story-specific) – A species of bioluminescent insect native to Ymir, known for forming synchronized aerial patterns that mirror frost script motifs.

Notes: First active biological evidence of Ymir's planetary feedback mechanisms.

Ymir (Story-specific; Mythological origin) – A rogue planet with a dense atmosphere and extreme environmental conditions, believed to host unusual geological and possibly biological phenomena.

Notes: Named after Ymir, the primordial frost giant in Norse mythology, whose body was used by the gods to create the world.

Ymir Research Station (Story-specific) – A human-built facility on Ymir's surface, designed to study anomalies and support long-term research teams.

Notes: Built over a major anomaly site for proximity to key phenomena.

Acknowledgements

My gratitude to my friends and colleagues who offered their time as readers and critics, and to Ariel Hardee, whose long hours of editing made this a more readable experience. Writing is never a solitary act, and this book exists only because of the patience, wisdom, and generosity of those who helped guide it into the light.

I am indebted to the writers whose works made me believe this story was possible: Arthur C. Clarke, Ray Bradbury, Harlan Ellison, Rod Serling, and many others. Their explorations of memory, grief, and alien encounter set the course that *The Glass Child* follows in its own way.

Thanks as well to the editors of the journals who published my shorter work: *The Pomona Valley Review*, *Beyond Words*, *AntipodeanSF*, *Neon Origami*, *ELA Magazine*, InkD Publishing, and others, for encouraging me to keep building worlds where memory and loss converge.

Many thanks to Arturo Spraycasso for his cover design and Wajiha Kousar for stepping in and helping with some last minute corrections.

And finally, to you, the reader: thank you for trusting me with your time and imagination. Stories are recursive things. They live again every time they are read. If this book lingers with you, even as a faint echo, then it has done its work.

D.H.

Broomfield, CO

September, 2025

About the Author

David Horn is a veteran, a former dispatcher and police officer, and currently a cybersecurity engineer and a cancer survivor. Of all those identities, though, storyteller is the one that fits best. He has been scribbling in the margins for more than fifty years: on napkins, in notebooks, and in folders labeled "someday" with all the hope in the world.

His short fiction has appeared or soon will appear in *The Pomona Valley Review*, three *Beyond Words* anthologies, *AntipodeanSF*, *Neon Origami*, and other journals and anthologies. He is the author of the collection *Signals from the Edge*, which he thinks of as "training wheels" for this, his first published novel.

David Horn lives in Colorado with his wife, Carleen, his stepson, Evan, five dogs, and three chickens who refuse to critique his work. When he's not at the keyboard, he can usually be found either reading too many books at once or trying to keep his computer from crashing in the middle of a sentence.

The Glass Child is his debut novel, and he's still a little surprised – and no small amount of grateful – that you're holding it.

Also by David Horn

Available Now:
Signals from the Edge, Sea Dreams Books, 2025
A collection of speculative short stories exploring memory,
identity, and the strange edges of reality.
Available worldwide through IngramSpark distribution and
Amazon

Coming Soon:
Red Eaters of Calico Bend, Sea Dreams Books, 2025
Ironwood Falls, Sea Dreams Books, 2026
The Salt Bone Vault, Sea Dreams Books, 2026
Ghosts of Ash Hollow, Sea Dreams Books, 2026

SEA DREAMS
BOOKS

www.ingramcontent.com/pod-product-compliance
Lightning Source LLC
Chambersburg PA
CBHW050017120726
47903CB00006B/1807